THE TIGHTROPE WALKERS

"I was born in a hovel on the banks of the Tyne . . ."

Dominic Hall grows up in the sixties on a brand-new estate, along with the other families who escaped the river. But the Tyne is still an overwhelming presence, and most of the fathers work in the shipyards. Dom is torn between his new mates: Holly Stroud, his enchanting neighbour, and Vincent McAlinden, who's something else altogether — a wild, dangerous boy with murderous instincts.

After his mother's death, Dom has to decide who he is, what he wants to be — and then face up to the consequences.

THE TIGHTROPE WALKERS

WALKERS

DAVID ALMOND

ISIS
LARGE
PRINT

First published in Great Britain 2014
by
Penguin Books Ltd.

First Isis Edition
published 2015
by arrangement with
Penguin Books Ltd.

The moral right of the author has been asserted

A catalogue record for this book is available
from the British Library.

ISBN 978–1–78541–038–3 (hb)
ISBN 978–1–78541–039–0 (pb)

Published by
F. A. Thorpe (Publishing)
Anstey, Leicestershire

Set by Words & Graphics Ltd.
Anstey, Leicestershire
Printed and bound in Great Britain by
T. J. International Ltd., Padstow, Cornwall

This book is printed on acid-free paper

to David Battye

I was born in a hovel on the banks of the Tyne, as so many of us were back then. It was a three-room dilapidated upstairs flat, in the same terraced row where Dad had been born, and just upriver from Simpson's Shipyard. Rats slunk under the floorboards, mice scuttled in the walls. The bath hung from a nail on the wall, the toilet was at the foot of steep steps outside. The river slopped against the banks and stank when the tide was low. There was the groan of engines and cranes from the yard, the din of riveters and caulkers. Sirens blared at the start and end of shifts. Gulls screamed, children laughed, dogs barked, parents yelled.

All hackneyed, all true.

By the time I remember anything clear, the slums were gone and we'd moved uphill into our pebbledashed estate built on a wilderness just above town.

It's said we travelled there like refugees. We came from crumbling terraces with tiny yards, from riverside shacks, from tumbledown cottages next to long-abandoned mines.

They were still completing it all when we arrived. There were trenches in the earth for pipes and cables. White markers showed where the pavements and roads would be. There were half-built garden walls and gateposts. Our dads roped furniture to their backs or pushed it there on handcarts. Our mams lugged rolled-up sheets and blankets. Retired pit ponies were used as cargo-carriers, Alsatians hauled pallets of boxes and bags. What did we have to bring anyway? A few sticks of furniture, enough clothes to dangle loosely in little wardrobes. Some brought animals on leads and in boxes or baskets: chickens and ferrets to house in back gardens. Ponies and pigeons and rabbits and dogs.

I was one year old when we arrived. Dad carried me there in a wooden box. The box became a cradle, then my bed in which I slept until I was three years old.

Men closed the holes and chasms in the earth as we settled in and as I grew. They laid kerbstones and paving stones. They raised lamp posts and telegraph poles. Men with scorched faces and with holes burned into their clothes tended fiery engines, braziers and steamrollers. They spread asphalt and tarmacadam with huge black brooms and great black shovels. Men in white overalls painted the doors and window frames. And kind men in brown with soft green caps stood on scaffolding by our walls and brought us pebbledash.

"True artists," Mam murmured, as we stood in the rubble garden to watch them work. I must have just begun to walk, but I believe I recall these things.

The pebbledashers laid tarpaulins beneath the wall. Then brought wet plaster in buckets and spread it on the wall. Then dug their trowels into sacks of tiny stones and flicked the stones towards the plaster. Beautiful sounds: the ring of the trowel, the chink of the flick, the dash of the stones against the wall, the scatter upon the tarpaulin of those that fell. Time and again and time and again they plastered, flicked and dashed, then gathered up the stones and began again until the wall was covered and they moved to other walls.

They kept turning, winking at me, proud of what they did.

I remember one of the men who came to me and tweaked my cheek.

"What do you think of that then, kidder?" he said.

"He thinks it is just marvellous," Mam answered. "Don't you, son?"

"Yes," I think I whispered as I turned my face into her skirt.

When I was small, I loved to press my palms against the walls, to feel the points and edges against my skin. I'd press until it was almost painful, then lift my hand to see the pattern of the stones on me, to see it slowly fade, then press again to bring it back. I'd touch tenderly with my fingertips to feel the tiny smooth and gleaming surfaces. The rectangles of the walls were lovely, with the flaring-outward at the foot of each one, the three-inch gap left between the pebbledash and the earth as protection from the damp.

It seemed so finished, so perfect, so modern, once the earth was closed, once the roads were laid, once the heaps of waste had disappeared, once all the men had gone away and we were left alone, to be ourselves, to grow together in our bright new world.

This is where these things happened, to me, to Holly Stroud, to Vincent McAlinden, in a time and place that seem so long ago but are not so long ago, in a time and place that lay halfway between the river and the sky.

Pebbledash

CHAPTER
ONE

McAlinden made his first mark when I was five years old. It was a bright spring day and I was with Holly Stroud. She lived across the narrow street, in a house that was a reflection of our own. We were walking on the garden walls. Her dad, Bill Stroud, was at our side, ready to catch us if we fell.

Holly high-stepped, danced and spread her arms like wings. I followed her, less certain.

At the two-foot gap between the gateposts, Bill lifted her up and carried her high in a perfect arc and put her down again.

She bowed to him, to the estate and to the sky.

Two kids trundled by on home-made stilts. A bunch of girls played hospitals, their orange boxes arranged against a garden wall.

"Now your turn, Dom," said Holly.

Bill helped me on to the gatepost. Invisible boys were yelling, playing football up on the high fields.

"Back straight," said Holly. "Pointed toes, head held high."

Bill held his palm against my back to help me understand.

"Like you're dancing, Dom!" cried Holly. "Yes, nearly right!"

She turned to the half-open first-floor window of the house. Dark curtains wafted on the breeze there.

"Mam!" she called. "I'm with Dominic Hall, Mam!"

"Wonderful!" replied her mother's voice.

"He's doing great, Mam!"

"Marvellous!"

Mrs Stroud began to sing.

O for the wings, for the wings of a dove...

Bill lifted me and swung me, and held me high and steady in the air. A bunch of boys ran past, screaming that they were off to bomb Berlin. A pony whinnied and a cockerel called. I stretched my arms and tried to lose myself in weightlessness.

The stone came spinning through the air and hit my brow. I flopped. Bill laid me down. He dabbed the blood with his handkerchief.

"What's your name?" he said.

"Vincent *McAlinden*!" yelled Holly.

"Dominic," I murmured to Bill Stroud.

"What on earth d'you think you're *doing*?" yelled Holly.

Vincent stood further down the street. He'd moved here just a few days ago. Squat, black-haired and filthy. He had his hands turned upwards in regret.

"I didn't mean it!" he shouted. "I aimed to miss!"

"Get back home," snapped Bill.

He held Holly back from running to him.

"Leave him," he said. "He's just a daft tinker."

His white handkerchief reddened with my blood. He spread his hand before my face.

"How many fingers?"

"Three."

"What month is it?"

"March."

"Good lad. Lie still."

Kids were gathering. *He's bust his skull. Is his eye out? He could've had his bliddy eye out.* Then Mam was here, reaching down to me.

"We'll have the bliddy polis on you!" someone called.

"Bugger off out of this estate, ye little sod!"

"How many fingers now?" said Bill.

"Two."

Mam held me and I sobbed.

"He needs a cuddle," said Bill. "And an Elastoplast, and a nice sweet cup of tea."

He stroked my brow.

"You'll be all right, son. You'll survive."

Then here was Dad in his black work clothes, with his knapsack hanging from his back.

"It was the new kid, Mr Hall," said some child.

"Him that just moved in the other day."

"Vincent McAlinden, Mr Hall."

"He threw a stone," said Bill. "The little sod."

"Are ye aal reet?" Dad said to me.

"Aye, Dad."

"And ye done nowt about it?" said Dad to Bill.

"Not yet," said Bill. "He's been . . ."

Dad took me from Mam and stood me up. He took the handkerchief from Bill and pressed it to the wound.

He set off down the street with me. I could smell the shipyard on him, the oil, the grease, the river, the filth. He drew furiously on a cigarette.

"What were ye up to?" he said.

"Just playing, Dad."

"With the Stroud lass?"

"Aye."

"Diyin what?"

"Walkin on the walls, Dad."

"Walkin on the bliddy *walls*?"

We came to the house at the foot of the estate. The rocky pathway that led out of the estate ran right beside it. A pair of dogs snarled through the fence. The back door of the house was open, a fire blazed in the grate inside.

"Where's that lad!" shouted Dad.

Mrs McAlinden came to the door. She wiped her hands on a piece of cloth. She lit a cigarette and drew on it.

"Look at this!" snapped Dad.

I lifted the handkerchief away.

She came to the fence and looked down at me. She yelled at the dogs to stop their bliddy snarling. Kids wailed inside the house and she yelled at them to stop as well.

"Vincent?" she said.

"If that's his name, that's him," said Dad.

I could smell the sweat on her. Could see the grease in her hair shining in the sun.

"Is it sore?" she said.

10

I squeezed back my tears and nodded. Yes. The blood was trickling down past my eyes now.

"The lad's a terror," she said.

"Get him here."

"Vincent!" she yelled at the house.

"Keep down!" she yelled at the dogs. "I dunno what to do with him," she said to Dad. "Be different if I had a man like you to give him a proper thrashin now and then."

"Get him out and I'll diy it now," said Dad. "At least I'll scare the little sod."

"I doubt it," she said. "Vincent! Vincent!"

She leaned closer and her huge breasts swung inside her loose black blouse.

"Would you like a cup of nice warm milk, son?" she said.

"No!" I gasped.

She looked at me fondly. Wiped blood from my cheek with her fingertips, then wiped them on her skirt.

"How d'ye get them to be so nice?" she said.

Dad threw the stub of his cigarette away. She gave him another and for a few seconds they just smoked, watching the fumes rise from their lips and towards the bright sky.

"Vincent!" she yelled.

He came to the door at last and stood just inside.

"It was just a bit of carry-on," he said. "I aimed to miss."

"Well bliddy miss better next time," she said. "Now howay here and say sorry to this bairn."

"Not while that bugger's standin there."

Dad snarled.

"Get here now!" he said. "Or I'll come and get ye and I'll bliddy swing for ye!"

Vincent shuffled out. He took one of the dogs by its collar and held it at his side.

"Have ye seen what ye've done?" said his mother.

"Aye," said Vincent.

"Just look at that bliddy blood," she said. "He's just a little lad. Ye should be lookin after him, not hoyin bliddy rocks at him."

"I aimed to miss!"

"Say yer sorry."

His shoulders slumped. He curled his lip and looked down at the ground.

"I'm sorry."

Dad grabbed his collar and dragged him close. The woman kicked the growling dog away. Dad hauled Vincent till he stood on tiptoe.

"Say it like ye *mean* it," he said.

"I diy mean it. I'm really sorry. What's yer name, kid?"

Dad elbowed me.

"Speak up for yerself. Tell him your name."

I looked into Vincent's eyes, looked down again.

"Dominic," I said.

"I'm really really sorry, Dominic."

"Are ye?" said Dad.

"Aye! Really. Aye!"

"So it won't happen again, will it?"

"No, mister."

"Cos if it does I swear I'll bliddy swing for ye. Do ye knaa what that means?"

"Aye, mister! Aye!"

"Good." He shoved Vincent away from us. "Now bugger off back into the house and diy something to help yer mother."

"Aye, mister. I will right now."

He scuttled back into the house.

Dad put his hand tenderly on my shoulder at last.

"Look at you," he said. "You'd think you'd been to bliddy war." He dabbed the tears and blood. "Ye'll need to toughen up, eh?"

"He'll learn," said Mrs McAlinden.

"Will he?" said Dad.

Mrs McAlinden shrugged. She shook her head.

"Kids!" she said.

We went back up through the estate. Holly and Bill and Mam were still standing there. Mrs Stroud still sang.

"That bugger there," Dad said softly. "That Stroud bloke. He's a conchie. You know what that means, don't you?"

"Yes, Dad."

"So he'll not be much use to you, will he? And just listen to the lunatic upstairs."

Morning has broken, like the first mo-o-o-orning . . .

"You ever heard owt like that?"

"No, Dad."

"No. Anyway they'll not be stayin much longer. This is a place for the likes of us and not the likes of them."

Mam came to us and cuddled me.

"Better now?" she said.

"Aye, Mam."

I lifted the handkerchief away.

"What a mess," she said. "But look, it's stopping now. Soon there'll be a scab and then a little scar, then it'll be like nothing happened at all."

"Better now?" said Bill.

I nodded.

"Brave lad," said Bill.

"Come out again soon," said Holly.

We went inside. Mam cleaned me up with Dettol and cotton wool and put an Elastoplast on me. Dad went upstairs and changed his clothes, and came back smelling of toothpaste and Old Spice. We had pork pie and chips and peas. We all sat together on the sofa and Dad smoked and Mam waved his smoke away.

Dad laughed at her, cuddled her, kissed her and sighed.

We watched *The Lone Ranger* and the picture fuzzed and faded and crackled in and out of view. Dad imitated the voices of the Indians and of Tonto.

"Kemosabe!" he said. "Ungawa!"

Mam clicked her tongue and laughed.

"That's from *Tarzan*!" she said.

"What is?"

"Ungawa. Isn't it, Dominic?"

"Aye," I said. "It means, Cheetah, go and get an elephant!"

Dad snorted and stood up, ready to go to the Iona Club. He kissed Mam, he stroked my hair.

"Hoy the rock back at him next time," he said.

14

"Don't say that!" said Mam.

He stood with his back to the fire and pondered.

"Why not?" he said. "Seems to me there should be a bit more of that Vincent McAlinden in him, and a little bit less of that Holly bliddy Stroud."

Mam rolled her eyes and he went away.

"More of Vincent McAlinden!" she scoffed.

We stayed together on the sofa. She clicked her tongue, for there was blood again, showing through the Elastoplast. She peeled it free.

"The skin's that thin," she said. "That's the trouble."

She tried dressing it again, and soon put me to bed.

"Don't forget your prayers," she said.

She kissed me and left me. I lay and listened to the night. Listened for the ghosts and monsters that all we children dreaded in this place. And then I slept, and Dad woke me: his footsteps, the click of the gate, the click and clash of the front door. I heard my parents talking softly together, then coming up the stairs.

I touched my brow, licked my fingers. Blood again. I imagined it bleeding forever, all the blood in me draining away through this narrow opening.

I slept again, woke again, heard more footsteps, rapid, soft.

Dared to go to the window and look out through my hands.

It was no ghost, no monster.

It was the tramp Jack Law. He leaned forward as he passed quickly beneath the orange street lights, heading towards the upper wasteland and the fields. His long fair hair, pale as the pebbledash, glinted in the moonlight, then he was just a shadow and then he was gone.

I lay back down.

"Our Father," I started, "who art in Heaven. Hallowed be thy . . ."

I licked my bloodied fingertips again. Put my fingers to the wound, whose mark would be with me for evermore.

"Our Father," I began again.

CHAPTER
TWO

Who made you?

Why did God make you?

Kind Miss Fagan said that these were the most important things we'd ever learn. We must learn the answers word by word. We must commit them to our heart.

"Who made you, Dominic Hall?"

"God made me, Miss Fagan."

"There is no need to include me in your answer. Who made you, Dominic Hall?"

"God made me."

"Good boy. And why did God make you, Holly Stroud?"

"God made me to know him, love him and serve him in this world, and to be happy with him forever in the next."

"Good girl. See how simple it is, children? We will learn a little every day until mistakes are made by none of us, until we can answer the most difficult questions deep inside the book. For we wish to have no blemishes on our souls, do we, children?"

"No, Miss Fagan."

"We wish to go to Heaven, don't we, children?"

"Yes, Miss Fagan."

"And we wish to please Miss O'Kane, don't we?"

"Yes, Miss Fagan."

"Yes indeed. Now, put away your catechisms and we will make some words and pictures. Would you like that?"

"Yes, Miss Fagan."

And she'd take a stick of chalk and reach up to the blackboard and start to write. Her fingers were slender. Her movements were deft. She curved the marks and angled them, and spoke the letters as she wrote, then spoke the word the letters made, then left a space and went on to the next word and the next until she dotted a stop, then spoke the words again to let us hear the meaning and the beauty of it all. And then we copied what she'd done, to make the shapes and sense and sentences for ourselves.

The grass is green.

The sky is blue.

The yellow sun is in the sky.

"No need to rush," she'd say. "Stay on the line. Remember your finger spaces. That's good, that's so lovely, children."

She'd gently tap the shoulders of some of us, and whisper that yes, we had it right. She'd lean down to the slow ones, sometimes take their hand in hers, guide their uncertain clumsy fingers into the right actions, the right marks.

"Yes," she'd murmur. "Well done. Practice makes perfect. Remember that."

She never lost her temper. Her classroom was benign. We sat on hard steel-and-timber benches bolted to steel-and-timber desks. There was a crucifix high up on the wall behind Miss Fagan's desk, and the alphabet, and numbers from one to a hundred, and a painting of poor St Lawrence being roasted on a fire. Through the high windows, we saw the scudding north-eastern sky, occasional songbirds flying past, tight flocks of rushing pigeons, and far away, for those of us who knew how and where to look, the tiny almost-invisible dots of distant larks.

Miss Fagan had us for our first three years.

I loved to be in there. I loved to copy the letters and make the shapes, to hear the sounds and rhythms, to see the visions that the words made in my brain. *The ship sails. The bird flies.* To write with chalk on slate. To be among the group allowed to write with dip pens, to dip the pen into my own little pot of blue ink, to write into neatly lined red exercise books, to copy prayers and hymns and Bible stories from the board, to dry the ink with bright white blotting paper. *Infant Jesus, meek and mild, look on me, a little child. In the middle of the night he came to them, walking upon the sea, and told them, Do not be afraid.* I loved the books we read. *Here is Janet. Here is John.*

And to write, to be allowed to write words of my own, sentences of my own, tales of my own. *Once there was a boy carled Dominic, who warked acros the waystland to have an advencher.* I loved to learn that *waystland* must turn to *wasteland*, to learn the power of a comma and a full stop, to love the patterns made

19

on paper by strings of sentences, blocks of paragraphs. There were many who couldn't do this. I sat for some time beside a boy called Norman Dobson. I was mystified by the way his words were scrawls across the page, no spaces between them, how they made no sense at all, how punctuation was random, meaningless, how he bent breathing wetly over his work as if in great pain. I would try to help him.

"Remember finger spaces, Norman," I'd whisper. "Stay on the lines."

He'd turn to me with furrowed brow and with snot trickling to his upper lip.

"You can do it, Norman," I'd whisper.

"I can't," he'd say. "I just bliddy cannot, Dom."

I'd watch his hands trembling with the struggle of it, the fear of it.

Holly knew the joy of it. I loved the times we were allowed to work together, to see the pictures that she drew to supplement and intensify my words, to make our shared creation. *Sum people said Don't go. It is too danjerus. But the boy was very brayv.* And to see a boy shaped just like me setting out across the page's snowy waste.

The school, St Lawrence's, was a stone-built place towards the river. It stood upon earth that was riddled with ancient mines. We were close to the wailing and shuddering of engines in the factories and shipyards down here. We could smell oil and weird sweet chemicals and the foulness of the river when it was low.

20

On hot days we gagged at the stench of the bone yard on the opposite bank.

The school was a place of ghosts. The older children told us tales of the children who had died below a hundred years ago, children killed in rockfalls and explosions. They rose to haunt this place above.

Beware of certain corridors, we were told.

Beware of that cupboard, of turning that corner.

Try this. Count the kids in your classroom. Sometimes you'll be counting more than there really are. You're counting ghosts. They come up from the dark to sit here in the light, especially with you, the younger ones. You haven't seen them yet? Keep your eyes peeled. Watch and be prepared. There, look! Oh no. Just a shadow. There! Run!

And worse. Monsters roamed the schoolyard at night when we children were away. They that hid in the daytime in lairs in the earth.

They're things half human and half beast.

We'd stare and wonder. How could that be so?

You'll come to understand, when you're old enough to know.

They sniggered, rolled their eyes.

Dogs and women, mares and men.

Ask your fathers, if you're brave enough, but be ready to get clouted.

Holly was a sceptic, even in her infancy.

"All a load of nonsense," she would say.

I didn't dare to contradict her, didn't dare agree.

She put her hand up in class one day.

"Yes, Holly?" said Miss Fagan.

"There are no such things as ghosts, are there, Miss Fagan?"

Miss Fagan smiled.

"Some say yes, some say no."

"But there *aren't*, are there, Miss?"

"Well, I don't believe so, Holly. I believe God sends us on our proper way once life is done."

"And there are no such things as monsters, are there? They're just things for stories, aren't they?"

"Hmm. Jesus himself encountered demons, Holly. In truth, there are things we cannot really know and understand. That is why we need the Church and prayer."

"The Church and prayer!" Holly muttered.

Miss Fagan's face darkened, a rare occurrence.

"Holly," she said.

"Sorry, Miss."

"Be careful, Holly Stroud."

"Yes, Miss Fagan."

St Lawrence's was the school of all Catholic children in that town. Vincent McAlinden was one of us. He was three years older than me. He had few friends. For a time he took Norman Dobson to his side, until Norman came into the classroom one afternoon with tears in his eyes and a cigarette burn on the back of his hand.

"Vincent?" I whispered.

"It was an accident," he said. "He didn't mean it, Dom."

Later, as we worked, tears fell to his book and made his page even messier than usual. I put my arm around him. I whispered to him to stay away from awful Vincent. By this time we'd left the room of kind Miss Fagan and were in the care of cold, strict Miss Mulvaney.

"Dominic Hall!" the teacher snapped. "What on earth do you think you're doing?"

I took my arm away.

"Sorry, Miss," I said.

"Sorry indeed," said Miss Mulvaney. "And stop that snivelling, Dobson. I can't bear a boy who snivels."

Fortunately for Norman, Vincent seemed to lose interest in him. He turned his attentions to a boy of his own age called Bernard, who lived on the far side of our estate. Bernard wore knee-length shorts and battered plimsolls and glasses with one lens blocked by grimy Elastoplast. It was said that he was even simpler than Norman, that he couldn't read, couldn't write, that even the kindness of Miss Fagan and the cruelties of Miss O'Kane had been unable to change him.

Like many children, Vincent and Bernard left the premises at dinnertime. But they did not go home like others did, to lunch on egg and chips or tomato soup. They played games with fires and knives. They dug down into the ancient pit heap nearby. Vincent forced Bernard into tunnels in the earth, seeking the entrances to the old workings below. Sometimes Bernard encountered ghosts and came out screaming. The two boys had been seen swimming naked together in the filthy Tyne. They'd been seen struggling, grunting, wrestling, groaning. We even heard that Vincent drank Bernard's blood. And it was said that they committed sins so awful that they were beyond forgiveness, sins that would consign them both to Hell for evermore.

One sun-filled day I caught sight of them. I was alone, gazing through a fence towards Simpson's Shipyard. I was lost in thoughts of Dad. I tried to imagine him crawling through darkness and fumes. Tried to pinpoint the noise of the caulking hammers hammering on steel. Tried to imagine his own hammer jumping and rattling in his hands. To imagine the showers of sparks that arose around the welders' rods, the red-hot fragments of flying metal. I saw the goggles he wore, the oily cap, the battered knee pads, battered boots, the cigarette that dangled at the corner of his mouth. I heard him wheezing, coughing, hawking, spitting. Imagined him grinning at his mates, snarling at the foremen, cursing the timekeepers, the gate controllers, the managers, the draughtsmen in their offices, the bliddy owners.

Then saw Vincent. He was kneeling in the field outside, just where it slanted down towards the river. Bernard was at his side, on all fours in the long pale grass. He was very still and his head was hanging downward like a beast's. Vincent leaned close to him, as if in tenderness, as if softly whispering something into his friend's ear. A few seconds of this, then Vincent touched Bernard's neck, and Bernard slumped into the grass and out of sight, as if he'd died. Vincent gazed down and watched. Then turned, and it was as if he knew I'd been watching. I could see him grinning even from this distance. He raised his hand and beckoned me. I wanted to run, but couldn't turn. Tried to see some movement in the place where Bernard had gone. Vincent stood up and started to wade through the grass towards me. I couldn't move. Said a rapid prayer in fright, then saw Bernard rising, and I ran, and heard Vincent laughing, and calling out, "I'm comin! I'm just behind ye, Dom! Aaaaah!"

Vincent was in the class of the dreaded Miss O'Kane. Once we had left Miss Fagan's, all of us were taken to that room each Friday morning to be tested. We walked along a stone-paved corridor and up an iron stairway to the heavy wooden half-glazed classroom door. One of the clever ones would be told to knock. Miss O'Kane's cold voice would call upon us to enter. And so we entered.

Miss O'Kane waited, sitting on her high chair. The cane of Miss O'Kane waited also, resting before her on her desk.

It was so easy. *Who made you? Why did God make you? Where is God?* These were simple things to recollect. And there was even a degree of kindness in the asking, for it was only we clever few — myself, Holly Stroud, a handful of others — who were ever called upon to respond to the complicated questions. *What were the chief sufferings of Christ? What is Hope? What does the Fifth Commandment forbid? In how many ways can we cause or share the guilt of another's sin?*

Despite that, many failed, and kept on failing. Of course it was often nervousness as much as dullness, or the expectation of failure, or an acceptance of the habit of suffering. There were those who knew perfectly well one week what was meant by a Mystery, only to have totally forgotten just a few short days later. Those who did not know their answer, or who had forgotten, were called to stand before us at the front. And it was then that the cane of Miss O'Kane was lifted from the desk.

"Yes, it is important," she would say, "to know your letters and your numbers. But it is more important to understand why it is that you were placed upon this earth, and it is essential to know what will happen when you die. Put out your hand."

One day when the sky outside was all tormented she turned with spite to Norman Dobson.

"What," she asked him, "will Christ say to the wicked?"

I and many others caught our breath. Surely Norman shouldn't be given such a question, which came from deep within the catechism and which needed such a complex answer. The school by now saw him as beyond help, or as one beyond the need of help, destined to become a labourer in the yard, or a cleaner, the lowest of the low.

But Miss O'Kane decided that day that his faith must be tested. Maybe her impatience was at a peak that day. Maybe there were troubles in her own life, a life that we children had no notion of.

"Come along, Norman Dobson!" she snapped. "What will Christ say to the wicked?"

Someone hissed the beginning of an answer. A glare from Miss O'Kane stopped that. Norman stuttered, stumbled, did not know.

"Oh, Norman," sighed Miss O'Kane. "Have you forgotten? Perhaps it is a sign that you are indeed one of those to whom God will refer on the Day of Judgement, when he says to you these words. Listen to them closely. Are you ready? 'Go away from me, with your curse upon you, to the eternal fire prepared for the Devil and his angels.' Did you listen, Norman? Did you understand?"

"Y-y . . ."

"Good boy. If you do not learn these things and live according to God's will, you will spend a lifetime building your own fire, and in death you will walk straight into it. Do you understand that?"

"Y-y . . ."

"You do not. You are too dull. God's words must be beaten into you. Now repeat them after me."

She spoke them again, phrase by phrase. He stammered the answer, phrase by phrase.

"Go away from me . . ."

"G-go away f-from me . . ."

"Well done," she said when they reached the end. "Perhaps you will be saved after all, Norman. Would you like to be saved? Good boy. Now put out your hand and we will help you in that purpose."

And Norman presented his obedient outstretched palm to her. And she raised the cane so high and brought it down so fast, and she hit Norman's hand in time to her chanting of the true response.

27

"Go away from me — *thrash* — with your curse upon you — *thrash* — to the eternal fire — *thrash* — prepared for the Devil — *thrash* — and his — *thrash* — angels!"

She put the cane of Miss O'Kane back upon the desk.

"On your deathbed," she said to Norman, "you may have reason to thank me for this day. Now go away from me."

It was known that Vincent McAlinden had never faltered and had never once been caned. It was said that he was asked exactly the same question every week.

"To whose image and likeness did God make you?"

"God made me to his own image and likeness."

"Correct, Vincent McAlinden."

CHAPTER
THREE

The McAlindens. Their ancestors fled from Cork during the Famine. They'd been cast out during the Clearances from the Western Isles. They'd been tinkers in Yorkshire, seacoalers in Durham, rag-and-boners in the Glasgow slums. They were vagabonds, wastrels, wanderers, thieves. The father was in Durham Jail for murder. Been murdered himself in the Jungle at Shields. He'd strangled a bairn of his own, chucked its body into a Pelaw cesspit. He was Mrs McAlinden's own damn brother, her own damn bliddy father. There wasn't just one dad but a clutch of them. Black-souled bliddy sinners, every single one of them. And her? Just had to look at her. Them whiskers on her cheeks, them moles, that sweat, that roll-up in the corner of the mouth. And that clutch of bairns that looked the same. The widow's peak that marked them out, the jet-black hair, the furrowed brows. Witchcraft in that family, had to be. Mebbe worse. Hey, mebbe they weren't true human at all. Mebbe some weird thing twixt man and beast.

In autumn and winter kids gathered beneath a certain street light as the night came on. Some of us were little more than toddlers, some were already in our teens. We told each other ghost tales and gave accounts of nightmares as the sun dropped down over the estate.

We shuddered as the sky darkened and reddened and true night came on. A boy called Colin Moss called us into a ring within the pool of light and began to speak.

"Now we will tell of the father McAlinden. Prepare yourselves. For the father and his dog will walk tonight."

We shivered and gasped, our breath plumed into the icy air. He looked from face to face.

We giggled, goggled, gasped and gaped.

"The McAlindens need their human flesh tonight. Is that correct?"

"That is correct," came the reply.

"Now Mrs Mac is turning on the oven."

"Click."

"Vincent Mac is sharpening the knives."

"Scrape scrape."

"Mr Mac is coming up from Hell."

"From damn and blasted bloody Hell."

"Now listen to the howling of the dogs."

"Aoooooo!"

"And listen to the gnashing of their teeth."

"Gnash gnash!"

"The father of the Macs will walk these very streets tonight."

"Tonight."

"He will wait till all bairns are asleep in bed."

"Asleep in bed."

"Whose door will he enter?

Whose stairs will he climb?

Whose bedroom will it be this night?
Which child will be taken to the oven?
Which child will be carried down to Hell?"

Colin raised his hand, extended his index finger and began to point to each of us in turn, one stab of the finger, one body to each syllable.

"They need a child to cook tonight. Will it be you? Will it be you? No — it — will — be — y-o-u!"

And, with one of us chosen, we suddenly separated and scampered below the inadequate street lights towards our doors, towards our parents, towards cups of cocoa and chairs by coal fires, towards the thrill of being in there with tingling skin and racing hearts, with the thrill of the night still seething within us, towards our desperate nightmares and our soothing dreams.

The lower wasteland, down the rocky path, between the pebble-dash and town, was left to Vincent. In the early years it had been a place for play. We dug our dens there, sledged in winter, we skipped and fought and dreamed that we were in a world far off from our homes, which were a few short footsteps away. But as we and Vincent grew, we used it warily.

He walked his dogs there, yanking at their throats with steel-and-leather chains. He squatted in holes in the dirt by smouldering fires. He wore a sheath knife at his waist. He smoked, he spat and snarled. When kids passed by he yelled that we were nancies, poofs, snobs, berks, teacher's pets and Holy bliddy Joes.

He gouged stones out of the earth and flung them at us. If we dared to face him he yelled, "Howay. Just bliddy try it, then."

One day I crossed the wasteland and heard wailing. Bernard was tied with a rope to a post. Vincent stood before him, snarling that he'd set the bliddy dogs on him if he ever dared do that again. Was he going to apologize? Was he going to bliddy apologize?

"What you lookin at?" snarled Vincent when he caught me watching. "What's it got to diy with bliddy ye?"

He laughed.

Untied the rope, set Bernard free.

"See? It's up to me exactly what I diy."

"Aye!" called Bernard in a frail and high-pitched voice. "What's it got to diy with bliddy ye?"

He giggled as Vincent put his arm around him. Bernard leaned on to him and they faced me, arm in arm, cheek to cheek.

Another day. Bernard stood against a door that leaned against a stunted hawthorn tree. He had his arms stretched wide like wings. Vincent had the sheath knife in his hand. I watched as he took aim and raised the knife, and threw, and the knife spun glittering from his hand to thud into the door six inches from Bernard's side. Vincent punched the air. Bernard punched the air as well, then spread his arms again.

"Come to see the show?" said Vincent to me.

He took the knife from the door, walked away, turned again and flung the knife without a hesitation. It thumped into the door six inches from Bernard's thigh.

32

"What about that, then, eh?" he said. "Pretty canny, eh?"

He called to Bernard, "That'll do, old son. Bring the knife and let's go off and have some fun."

Bernard twisted the knife out from the timber, went to his friend.

McAlinden hugged him tight.

"Good lad, Bernard," he said. "Good brave bliddy lad. Howay, let's gan."

They passed close by. Vincent looked me in the eye.

"Why not come alang with us?" he said.

I didn't move.

"We'll have a laugh, eh? Me and you and Bernard."

"He hasn't got the guts," squeaked Bernard. "Not to come to play with Vincent McAlinden and his pal."

Vincent winked at me. He put one arm around Bernard's shoulders and raised his other arm, as if to take me to his side.

He lowered his voice, softened it.

"Naebody would knaa, Dom," he said.

He held my gaze.

"You want to, don't you, Dom? You really want to."

He shrugged.

"Ah, well. Mebbe another time, eh?"

"He's just a chicken," said Bernard as they turned away. "Squawk squawk bliddy squawk."

Vincent tightened his arm around Bernard's throat.

"No, he's not," he snarled.

He turned back towards me. He held Bernard's head down.

"No, he's bliddy not," he said into my eyes. "This one's got something special, Bernard. Haven't you, Dom?"

I said nothing.

"And one day he'll see it," he continued. "And he'll come to me just like you did, little Bernard."

He grinned, he turned the grip into a hug, held Bernard to his side. Then turned away downhill, towards the town and river.

Days later I was in town buying bread for my mam. I was beside Dragone's coffee shop. Here came Bernard, passing by.

I grabbed his arm.

Stared into his frightened eyes.

"What do ye want?" he said. "Let me bliddy go."

"Why do you let him do it to you?" I said.

"Let who diy what?"

"You know what I mean. Why do you let him treat you like dirt?"

"What he does and what I diy is nowt to diy with bliddy ye."

"He could have killed you with that knife!"

"Oh no! Vincent could have killed his poor ickle Bernard!"

He sniggered. He pulled away, walked away.

"Squawk squawk!" he squeaked. "Squawk squawk bliddy squawk."

He turned.

"And you're jealous!" he said.

"What?"

"Aye. Cos I've got a proper pal in him and Vincent's got a proper pal in me."

I laughed at the stupid idea.

"And who've ye got, chicken?" he said. "That locked-up crazy witch's daughter! And I've got the one and only hard as nails and scary Vincent bliddy McAlinden." He pointed at me. "And I'll set him on you if you divent bliddy let me be."

He laughed.

"Mebbe you're the one he gets to kill!"

Then off he ran, uphill towards the waste.

And I walked by Vincent with Holly Stroud one day, and he was sitting on a stone, and fondling his dog.

"Dom!" he cried. "And his bonny lass!"

He jumped to his feet.

"Watch this!" he cried.

A hen must have escaped from his garden. He ran to it, lifted it up in both hands and held it squawking and frantic in the air above his head. Then crouched and slammed the bird across his knee, twisted its neck, and strangled it right there in front of us. Then held it out to us again as it jerked and shuddered in its post-death throes.

"Tek it!" he said. "Tek it home and cook it for your tea!"

He giggled.

"You're horrible, Vincent McAlinden," said Holly, looking calmly at him.

"Ah well," he answered. "Nen of us is perfect, eh?"

And he lifted the hen to his open mouth as if about to eat it feathered and raw. He went on giggling as we walked away.

"Gannin for a little shag?" he yelled.

We were seven or eight years old.

"Yes!" yelled Holly, laughing loud. "We're gannin for a little shag!"

"I'll come!" he called. "Let me come and I'll join in!"

Holly went on laughing.

"Don't leave me!" yelled Vincent. "You're me mate, Dom! And oh how I love you, lovely Holly Stroud!"

CHAPTER
FOUR

"What he really needs is a war," said Dad.

He swigged from a can of McEwan's Export.

"You can't say that," said Mam.

"Course I can. He's the kind of lad that should be battling, a lad that *needs* a war."

I had a notebook on my knees, a biro in my hand.

"War!" scoffed Mam.

"Aye, war. Ye'd be in a fine damn fettle if we hadn't fought it for ye, wouldn't ye? You'd not be writing in notebooks if me and them like me hadn't killed and died for you. Ye'd be a caulker just like me. Ye'd be a bliddy tank cleaner like me father, the lowest of the bliddy low."

Mam winked at me.

"Your father's such a hero, Dominic."

He shrugged.

"What I say is true. It's thanks to war we've been raised up. And it's thanks to lads like Vincent. He'd have been fine out there in the jungle in the heat with the terror of the bliddy Japs. I knew lads like him, and no, you wouldn't want to come across them in a pitch-black alley late at night, but out there they were worth their weight in bliddy gold."

He threw his cigarette into the fire.

"Mebbe war'll be back soon, and Vincent's time'll come."

"Let's pray not," said Mam.

"There's some that want it. There's some can't bliddy wait for it."

He swigged off the last of the Export. He held up the can to the light and twisted his face.

"It's not the same," he said. "A proper pint of beer is a thing of joy."

Mam laughed.

"Is that right?" she said.

He crunched the can in his fist.

"How we used to talk about it, out there in the stinking heat. Just wait till we get back, we used to say."

"To get a pint of beer?"

"Aye, a pint of beer. Nowt else! And I'm off to get one now."

He winked at me. He kissed Mam and stroked my hair.

He hesitated.

"One day I'll find a way to let you know what you've been rescued from," he said, then went into the dusk.

Mam asked to see my writing, turned it towards the fire's flames to see it better.

"Where do you get it from?" she said.

"Thin air."

"Ha!"

She read to the end, to the place where the flow of words met empty space.

"What happens next?" she said.

"Dunno."

"Like life."

She looked out. Large silhouetted birds flapped through the sky. We heard the voice of Mrs Stroud coming from across the street.

What is life to me without thee?

What is life if thou art dead?

"Kathleen Ferrier," Mam said. "Poor soul."

"Poor soul?"

"To keep herself locked away like that . . ."

"Why does she lock herself away like that?"

"Maybe there's no answer. Maybe she's just happier like that. And Kathleen Ferrier herself was a poor soul, of course."

She sang again, so beautiful.

"Died far too young," Mam said.

"Did she?"

"Aye. And where's the sense in that?"

What is life, life without thee?

What is life if thou art dead?

"I know! Maybe I should take your story for Mrs Charlton to read. Would you like that? I'm sure *she* would."

Mrs Charlton. She lived over the hill in Low Fell. Once a week Mam cleaned for her. She brought back tales of a garden with apple and oak trees in it, of dark furniture, softly lit rooms, of high ceilings, of walls filled with books, two cars in the driveway.

"Would you like that?" she said again.

"Dunno."

"Dunno! Dunno! What a lad for your dunnos!"

Mrs Charlton sent us gifts: packets of teas with names like Darjeeling and Lapsang Souchong; a tin of green olives that we nibbled suspiciously and spat straight out; a cracked green Oriental table lamp with a shade showing horsemen playing polo against a landscape of castles and domes and minarets.

Each year she sent a birthday card.

Happy Birthday, Dominic. To the lovely son of a lovely mother. Work hard, be good, I'm sure you will go far.

"Well, I do know," said Mam. "She'd love it and so would you. Get it finished and I'll take it to her."

"OK."

I continued writing. I led the words into the empty space. This was new for me, to write for an unseen audience. I wrote about two boys who climb through the window of a huge abandoned house. They find a chest of treasure in the attic. They wonder if they can keep it. Maybe we should give it to the police, they say. And if no one claims it, it will be ours. They tell nobody. They turn the treasure into cash and buy beautiful houses for their families. But it's just a dream, a trick of the mind. The two boys wake in their separate beds in their tiny houses, penniless as ever.

I marked the last full stop with disappointment.

I wanted to write a savage sweaty violent tale, the kind of tale that Vincent McAlinden might have made if he was interested in writing. But I could not do it. Because I was me? Because I wasn't up to it? Too nice, too good? Because the tale was to go to a woman I'd never seen, to a house in Low Fell?

Mam took it from me.

"So clever," she murmured.

She gazed out at the sky and sang along.

Blow the wind southerly, southerly, southerly,
Blow the wind south o'er the bonny blue sea.

"Thank God there's no war to send you to," she said. "And thank God you won't be going down into the yard."

She folded the story carefully, slid it into an envelope.

"Who knows what you'll come to do," she sighed.

She sang again.

Blow bonny breeze, my lover to me.

CHAPTER
FIVE

"She says it's the angels," said Holly.

"Angels?"

"She hears them, the sound of them singing within everything. She tries to sing with them."

We stood listening. A light breeze blew dust along the pavements, over our feet.

"Do you believe her?" I said.

"She says sometimes they're far away and sometimes they're very close. Sometimes they're right here, with us, but we can't see."

Today there were no words, just a weird wailing.

"She says one day we'll all be drawn to the heart of it and we will see the glory."

"The glory?"

"Yes. She says the glory of Heaven is very close to us. She says the angels wish to share it with us."

"Do you believe her?"

"She seems happy, Dom. She says she hears the music of the spheres, too. The music made by the stars and planets as they turn. She sometimes asks me to listen with her, but I can hear nothing."

"Why won't she come out?"

"She says someone has to be still, and to pay attention."

I listened. Engines, birdsong, breeze.

"But sometimes I think she's just dead scared," said Holly.

CHAPTER
SIX

I did go to the yard one Christmas, to the heart of all the sound, to see what I'd been rescued from. There was a party for the draughtsmen's kids. As a single child, Holly could take a guest and she chose me.

She brought the invitation across the street: a gilt-rimmed card with a picture of three sailing ships upon it.

"My dad got the secretary to type your name on it, Dom! Look!"

The Management and Draughtsmen of Simpson's Shipyard wish to invite Master Dominic Hall to celebrate Christmas in the Drawing Office with them.

"Master!" said Mam. "How exciting! Oh, doesn't it look grand."

"You'll come?" said Holly.

"Of course he will!" said Mam.

She put it at the centre of the mantelpiece.

Dad spat and cursed when he came home and saw it.

"The Management and Draughtsmen!" he sneered.

"Don't," said Mam.

"Don't what? You've said he'll go?"

"Of course he'll go."

"Of course he'll go. Of course he'll swan about with the bosses and their bliddy bairns."

"It's Christmas, Francis."

"An where's the bliddy parties for the caulkers' and the cleaners' bairns? What about the parties in the double bottoms and the bliddy tanks?"

She clicked her tongue. She put the card back above the fire.

"Take no notice, son," Mam said. "I'm very pleased for you."

Dad muttered, cursed under his breath.

"Christmas in the bliddy drawing office."

Mam bought me a new white shirt and tie and a cardigan from the Co-op. She took me to Laurie's Barbers in the town square for a haircut. On the day of the party, Dad woke me up. He'd calmed down by now.

"Have a good time," he said. "But divent get conned by them. Remember who you are and where you're from and remember your own dad's outside crawling in the vessel's guts."

He grinned and kissed my brow.

"Look out for me," he said. "I'll be looking out for you."

And he hurried out and I heard his running footsteps in the street.

Bill and Holly came for me at lunchtime. She had a silver ribbon in her hair. Bill was in a tweed overcoat and trilby. We walked downhill, past the Christmas tree in the square, the turkeys in the window of Dodds Butchers, the piles of apples and tangerines in

Bamling's fruit shop. We waved to people we knew. We headed lower, across the footbridge over the railway line, towards the scents of the river, the din of the factories and yards, to the jibs of the great cranes that stood above the river. There were other fathers with other children, all washed and brushed like us. The pavements turned to cobblestones. We approached the high shipyard gates, the great arch above them bearing the name, SIMPSON'S, upon it. Beyond it were dark brick buildings, and then the cranes and the huge dark wall of a ship.

The gatekeeper in his boiler suit came out of a cabin to us.

"What do you think *you're* diyin here?" he asked. "Get yersels back yem!"

The children giggled.

"Ye know what we're here for, Mr Martin," called some keen-eyed girl.

"What's that, then?"

"The *party*, Mr Martin!"

"Oh. It's for the party, is it? Then ye'd better get yerselves inside."

He slid great bolts and locks and pulled the gates. They groaned and clanked and screeched as they opened.

"Howay in," said Mr Martin. "Mek yerselves at yem."

We started going through.

"Tek care, though," he said. "There's some lads in here that'll gobble ye up if ye don't watch oot!"

Bill led us all up ornate metal steps. We came to a wooden door with AUTHORIZED PERSONNEL ONLY printed on it.

"Ready?" said Bill.

"Yes," we said.

"Then come inside."

We went through the door. The others filed in behind us. We entered a huge room with wide windows that overlooked the yard. The men grinned as the kids gasped: the half-built ship outside, so huge, so dark, so close. It blotted out the river, obscured the opposite bank, filled half the sky, filled half the world.

There were decorations strung across the ceiling, a bright-lit Christmas tree in a corner. There were framed drawings on the walls: splendid finished ships that now sailed the seven seas, some of them a century or more old. There were photographs of famous launches.

The draughtsmen unrolled great sheets of paper for us on massive room-long tables. They bore drawings: ships and bits of ships; hulls and decks and funnels and anchors and chains and gantries.

Bill stood with us and directed us to see.

"See?" he said. "Everything must be drawn before it can be made. We draw every single step in every single stairway. Every water pipe, each single electric switch. We show where every single rivet goes."

Holly traced the lines with her fingertips. Everything was so clear, so accurate.

"Proper art," said Holly.

Bill smiled.

"Ah, no," he said. "We're copiers. We draw the plans but we're just followers of other plans. We draw the things we're told to draw."

He laughed.

"We draw bits and pieces, fragments. We make them exactly right. No room for any imagination."

He pointed through the window.

"And the fragments turn to steel and men turn steel to ships."

We all looked out at the wondrous work.

"And if we all do it right," he said, "the ship goes out on to the sea and doesn't sink. And then we move on to another ship."

The drawings were rolled up again. Sandwiches and cakes and lemonade and orange squash were brought into the room by waitresses in black-and-white and laid out on the tables.

I chewed a ham sandwich. It was crustless and triangular. I drank a glass of orange squash.

"Does somebody," said Holly, "have the whole ship in their head? Every bit of it, right from the start, everything in order?"

"I guess they must have an idea of it," said Bill. "Not all the detail, maybe. But it must be like they have a vision."

We looked out at the ship again.

"So that great metal thing outside started as something like a dream. And look at the damn thing now. Pretty solid, eh?"

We went on eating, drinking.

"Mebbe the dreamers are the true artists of this place," said Bill.

I kept looking out. Dark-dressed men lugged machinery and tools through the December winds, they clambered across frail-looking scaffolding, they crawled into gaping holes in the ship's side, they bent to the decks like they were praying. I went closer to the window.

"Looking for your dad?" said Bill.

"Aye."

"He'll be one of them with sparks flying all around him," he said.

But there were so many of them like that, and so many of them walking, crawling, squirming, praying. Was *that* him? Or that? Or *that?* They were like ghosts, like devils, like a living part of the ship itself.

"No?" said Bill.

I shook my head.

"Mebbe he's inside it," said Bill.

A fat man in a black suit entered. He spoke into a microphone. He was so very proud of us all, he said.

He spoke directly to the children.

"Are you proud of the work of your fathers, boys and girls?" he asked.

"Yes!" was called.

"Yes indeed. Where would we be without them?" He snorted. "Without these fine artists, that ship out there could sink! And we don't want that, do we, children?"

"No! No!"

"No indeed!"

He told us he was thankful for the achievements of the past. So hopeful for the days that were to come. So delighted to see us here, the citizens and shipbuilders of the future.

He pointed out towards the ship.

"Look at that," he said. "One of the great achievements of mankind. And it is made here, on this river, by us."

He raised a glass of champagne towards the ship, then towards the draughtsmen, then towards the children.

"You should be very proud," he said to us. "Will you be the ones who will help us build the ships of the future?"

"Yes!" some called.

Even with the windows closed, the din and clatter from outside were immense. Dark bodies in dark clothes in the deepening dusk. Soon they blended with the colour of the ship. Long fluorescent lights were turned on in the drawing office and spotlights began to shine outside.

The ship became truly beautiful then, truly like a vision. The sparks from welding rods and caulking hammers were like fireworks. Strings of light dangled as on Christmas trees. Tiny jets of acetylene burned bright blue. Light shone out from trapdoors and portholes and holes and cracks and gaps. The sky above became deep red, and black smoke from braziers on the deck swirled across it. The dark figures climbed, clambered, slithered, emerged and disappeared.

We all got a selection box with chocolates inside. I was given a biro with four colours in it. Holly's gift was a little set of drawing pencils.

We were told we had to leave before the workers were let out, or we'd be crushed in the stampede. We went back through the gates and walked uphill again. After five minutes we heard the grinding of the gates, and the hectic clatter of running men in heavy boots on cobblestones.

"Run!" we giggled. "Run!"

"Did it gan well?" said Dad when he returned home.

He stood before the fire, warming his legs and backside at it.

"Yes," I said.

"They looked after ye aal reet?"

"Yes." I showed him the biro. "They gave me this."

"I seen you," he said. "I seen you lookin out. I even waved at you."

I clicked the biro.

"Did ye see me?" he said.

"I don't think so," I said.

I wrote a green word, a black word, a blue word, a red.

The lights flickered on our little Christmas tree.

"You divent bliddy think so?"

"No. I couldn't make you out, Dad."

He spat into the flames, lit a cigarette, cracked a can of Export. He gulped as he drank. His throat crackled as he sucked smoke down into his lungs.

"Dom said it looked beautiful, love," said Mam.

"Did he now?"

He paused while he drank and smoked, then he came at me. He dragged me from the sofa, across the room, pushed me down on to the floor beside the fire.

"Kneel!" he snarled. "Stare down into them bliddy flames."

He pushed my face close to the heat. With his free hand he lifted the steel poker and hammered it against the metal grate, faster faster, louder louder.

"Francis," said Mam, but he took no notice.

"Listen to the thunder, boy," he roared.

I smelt the drink and tobacco on his breath, felt his rough hand on my neck.

"Listen to the din and breathe the bliddy fumes!" he yelled.

I could do nothing but what I was told.

"This is what's called being cruel to be kind," he shouted. "This is what I bliddy do!"

The heat of the fire began to scorch me.

"How do you like it?" he said. "How do you bliddy like it?"

"I don't!" I said.

"Do you think it's beautiful now, then?"

"No, Dad! No!"

"Bliddy no!"

He released me and I knelt up.

"I'm a man," he said, "who has taken great sea journeys and who has fought for freedom and who has come home to marry and to have a boy and to work for the good of the country and to believe in the future and now I crawl around ships in hail and sleet and I hammer at seams of steel inch by bliddy inch. I do it every day and I will do it every day until I'm done."

I backed away to Mam's side.

He showed me the scars on his hands, the rips in his clothes.

"This is what I diy!" he said. "Never forget it and never forget where you come from."

"He won't, Francis. Will you, son? No matter how far you go."

"How far he'll go! Mebbe he won't go anywhere!"

"He will. We have come far already, he will go further."

Dad cursed, grimaced.

"But he has me in him. And he has his wretched grandfather in him. And all the mes and all the bliddy grandfathers."

"Don't fret so, Francis. He's clever. And there's so many opportunities . . ."

"Opportunities for them like us to fall right back to where we started. There's them that want it. They need us to build their ships and dig their coal and lick their boots and arses, but when things get tough they won't give a thought to kickin us all back down again."

He threw his cigarette into the flames. He lit another.

"I'm sorry, son," he muttered.

And he left us for the Iona.

CHAPTER
SEVEN

I got a knife that Christmas. A copy of a bowie knife, made on the sly by one of Dad's mates in the yard. Wooden handle, ship-steel blade. Lots of the welders' and caulkers' sons had ordered them.

Dad laughed.

"Divent let the bosses know," he said. "They'd have our guts for garters."

I wore it in its leather sheath on my belt. Dad said it looked great, but Mam said it made me look the opposite of me. She bought me books and pens.

There was a card from Mrs Charlton. A note inside praised my style and my cleverness.

How proud your parents must be, she wrote. *And how proud I am, too. Your story has pride of place on our library table, Dominic.*

There was a folded pound note with it.

I spent it on pop and crisps and sweets and a single cigarette and match from Dixon's newsagent's. I held the knife in my hand as I smoked the cigarette in a narrow alley beneath the town square. I dreamed of being hard as Vincent McAlinden, of caring about nothing, and I coughed, gagged and spewed the crisps and sweets on to the concrete at my feet.

CHAPTER
EIGHT

I touched Holly's tongue with mine. We were in Bill Stroud's allotment, one of many beyond the upper limits of the estate, before the sloping playing fields began.

Holly had paint and paper spread out on an ancient table by the greenhouse. The table's cracked timber was hot in the sun. She was drawing me, painting me.

"Keep still," she said.

Brilliant red tomatoes hung from bright green stems and leaves just inside the greenhouse glass.

The sun glared on the glass, on us.

Bill leaned down over an open cold frame, picked tiny weeds from among the cabbages growing in there.

"Now this is proper art," he said. "The work of skill and the imagination. A blending of the seen and never-been-seen-before."

He turned his face to the sun.

"And this is the life," he said.

Skylarks singing, chickens clucking, kids yelling on the playing fields. The air was filled with the scents of earth, with the talk and laughter of the men in other allotments, with the endless engine din.

Holly gave me sharp teeth and claws, a hunched and lumpen body. She dressed me in a long black coat. In some of her pictures I filled the space, in others I was a distant dark shape in a broad green landscape. The work was lifelike, dream-like.

"Keep still," she said.

"What's the point, when you make me nowt like me?"

Bill laughed without turning to us.

"She draws the inner you!" he said. "She draws an ideal you."

I left my bench. I dug in the earth with my knife. I stabbed a beetle, sliced a worm. I thought of going to play football with the lads. Sometimes these people tired me. I was just a kid. I wanted to run free with other kids, to yell, to fight. I wanted to fling the knife at something.

Holly drew on. Bill had been teaching her since she was a baby, guiding her hands and fingers across the pages. Now she drew fluently, gracefully. Things she saw merged with things she dreamed, things she imagined.

"She draws the beast within!" said Bill. "And the beast needs to be watered."

He opened a bottle of lemonade and we all glugged from it. We wiped away the droplets from our lips and chins.

"Hungry?" said Bill.

"Aye," we said.

"Then go and plunder those fruits in there."

He turned back to his weeds.

We went into the greenhouse glare and heat. I could hardly breathe at first. Wasps and flies droned and rattled at the apex of the glass. Tall plants and brilliant fruit crowded against the walls and us. We reached into the plants, twisted warm tomatoes from their stems, weighed them in our fingers, lifted them, bit into them. I halved one with my knife, the sharp blade sliding smoothly through the skin and flesh. I gave her one half, bit into the other. So delicious. Juice and seeds dribbled from my lips. I swiped them with my fist, bit again, picked again, cut again, bit again. We laughed at the mess on each other's face. Suddenly we both leaned forward to lick each other's chin and our tongues touched. We stepped back, caught our breath, stunned by the sudden soft electrifying roughness there.

We turned our eyes away from each other. I closed them for an instant to retain the taste of her.

Then a knocking on the glass. Bill beckoning: come quick!

We hurried out.

"There!" he said.

Jack Law, striding on the footpath that ran alongside the allotments. Jack Law, heading towards the hills that were said to be his home. He moved swiftly, feet padding on the earth, hair bobbing in the breeze, little knapsack bouncing at his back. He moved swiftly away, on to the fields, heading upwards.

"*Jack Law?*" breathed Holly.

"Jack Law," breathed Bill.

I often dreamed of him. Dreamed of being him, an explorer, a wanderer, without a home, with hardly anything at all.

We watched him blur into the landscape that shuddered in the light.

"Who *is* Jack Law?" said Holly.

"No one knows," said Bill. "A tramp, like all the other tramps."

"Mebbe it was the war," I said, repeating what my mother had said one day.

"Aye. Mebbe he simply couldn't settle after it."

Holly drew him as he disappeared.

Bill found the keys and closed the greenhouse door.

We walked to the allotment gate.

"He's a good man, so they say," said Bill. "He'll do no harm to anyone, they say."

I was already beginning to write him in my mind.

Today we saw the silent tramp, Jack Law.

CHAPTER
NINE

Jack Law. He'd been with us always, from the days I first remember. He lived nowhere, or nowhere that anyone seemed to know. Somewhere high up, it was said. Somewhere beyond the fields over the brow of the hill. Somewhere distant from rivers and ships and the din of engines and the stench of bones. Some said that he had no single resting place, that he slept whenever darkness fell, in whichever place he found himself. He was the fair-haired man in black with the rucksack on his back who seemed to be forever walking walking walking. Sometimes we'd see him striding uphill on weekend afternoons as we played football on the fields. We'd see him crossing the town square with a bag of bruised apples or broken biscuits in his hand. Only once did I ever see him sitting motionless, when I looked into the window of Dragone's coffee shop and saw him at a table, gazing down at the mug of Horlicks between his hands.

My mother said he was a figure to be pitied.

Damaged goods, said Dad, twisting a finger at his temple to suggest Jack Law was mad.

There were rumours that he had a sister in Canada who sent a little money for him each year. There were tales that he'd once started training to be a priest but the Church took a dislike to him and cast him out. Some said he had been wild forever, that he'd been thrown out as an infant, that he'd grown like an animal, without family or home, in the fields and woods of County Durham. They said that his body had grown but his mind had not. Some kids said that he'd had his tongue torn out in the war, that he'd seen sights so dreadful that he never dared speak of anything again. Some said that the only creatures he could communicate with were animals. They said he'd been seen sleeping in farm fields with cattle, whispering into the ears of ponies, singing with the birds. Once I heard a friend of my mother's say that he must have chosen silence, that he lived in an attempt to be close to the earth and close to God, that he was some kind of saint.

No children feared him. The dreams we had of him were all benign.

Once, when I was small, Mam opened our door and there he was. He did not speak, he would not come inside. He stood waiting there as my mam prepared him a bottle of cold tea, a packet of cheese sandwiches. He must have known that I was just inside, watching from the foot of the stairs, but he would not raise his head, would not meet my eye. I saw the layer of dirt on his elegant hands and elegant face, the grass stains on his knees, the blue eyes shining, the thick fair beard, the waving, slightly matted hair. I saw that he was a handsome man. I wanted to go to him and ask something, anything, get him to tell me something of himself. I wanted to see his tongue and to hear what it said when it moved. I wanted to address him, to meet his eye and to explore the mystery of what was within him. But, like Jack Law, I dared not speak, dared not move. He was like a statue, framed by the doorway with his head bowed, like the statues we had in church, and maybe I was too. I stayed in the shadow of the little hallway while the sun between the houses poured down upon him. Mam came with the tea and sandwiches, and even then he did not look up. He bowed slightly, turned away and headed upwards through the estate.

"There but for the grace of God," she murmured as he disappeared.

Jack seemed so beautiful to me. Sometimes on dull afternoons in school, bored by trigonometry or stories of ancient saints, or trying to turn my thoughts from tales of Hell, I'd close my eyes and see him wandering through the town as if he wandered through myself. That's the way to live, I'd think, to be footloose and free, to have nothing, to be Jack Law.

CHAPTER
TEN

We were in the allotment again when we saw the circus. It appeared like something in a dream, a line of coloured trucks and horse-drawn carriages and caravans making their way across the playing fields, shimmering in the sunlight. We heard the distant drone of engines, the creak of gears, the whinnying of horses. The convoy halted in an untidy circle on the grass. We held our hands as shields against the sun. We narrowed our eyes and strained to see. People spilled out from the carriages. Dogs and ponies and children began to run across the open spaces. And then the music started, familiar, hackneyed, unmistakable, wavering in the breeze on its way downhill to us.

"A blooming circus," said Bill. "How did that get here?"

It only stayed a day or two. It was maybe during the summer holiday, maybe some half-term. We walked to it on a breezy day, a little bunch of kids of all ages from the estate. Mothers came with us. Other kids, other families walked across the great green spaces from other estates and from streets of terraced houses and Tyneside flats to gather at the red tent. There was a little zoo of beasts: goats and a llama and a group of tiny, gorgeously maned white ponies. And a pair of peacocks, and a green parrot in a silver cage that called out, "Hurry along! No time to waste." I remember the feel of fur against my fingers as I reached into the little pens and cages, the feel of hot breath across my wrist, the smell of beast and dung and straw. Inside, the tent was like the night — tiny holes in the fabric letting in light like a million scattered stars. It must have been a sad and run-down thing but it seemed a thing of power, transporting us into an astonishing night while an ordinary afternoon passed by in our ordinary town outside.

I sat with Holly on the hard bench. Tumblers performed. Dogs leapt through hoops of fire. A girl who seemed little older than Holly climbed a rope high towards the apex and danced above us in the air. Clowns sprayed us with water from the flowers on their lapels. The lovely ponies trotted round and round the ring under the guidance of a girl with broken feathers in her hair. A strongman in black trunks and white vest posed before us to show the mightiness of his biceps and thighs and chest, then lifted rocks and dumbbells and thumped himself with metal bars and allowed circus workers to jump up and down on boards laid across his chest. Rudolfo, I think he was called, for I remember a woman named Mrs Thompson saying afterwards, Yes, he was indeed quite rude.

The tightrope walker came on last. His rope was strung between two poles. He danced into the ring. He had a sky-blue cloak on his back. He too roamed the ring to show himself to everyone.

He called out to us in an accent none of us suspected could exist in our world.

"I am Gabrielli. I dare to do what no other dares to do. I dare to walk with nothing beneath, just empty space and then the hard and deadly earth." He pointed up to the rope. "Do you believe I can do this thing, that I can walk from this point to this point and not fall?"

"Yes," Holly whispered. "Of course you can!" She grinned. "I bet he pretends he can't. I bet he seems about to fall. I bet he makes it to the end."

"Yes," I whispered too, but with less belief. I stared up at the narrow cord across the emptiness. How could a man do such a thing?

"Can I?" Gabrielli called again. "I can't hear you!"

"Yes! Yes!" the young ones yelled.

"Yes," called Holly. "Yes, you can!"

Gabrielli calmed down.

"That is good," he told us. "For if you truly believe in me, children, then I will not fall."

He threw his cloak into the gathering silence. He climbed up to his rope. A spotlight shone upon him and cast his silhouette on to the cloth above. An assistant stretched up to hand him a long balancing pole. He took the pole, weighed it between his hands, slipped them across it so that it was balanced, held it horizontally across himself, breathed deeply and stepped out.

There were screams and cheers from the little ones. Adult voices hushed them.

And so he walked, and yes, there was a moment when he swayed, when the rope seemed to lurch beneath him, when he leaned right over, when he truly seemed to be right on the point of tottering, but he corrected himself, and he didn't fall.

We cheered so loudly. He grinned in joy and triumph and relief. He posed for us with his chest held out.

"Thank you, children!" he called. "You kept me safe. Now keep me safe again. Keep me on my tightrope."

And off he set again, and then again, and then again. The tent was small. It seemed that we could almost reach out to touch him, that we could almost guide him with our hands across the spaces above us. But we held him there with our breath, with our hope, with our faith. He walked, he teetered, he smiled. He didn't fall.

And he came to earth at last, leaping the final inches to the circus ring. He gathered up his cloak of sky.

"Thank you," he said again.

He waved. And I was certain that he looked directly at Holly Stroud and me as he gave us thanks again.

"Without you, children," he said, "I am as nothing."

Then went from sight into the darkness beyond the circus curtains, and the top-hatted ringmaster came in. There was a llama at his side. He held his arm around its peculiar neck as he spoke to us.

"Did you enjoy our show?" he called.

"Yes! Yes!"

"So who wants to be a strongman, who wants to be a trapeze girl, who wants to be a clown, a tightrope walker?"

"Me! Me! Me!" was yelled by many voices.

He held his ear to the llama's lips.

"Not you, you silly," he said. "It's only people who could do such things."

"Me!" was yelled again.

"Me," was whispered by Holly Stroud.

We went out into the shining day. Our eyes stung as they adjusted to the light.

"We could do that, Dominic," Holly told me as we headed back towards the estate. "We could be brilliant tightrope walkers."

She stepped across the earth as if it were nothing but a half-inch of rope across the void. She teetered, laughed, straightened again.

"Couldn't we?" she said. "We're light, we're strong, we're young."

I thought it was a joke, but next morning she was at our door with a rolled-up washing line in her hands.

"I've been dreaming about it all night, Dominic!" she said.

CHAPTER
ELEVEN

The rope was useless. Too soft, too weak, too flexible. We couldn't get it tight enough. We tied it to the drainpipe at the corner of the house, the other end to the drainpipe on the outhouse, a distance of four feet or so, two feet or so off the ground. But it sagged, sank. No way it could take the weight of one of us. So we tried again. We doubled the rope and tripled it and twisted it and hauled on it with all our might before we tied it. A little better, still no good. Holly fell, I fell.

Someone called, "They're playing monkeys!"

A clutch of kids had gathered at the gate.

Holly bowed to them. She shinned up the drainpipe and stood holding it with one hand. Slid one foot across the rope, then another, tried to stand up straight with her arms held wide, fell, turned the fall into a leap and thumped down on to the concrete.

Applause from outside.

She stepped on to the rope again and fell again.

Mam came to the back door with her arms folded.

"Gabrielli mebbe had a trainer," she said. "Have you thought about that?"

"Yes," said Holly. "But I don't think there are many tightrope-walking trainers in these parts."

"Indeed not," said Mam. "But it looks to me that you should be using two ropes, one to walk on, one to hang on to."

I looked at her.

"I'm not as daft as I might look. I'm quite a dancer, for instance. Ask your father. I know something about balance."

We took her advice and tried again.

We tied the first rope again, just a couple of feet above the ground. Then we twisted together another rope and tied it from the end of the outhouse gutter to the drainpipe on the house wall. Mam got a stool from the house. Holly stood on it, reached up to the high rope and stepped on to the other. Both ropes jerked and swayed, but she stayed there, and they calmed, and she began edging sideways towards the outhouse, sliding her hands over the high rope, stepping foot over foot on the low one.

She turned and went back to where she'd started from. Now she stilled herself, put one foot in front of the rope, flexed her legs gently, opened her hands so that they were hardly touching the top rope. Then dared to take both hands away and turned her fall into a leap of joy. She beamed and clapped her hands.

"Just for the teeniest tiniest second, I knew what it must feel like! Go on, Dominic."

So up I reached for the high rope, stepped on to the low, panicked, fell, cracked my knees. I kept on trying. Stepping up, stepping out, falling. Holly was getting the hang of it. She even achieved a two-second balance before she had to jump free.

Then Mam walked on the rope, and what she said about her balance was true. She slid easily across between the drainpipes, and on the very first crossing, she balanced just about as long as Holly had.

"Told you, didn't I?" she said. "So maybe there is a tightrope-walking trainer around here."

We went on. We talked about using a balancing pole. I weighed a six-foot-long clothes prop in my hands and could feel that it didn't have the weight for the job. It'd need to be something that pressed down upon the palms, something that felt as if it was falling itself.

And the rope. It needed to be thicker, stronger, something that felt as if it pressed upwards, against the body's downward force.

We wrapped scarves around our knees and elbows. Kept having to tighten the ropes. Began to get a deeper sense of how it might feel to stay there, to walk there, to be free of trepidation.

By the afternoon's end, blood trickled from Holly and me. Even Mam had a bloody scrape on her knee.

The kids kept coming to watch. Doreen Minto, an older girl from the far side of the ring of houses, stood with her mam beside the gate.

"What's the point of that?" shouted Mrs Minto.

"Good question," said Doreen. "What's the bliddy point of that?"

"There is," said Holly, "no bliddy point at all. And that *is* the bliddy point of it."

Doreen laughed.

"And them two are reckoned to be the brainy ones!" she said.

Then Vincent McAlinden was there, with Bernard at his side. Bernard squeaked some mockery. Vincent slapped him, and slapped him again. He watched us silently. Then went away, with his friend a footstep behind.

Finally, we dabbed our knees with cotton wool soaked with Dettol. Mam made cheese sandwiches and we sat on the concrete with our backs against the pebbledash and ate there with the late sun falling upon us, and a blackbird singing somewhere in the back garden.

Soon the working men began returning to the estate. They headed home to wives and families and dinners. Dad entered the gate. He had his jacket slung across his shoulder. His eyes were weary, his face was black, burns were spattered on his hands and wrists.

"Been to war?" he said.

"We've been tightrope walking!" said Holly.

"Have you now?"

"Me and all," said Mam. "I was the trainer."

She kissed his cheek, brushed a spot of soot from it.

Dad looked down at me.

"Tightrope walking, eh? That's a fine activity for a caulker's son."

He stepped over it.

"More like a thing to trip you up than a thing to walk upon," he said, and went into the house.

That night I dreamed there was a rope stretching from the deck of a half-built ship in the yard, over the school and the church, over the pebbledashed estate and the playing fields, a proper tightly fastened tightrope. I held a long, bending balancing pole and walked upwards step by step by tremulous step, and the larks hovered and sang loudly around my head. I saw Vincent McAlinden watching me from the wasteland below. I turned my eyes from him. I would not fall off.

CHAPTER
TWELVE

Holly was bolder than me. She turned her eyes to Vincent. She stepped many times into his wasteland. She carried easel, paints and paper.

"Are ye not scared?" he'd ask her.

"No," she'd say.

She told him she made pictures of him to show to her mam. She laughed when he said he could just go up the stairs and show himself in the flesh.

She painted him with the knife in his hand, with his dog at his feet, with Bernard at his side. She drew him all alone wreathed in smoke from his fires and with his face shining in the light of the setting sun. She drew him close up to show the dark eyes, dark hair, dark pointed widow's peak. Sometimes he looked exactly like Vincent, sometimes like a character from a story book of ancient times — a Celtic warrior, an Apache brave, a Stone Age man. Sometimes his face was sunken, brutal, ugly, old. Sometimes it was strong and young, the face of a child.

Sometimes, she said, his voice was low and guttural, sometimes softer, almost sweet.

72

He asked her why I didn't come with her. Too scared? I thought he'd hurt me? He stroked the edge of his knife blade. Was I mebbe scared he'd kill me?

"I don't think you'd kill anybody," she told him.

"There's some would not agree with you. There's some say I am bad and nowt but bad. Ye seen me kill a chicken. D'ye not think somebody that could do that could go on to kill a man?"

"No. That was showing off. And there's good in everyone."

"You think so?"

"Yes."

"Paint on."

She drew him as a tiny figure in a great wasteland. She drew the towers and bridges of a city far beyond. She drew the flocks of birds overhead. She drew the children at their skipping games and wrote the relentlessly repeated words that spiralled upwards from their mouths. *January, February, March, April, Ma-ay* . . . She drew herself with him, side by side with him against the pebbledashed estate. She drew herself at her easel painting him. She drew children who looked on in amazement to see Holly Stroud and Vincent McAlinden in such a strange formation.

She told me that he asked how she could draw and paint like this when she was so young. She answered that children were capable of great things. Did he not know that?

She said that one day Vincent came to her and asked if she'd give him a little kiss to thank him. She told him no. She gave him some of the pictures. He said he stuck them on his wall. She said he said he'd show them to his kids one day.

"If I ever have any, that is," he said.

"If you ever do," she said.

"D'you think I ever will?" he said.

"How would I know?"

He laughed.

"If I do have them," he said, "it'd be good to have them bonny, just like you."

She turned away.

"What d'ye think it'd be like?" he asked. "A bairn born of Holly Stroud and me?"

Again he came in close and asked to kiss her. She said she told him he was showing off again, and she walked away.

She took the best of the pictures to her mother's shadowed room.

"This is Vincent McAlinden," she said.

This one showed Vincent in the guise of an ancient chieftain. He wore animal skins. There were tattoos all over him. He bore a knife and an axe in his hands.

"He's a boy who lives just down the street, Mam," Holly said.

"Is he?" whispered her mam.

"He's older than me but still a boy."

Mrs Stroud angled the paper to the light.

"So," she breathed. "There are still things like that out there?"

CHAPTER
THIRTEEN

October. My last year of primary school. Vincent and Bernard came to the door. There were a dog and a handcart at the gate outside.

"Owt for the bonfire?" Vincent grunted. "Boxes, boards, broke old chairs?"

"Owt that'll burn," smirked Bernard.

Mam came to my side.

"That time of year again," she said. "Doesn't time fly by!"

"We're ganna make it the biggest one in town, Mrs Hall," said Vincent.

"Bliddy massive," said Bernard.

"And aren't you getting tall, young Vincent?"

"Aye, Mrs Hall."

"And rather handsome, too."

He grinned. He winked at me.

"You could come and help," he said.

Mam nudged me.

"Yes," she said. "Why not?"

I gave no answer. Bernard sneered, Vincent shrugged, Mam smiled.

We gave them a bag of our own kindling and a stool that had lost a leg.

"Thank ye kindly," said Vincent.

They walked away.

"You could join in," said Mam. "It might be fun."

Bernard dropped the kindling and stool into the cart, then took the handles, leaned forward, lowered his head. Vincent slapped his arse and Bernard shoved. Vincent waved and Mam waved back.

"He's not the monster of your dreams," she said. "He's growing up, like all you bairns. We have a duty to make sure that the Vincents of the world feel that they are part of us."

The bonfire on the wasteland grew. They spent weeks gathering material for it. They came to houses, they ripped branches from trees at the top of town, they got wooden boxes from Bamling's fruit shop and the Co-op and Walter Willson's. They stole wood from other bonfires, they snapped railing and fences in other parts of town. Somehow they found doors and floorboards and mattresses and a wooden bedstead and a battered armchair. They hauled them and pushed these in the handcart through the street. Vincent laid a ladder against the fire as it grew, so that he could haul the material to the top. They built neatly, carefully. They put the shapeless lumpy stuff inside, with planks and boards and branches on the outside, turning it to a tepee shape. It grew almost as high as a house. Quite an achievement, said Dad. Shows what lads like that are capable of when they have a proper job to do. I saw it was a place to play as well. One day I saw Vincent slipping into the bonfire, through a doorway made with boards.

He saw me and he laughed.

"Anybody that comes trying to nick stuff had better watch out," he said. "There'll always be one of us hid in here, waiting for the plunderers."

It was what many did, made dens inside their own bonfires, for there were always robbers and plunderers around at Guy Fawkes time, always those who wanted to make sure that their own bonfire would be the best in town. And they were children's places, hiding places, dens, places to play.

Bonfires appeared everywhere, on patches of waste ground, in back gardens, high up on the playing fields.

We looked forward to the thrill of the night itself, when we'd gather to see Vincent's bonfire burn, to see its flames and sparks raging across the waste, to see the black fumes stream across the sky, to feel the scorch of it, the thrill of it. To see the other fires burning all across Tyneside, to see the glow of fires by the sea that blended with the sky, the glow of fires beyond the hill, to see rockets screeching up into the night, the cascades of Roman candles, the whiz of Catherine wheels, to hear the snap and crack of bangers, to leap away when a jumping jack came snapping at your feet. To be with a crowd of adults and kids, all with faces shining in the light, all of them amazed, all of them excited and alive.

CHAPTER
FOURTEEN

Vincent's wasteland turned to war zone. He patrolled with a stick through his belt like a sword. He wore his sheath knife at his hip. He put warnings on the fire itself. Keep Off. Property of the McAlindens. Get Lost. Danjer of Death! He had a snarling dog on a bright steel chain. He had Bernard at his side. He sat by one of his holes in the far corner, from where he could scan it all. He had a little fire burning there. He cooked sausages on sticks, beans in billy cans, potatoes in the embers. He smoked little cigarettes, No. 6. He coughed and spat and glared at anyone who dared come near. He and Bernard took turns in the hiding place within the bonfire, ready to leap out and scare any plunderer.

It was on a Saturday afternoon, when the light was quickly falling, that the burners came. How did Vincent not see them? Perhaps he just wasn't as perceptive as he thought. Perhaps he was asleep and dreaming. Perhaps he had become complacent: surely nobody would ever truly dare to trespass against the McAlindens. Perhaps it was simply the lack of light. But why did the dog not bark? Because it was sleeping, too? But the dogs of the McAlindens had never been known to sleep, had never been known to miss a chance to slaver and howl and bark.

The intruders didn't come to steal. They simply came to burn, to set the bonfire alight days before its proper date, and to quickly disappear into the gathering night. What a lark! Just a joke. Just a way of getting a one-up on Vincent McAlinden. They must have been silent as death as they approached, as they crawled through the shadows to trickle their fuel, to empty their can, to strike a match, to slip away.

How were they to know that poor Bernard was inside?

I was in the kitchen with Mam. There was a sudden shudder in the air. There was a sudden glare above the wasteland. Flames leapt towards the sky. We didn't know what it was, but we ran, and as we ran others were running at our side. The air raged and crackled. There was the stench of blazing petrol. We found the fire roaring.

Vincent danced at the edges of the flames, screaming the name of Bernard, his only pal. A dog howled at his side. Vincent's mother stood further back, holding her arm against the heat, yelling for Vincent to retreat.

Bill Stroud phoned the fire service. Minutes later the fire engine could be heard roaring through town with its bells ringing, minutes after that here it came into the estate, and here came the firemen running, unrolling great hosepipes, then unleashing streams of water on to the flames.

Holly arrived, and we stood there useless, holding hands.

"He was in there?" she said.

"He must have been."

"I saw him just yesterday."

"Get back!" the firemen called to all of us. "Go home."

The fire became a soaked and sunken hissing smouldering thing. The firemen began carefully lifting ashes and half-burnt stuff away. We were told again to leave. This was not a thing that children should see.

"Come on," said Mam. "There's nothing we can do."

She crossed herself and turned her eyes to Heaven.

"Who'd do such a thing?"

"Kids," said Dad. "Just bliddy kids doing kids' daft bliddy stuff."

Then Vincent was beside us.

"I'll get them," he told us through his tears and snot. "I'll catch the buggers and I'll make them pay."

He ran away, ran back again.

"Is this what it'll be like in Hell?" he said. He glared at Holly: wild eyes, bared teeth, skin blotched with soot and tears. "Draw me now! Draw me now! Draw Vincent bliddy McAlinden now!"

"Oh, Vincent," she said. "Not now."

She reached out to him. He glared.

"Go back to your mam," she said.

It was then that we saw Jack Law, at the far side of the fire with the smoke swirling around him. His mouth was opening, closing, opening, closing, as if in a ceaseless stream of sounds or words.

Vincent ran through the smouldering waste to him.

"How come you're the one that's always there?" he screamed. "How come it's always you that's always lookin with your beady bliddy stupid eyes?"

He picked up a rock and raised it high as if to bring it down on Jack's head. Jack backed away, backed away. Then turned and walked, strode quickly past us. He met my eye, he opened his mouth as if to speak, and nothing came. Then was gone, and Vincent was on the earth, beating it as if it were some great enemy.

His mam stood uselessly over him.

"Nothing we can do," said Dad.

We went back into the estate, past the police cars, the fire engine, the ambulance. Here came kind Dr Molly in distress, with her doctor's bag in her hand, and then the priest, with his hand against his heart and his black cloak flapping as he ran.

CHAPTER
FIFTEEN

No one was ever found. Nobody ever confessed. There were tales of a gang of scorched and gleeful boys running across the square that dusk. There was talk that the burners were wild kids from down Wardley way. But nobody came forward. No parents gave up their children. How could they live with themselves, knowing what they'd done? How could they live with such sin on their souls? And what would await them after their own deaths?

An evil act, some said.

No, said others. Just a prank that went wrong.

But what was the name for a prank with such effects?

How bitter that winter was, how beautiful. For weeks the temperature hardly rose above zero. Snow fell, it hardened, frost formed on the snow and turned to ice, snow fell again and hardened hardened. I woke each morning to flowers of frost on the window. We scattered sand and salt on to the paths and pavements. We made thirty-yard-long slides in the schoolyard. In the estate, we carved out blocks of ice and formed igloos against the walls. We raced across the playing fields on sledges.

Bernard didn't leave us. He was there in all our minds. We prayed for him in church. We prayed for

Vincent, his friend. Vincent was rarely in his wasteland now, and when he was he had forgotten all about his name-calling and threatening. His body slumped, he kept his eyes downcast. Even the dogs became subdued. We saw an ambulance draw up at his house one day. It was to take him away to the mental hospital in Prudhoe, we heard. But Vincent screamed and fought and would not go and the ambulance drove away again.

Once, Holly and I found him in his shirtsleeves, scratching the earth with a stick. Frozen mist hung over the wasteland. Foghorns sounded far away.

He didn't turn as we approached.

"I see him," he said.

"See who?"

"Bernard. He walks out here where the fire was."

He scraped the earth, lit a cigarette.

"Do you think he does? Or d'you think his soul's at peace?"

"Vincent," I said. "Do you want to come with us?"

"Where to?"

"Dunno," I answered. "Anywhere."

He pointed into the mist, towards the blurred lights of the estate.

"There," he said. "And over there. He doesn't look at me."

I looked where he pointed. Nothing.

"I hear him comin up the stairs at night. Hear him comin in the room, see him standin there beside me bed. You think that's possible?"

"No," said Holly. "It's nothing but a troubled dream."

"You believe in what comes afterwards? In Hell?"

"That's all nonsense, Vincent," Holly said.

"Go *away* from me, with your curse upon *you*, to the eternal fire."

"It's just a tale to scare us, Vincent."

"Fire and flames and smoke for evermore. Burnin burnin bliddy burnin."

"Oh, Vincent."

He laughed bitterly.

"Oh, Vincent!" he mocked. "Oh, Vincent, come and play."

And suddenly he grabbed Holly, wrapped her in his arms, started kissing her and licking her. He got me too as I tried to separate them.

"You as well!" he snarled. "Oh, two lovely little bairns!"

I caught the scent of him, felt the stubble on his chin, the icy wetness of his lips, felt his body thrusting itself at us.

"Is this it?" he snarled. "Yes? Yes? Is this the kind of bliddy thing you want?"

Then threw us free.

"Go away, little innocents," he said. "Go away, young bairns."

That night I dreamed him coming up the stairs and through my door. The stench of fire was on him. He stood in the doorway.

"Leave the lass," he said. "Come out with me and play in Hell."

CHAPTER
SIXTEEN

We went on with our rope walking on clear days beneath astounding winter skies. Maybe the death of Bernard was a weird inspiration. We were ungainly, our ropes were inadequate, but we walked for life, we walked against death. Soft-soled shoes were best. In them, our feet could grip the rope, could hold it, making the rope less alien, less threatening, almost an extension of ourselves. We knew that at the best of times the rope and the walker and the air through which the walker walked would become one single thing.

"Each time we walk," said Holly, "we make a work of art."

She became braver, bolder, was soon leaving me far behind. Soon she could walk the whole rope without a fall, whereas I would always stagger, grab the upper rope to stabilize myself. It was failure of confidence, of faith, as much as of balance and skill. But I improved. I began to complete the walk without needing the upper rope, without a fall, and as the winter passed we knew we'd need greater challenges once spring arrived.

Tyneside became monochrome: white patches of roofs and fields and tracks, black roads, dark walls, dark river, dark distant sea. Dad told of the freezing shipyards, of men in pullovers and hats and gloves and scarves working and cursing beside fiercely burning braziers. The men slithered across the salted decks and over salted gangways. There were many accidents: falls, stumbles. There were sprains, broken legs, even a couple of fractured skulls. Donny Linn got frostbite that turned to gangrene and he lost three toes. Many got the shakes. There were extra small allowances for working in such weather. But there was much absenteeism, of course. And some days the yard was closed down — everything seized up with snow and ice, and just too bliddy cold for work. And no overtime, no more extra shifts to bulk the pay packet out. The drawing office stayed open, Bill Stroud continued to draw his bits of ship, continued to get properly paid. Dad glared across the street at him, snarled at his overcoat, his scarf, his trilby, his leather gloves.

"Why don't they just bliddy bugger off out of here?" he snapped.

Pensioners died in their homes. Chesty babies died in their cots. We found birds lying dead in frozen gardens. Cars skidded and crashed. Diesel froze in the tanks of buses. Trains didn't run. Schools were closed. Kids slid and sledged through the streets and lanes. Our skin was chafed and scorched. We knew chilblains and delight.

Holly and her dad joined CND that winter. They raged against the Russians and the USA. Atomic weapons? Hydrogen bombs? Didn't people know there was quite enough of death without the need of such stupid things? They marched for peace and disarmament in the Haymarket in Newcastle. Bill and Holly distributed campaigning leaflets. They showed mock-ups of a blasted world. Is This What You Want the World to Be? Join Now. March for Peace. Speak Out Against Bombs and War. Save the World for Your Children.

"Typical conchie crap!" grunted Dad. "We've been battling each other since time began and we'll be battling each other for ever-bliddymore."

"You can't believe that!" said Mam.

"Can't I? Mebbe war is all there ever really is. Mebbe peace is just a gap, a time to count the ammo and gather your strength before getting back for a proper kill. And this time if it happens it'll be a proper kill. This time it'll be the bliddy cataclysm!"

"So we shouldn't try to stop it?" I said.

"How? With a bunch of long-hairs and beatniks and bliddy draughtsmen and their bairns walking the streets and singing happy-clappy crap? How do they think they know better than them that's really in the know? Do what they say, and we really are wide open for the kill. Here we are! There's no defences! Come along and bomb us now! You thought of that? No, you haven't. It's not the bliddy fairies that we're dealing with. It's warmongers that know how to go to bliddy war and *want* to go to bliddy war. Now shut yourself up and do something proper with your time. And keep yourself free of the daft ideas of your bliddy Strouds."

Later he came to me more sadly, with the scent of beer on his breath.

"War's inside us, son. We might not want it, but we'll never be bliddy rid of it. I'm your dad. I got to tell you what I think is truth."

At school, Miss O'Kane stabbed her finger towards the CND badge on Holly's pullover.

"What," she said, "is that?"

"A badge, Miss O'Kane. It stands for the Campaign for Nuclear Disarmament. It is a statement against the evil in the world."

"I know what it stands for, Holly Stroud. It's not allowed."

She reached for the cane of Miss O'Kane.

Holly dared.

"You wear a badge, Miss O'Kane."

"Yes, Holly Stroud. A badge for the Legion of Mary, which is a rather different matter. Now take yours off."

Even Holly wasn't brave enough to continue to speak out against Miss O'Kane and the cane of Miss O'Kane.

She unclipped her badge, held it in her closed hand.

"Let that be a lesson to you all," said Miss O'Kane. "There is naught to be gained by following the fashionable and flawed ideas of the time. Stand up for the eternal truths. Now put your hands together and we will pray for the conversion of Russia."

She put the cane of Miss O'Kane back upon her desk.

CHAPTER
SEVENTEEN

The ice retreated. Even the kids were glad. We were sick of chilblains and chafed skin and sodden socks and wet jeans. Sick of the sniff and the cough. Sick of icy-cold sheets when you got into bed. Sick of teetering, slithering, sliding, falling. We wanted to walk and run with confidence across the earth. Wanted the sun to haul itself up from its sullen place low over the horizon, to get into the air above us and bliddy shine. Which it started to do of course. For the world turns, and keeps on turning, no matter how things might feel in the darkest of times. And carpets of ice on ponds retreated, and flowers of frost on windows faded, and pipes burst and homes were flooded, and gardens turned to muddy patches, and the whole world started to relax, to sigh.

At last, at last. It was nice when it started but . . . Ee, we'll remember this one a long time. It's just like the one in — when was it? — '47? Just a short time after the war.

We stopped hugging our own bodies and swaddling them in too many inadequate clothes. And the grass showed bright new shoots and here were the snowdrops, and even the buds on hawthorn and roses began to swell. And there were days when you could turn your face to the sun and at last feel some heat coming through all that blue emptiness from a hundred million miles away. And relentless work resumed in the yard, and the men knew the work was there and they'd be able to do an extra shift or two and they knew there'd be a packet of proper pay at the end of the week. They'd be able to feed the bairns and get a few pints in the Iona Club. The spring was coming back. Bliddy phew!

Now at school we did endless English Progress Papers and endless Maths Progress Papers. Or the brainy ones did. The school had given up on the Norman Dobsons. No way a kid like that'd get the eleven-plus. Leave him to do his scrawl and mess and keep on spelling wrong and keep on adding and subtracting wrong. And fractions! What's he going to turn out to be? A labourer in Reyrolle's, a tank cleaner in the yard. What need of learning will he have there? Enough to count his meagre wages, enough to read the team sheet on a football programme, enough to listen to and bow down before the word of God. No need for deep understanding for any of that. No outcome for him and kids like him except St Timothy's Secondary Modern. And anyway, in the end, what does God really care about the brains of Norman Dobson? Those of the simplest faith, the poor, are perhaps those that are dearest to his heart, those that will slip the most easily through that needle's eye. Maybe it was an act of charity to allow the Norman Dobsons to stay dull.

The clutch that Holly and I were in, the clutch of seven or eight or so, we were the ones brought forward to the front of the class. We were the ones that got Miss O'Kane's attention. We did comprehension and precis and we worked out how quickly a bathtub filled when a tap was running and a plug removed. We learned how to turn the word RISE into the word FALL with a single change of letter at each step. We learned the lines of kings and queens and popes. And we hated it. It was so dull dull bliddy dull. But we did it.

Bill Stroud laughed at our complaints.

"What would you like to do instead? Paint all day?"

"Yes!" said Holly.

"As would I. But I cannot. But for you, if you work hard now, and do the things that you are asked to, the world will be your oyster. You will be educated, you will have qualifications, you will be free of all impediments. You will explore your talents, and if it turns out as you wish it to, you will paint and paint to your heart's content."

"I want to be a tightrope walker, too!"

"Which you are, and which you will be." He grinned. "Have you told Miss O'Kane about such ambitions?"

"Ha!"

The spring kept coming and making us glad. And we grew, we learned, we wondered. We knew our universe was endless. We knew that there was such a thing as evolution. We knew that our bodies were as the bodies of beasts were. We knew that we were as nothing in the chasms of space and time. We had begun to suspect there was no God. I quaked before that idea, but Holly simply laughed.

"We are free!" she cried.

CHAPTER
EIGHTEEN

We'd taken the test. We were waiting for the results. I was by the outhouse. Clouds streamed across the dead-straight edge of its roof, making it seem that the whole building toppled endlessly backwards. A summer morning and the air was cold. My breath condensed around me.

I heard footsteps, and Bill and Holly Stroud were there. Bill carried a rolled-up cable in his hand.

"It's a proper tightrope, Dominic," said Holly. "Made of steel. A wire."

Bill held it out to me. It was gleaming, grey-black. The filaments that formed it were wound beautifully around each other. It was half an inch thick. Each end was formed into a loop, with a tightening ratchet at one end. I took it from him, closed my hand around it, ran my hand across it. So smooth, such weight in it.

"Isn't it beautiful?" said Holly.

"Had it made in the steel shop," said Bill. "Should be a perfect fit."

He took it from me, knelt down, told me to hold one end against the house, he held the other against the outhouse.

"Yes," he said. He showed me a pair of steel hooks. "Maybe your dad could put these in the wall for it, Dominic."

We stretched it out on the earth. We stepped along it. Felt the strength of it, the solidity of it. Then Bill lifted it, held it out between his hands, held it up across the sky. The clouds streamed and the cable seemed to sweep in the opposite direction, ready to raise Bill from the earth.

"Imagine," he said. "Some folk walk across canyons, across rivers, between buildings, with nothing but this between them and death." He laughed. "But two feet up's a decent place to start."

Dad came through the gate. He hesitated as it clanked shut behind him.

"Hello, Frank," said Bill, lowering the wire.

Dad grunted a reply.

"Thought we might ask you to do a little job," said Bill.

"Aye?" said Dad.

"Aye. If you don't mind. It's for these tightrope walkers here."

"Bliddy tightrope!" said Dad.

"Couple of hooks to put in, that's all," said Bill. "Keep 'em safe and secure while they're dancing in the sky."

Dad took the cable in his hands and touched it like I had. His scarred hands were coarse against the smooth cold manufactured steel.

"It's lovely work," he said.

"Indeed," said Bill.

Dad didn't look up.

"If I carried out a thing like this they'd have me neck."

Bill said nothing.

"There's times they check our bags and pockets at the gate."

"I know that, Frank."

"That Hector Minton spat on Solly Hull and called him a thieving bastard. Fined him two days' wages for two tins of paint. Joe Robson was chucked out for a hammer and a bag of nails."

"I know, Frank," said Bill. "I don't approve of it."

"Do you not? Where do the bliddy hooks go, then?"

Bill crouched and pointed.

"I thought about this high. I thought about just here. What do you think?"

"Aye, that sounds just right. Shall I do it now?"

"It's not urgent. You'll want your dinner maybe."

"No need for that to get in the way, Mr Stroud."

"Bill. I just thought it might be nice to update the equipment and keep these two moving forward. The holes'll need to be deep. The hooks'll need to be really secure."

"Is that right? I'll do it now."

He got a bag of tools from the outhouse. He drilled through the pebbledash with a crank drill. Tiny stones and mortar tumbled down. He drilled deep. He bent down and blew dust out from the hole, brushed its edges with his fingertips. He rolled some fibre filler to a point between his fingers then pushed it in. He forced it deep with his thumb, then with a piece of dowelling

94

that he struck with a mallet. He kept filling until the fibre was at the surface, then carefully put the point of the hook to it and turned. The hook went tight and deep. He put his finger into it and pulled.

"That's not going anywhere," he said.

Then he checked with Bill — how high? Exactly where? — and he did the other one. By now, Mam was watching from the doorway.

He swept up the fallen pebbledash with a dustpan and brush. Stood up, hands on hips, looked down at what he'd done.

"Nice work," said Bill Stroud. "It's a perfect horizontal, Frank."

Dad touched his finger to his brow.

"Thank you, Mr Stroud."

Bill opened a pack of cigarettes and held them out to Dad.

"I've got me own," said Dad.

Both men lit up, breathed their smoke into the sky, and Holly and I fixed the wire. I ratcheted it tight. We fastened the top rope as before.

"Look how straight it is," Holly murmured. "Look how beautiful it is."

"You first," I said.

Mam brought the stool. Holly stepped on to it, reached for the top rope, stepped on to the steel.

"Oh!" she gasped. "Oh, wait till you feel it under you, Dominic!"

It moved ever so slightly as she stepped along it. A slight give and then a slight recoil. It shuddered if she trembled. She closed her eyes and stood dead still. She opened them and dared take her hands from the rope above. She balanced, swayed, then dropped.

Then it was me. My turn to feel the narrow tight line below, the line that seemed to push me up as I pushed down, the line that made me feel for the first time that I might be able to do this thing.

Mam applauded us all.

"What a team!" she said. "And all for the benefit of two daft kids."

She walked the wire, of course, and showed again how fine she was, how balanced.

Bill Stroud left us then. He told Dad he'd be going to the Queen's Head tonight. Care to join him?

Dad looked away.

"Aye, mebbe," he said.

I knew he wouldn't. I knew he'd be in the Iona with his mates. He went inside to eat. Mam went with him.

Holly and I stayed till dusk, crossing and recrossing the wonderful wire. We praised each other, encouraged each other. We laughed, we smiled, we caught each other when it seemed we'd fall too hard. At times we held each other longer than we needed to. Vincent McAlinden appeared for a few moments at the gate. Holly waved, she moved a few steps towards him, she asked him if he'd like to try. He did not answer, just stared, with the red of the setting sun reflected in his eyes, then slowly turned and went away.

"It's his loss," she said.

The first stars started to appear above the estate. We lay down beneath the wire and stared at the firm black line that crossed the darkening reddening sky, the pale, hardly moving clouds, those first stars, those voids of space and time. We held each other's hand, just two plain kids from a pebbledashed estate, astonished by the wondrous place in which they'd grown.

The Mask

CHAPTER
NINETEEN

We passed. We became pupils of the English Martyrs. The Norman Dobsons of the world were culled and sent down to St Tim's.

One evening in the first week, parents gathered with their children in the hall. I was in my brand-new uniform: grey, blue, black, with golden battlements upon the blazer pocket. Mam was in a pretty floral dress. Dad was in his only suit, thick navy serge, the one he wore for funerals. His white shirt collar was tight around his throat.

The head teacher, Dr Creel, stood before us with his deputy and his heads of department lined up on either side. Some of us may not appear to be the most privileged of children, he said. We must know that. But times were changing. It was our good fortune to be young in these days of optimism and growth. We had the opportunity to turn our disadvantages into privileges. We must work hard, we must develop an inner strength, we must reshape ourselves, we must become more than we appeared to be.

"Hear, hear!" called out Bill Stroud at these words. "Hear, hear!"

Afterwards there were cups of tea and slices of Battenberg cake. Holly moved easily among groups of new children. Her father shook the teachers' hands so easily, spoke with them so easily.

My dad blushed when Creel came to him and asked him, "Which is your child, sir?"

Dad couldn't look him in the eye. He pointed to me.

"Dominic Hall," said Mam.

"Ah," said Creel. "We have heard good things. An exceptional eleven-plus paper, we were told."

He reached out and shook my hand.

His grip was firm, his skin was cold.

"Welcome to our school, Dominic Hall."

"Thank you, sir."

"You will grasp your opportunities here. I am sure of it."

"Thank you, sir."

"Look me in the eye and tell me that you will grasp your opportunities."

"Yes, sir," I said.

"Yes, sir, what?"

"Yes, sir. I will grasp my opportunities."

"Good. It is best to state these things. It helps them to come true. And what ambitions do you have, Dominic Hall?"

I did not know what to say.

"Perhaps there is some dream, some vision, burning in your heart." He laughed. "Or do you dream only of playing for Newcastle United, as so many boys of your age do?"

"I don't know, sir. Not that, sir."

"Maybe there's a secret something that you confess to no one. Or maybe there is something that is hidden even from yourself. Whatever it is, wherever it is, we'll help you to find it, and to state it, and help it to burn bright."

"Thank you, sir."

"Good lad."

He shook my hand again.

"We'll make you proud of this boy, Mr Hall, Mrs Hall," he said.

"Thank you, sir," said Mam.

An English teacher, Mr Joyce, asked did I like reading? I mumbled yes. He said that was excellent. He said that in the very first year we would be reading Conrad. Did I know him? I shook my head. One of our finest, he said. An artist in prose. "The Secret Sharer", he said. I would love it, he was sure.

"I hear that you're something of a wordsmith yourself," he said. "Is that correct?"

I looked blankly back at him.

"A whisper from your old school," he said.

He winked.

"Sometimes," he said, "we aren't even aware of our own strengths, and the effects that we have on others."

He shook Dad's hand.

"Congratulations on your son's success," he said. "A credit to the whole family, I'm sure."

"Thank you, sir," Dad muttered.

He trembled as he spoke. I knew he couldn't wait to get away.

We stood close together. There were other inward-turning trios just like us. A couple of the other trios approached. Families like us, fathers who worked in the yard with Dad, welders and caulkers and electricians. The men passed cigarettes around, held them in cupped hands, smoked, tapped the cigarettes nervously on ashtrays, sipped coffee and tea, twisted their faces at each other with the embarrassment of it all.

"I can't bliddy believe it," I heard Dad say. "A man like me, in a place like this, taalking to a man like that."

"Thanks to our bairns," said one of his friends.

"Aye," said Dad. "Our bairns."

He glanced shyly at me, as if I'd become some alien creature to him.

Holly laughed. She was with a music teacher. She started singing happily and the teacher's face was wreathed in smiles.

CHAPTER
TWENTY

The school was red brick with a tarmac yard around it, then a broad field with football pitch and running track. The teachers wore black gowns over dark suits, white shirts and ties. Several carried a black strap, which curled out from their top jacket pocket. These straps were used coldly, matter-of-factly, rather sadly. Why are you making such a noise, child? Put out your hand. How dare you look at me like that, boy? Put out your hand. Why are you not paying attention to what I say? Put out your hand.

It was another Catholic school, so yes, there were statues and crucifixes, but they were perched on shelves high up on walls, screwed to the wall above the stage used for assemblies. They were hardly ever mentioned. Prayers were said, but more brusquely than before. No lessons were drawn from them. Priests were to be seen in the corridors, and sometimes one of them led a recitation of Our Fathers, Hail Marys and Glory Bes in school assembly, but in their black clothes and their white collars, they carried an aura of loneliness, of ineffectiveness, and they seemed out of place here.

The first terms passed by quickly. I learned to become a grammar school boy. I was polite to the teachers, I worked hard. I kept my shoes polished, my hair combed, my uniform neat. I did my homework diligently. I was praised for my attitude, my application, my cleverness. Unlike many others, I avoided the strap. I went to football trials and became the school team's centre half. I went to lunchtime discos and danced to Chubby Checker. We were told that it was essential to play hard as well as to work hard, and that moral fibre must be matched to our intelligence.

I learned about the rivers and mountains of South America, about the savage rituals of the Aztec priests, how they'd cut out the still-beating hearts of sacrificial girls and boys. I learned that different metals expanded and contracted at different rates, that frozen rubber tubing could be snapped like glass, that the exposed heart of a dead frog could be made to beat again by the simple application of a weak electric current. We did elocution and we learned about articulation and pronunciation. We were told that it was fine to retain an element of our own tongue, but it would be better to reach towards an accent more suited to the world beyond these local horizons. In speaking French, however, it could be beneficial to speak in Geordie. *Say it as if you were a pupil at St Tim's*, we were told. *Say it as you would to your pals on your estate.* And we did so, and we giggled at the strange words attached to our familiar sounds. *L'eau. L'oeuf. Le ruisseau.* In class we read Conrad and the poems of Edward Thomas. We were told that Adlestrop, and *all the birds of Oxfordshire and Gloucestershire*, was beautiful. In the playground we searched D. H. Lawrence for cunt and

106

John Thomas and Lady Jane, leafed through Henry Miller for fuck and prick. In second year, we were guided into Shakespeare by Joyce. He stared hard at those who repeated the dreaded word, Shakespeare, under their breath.

"You think that Shakespeare is not for you?" he said to us. "You think he is above you? Or, dare we say it, you think you are above *him?*"

"Double, double toil and trouble," said Holly.

Joyce laughed.

"Indeed," he said. "And fire burn and cauldron bubble. Such language sings to all of us, no matter what our age."

He leaned forward, as if passing on some whispered secret.

"Shakespeare, of all the greats, speaks to us in a common tongue. Fair is foul and foul is fair. Is this a dagger which I see before me? One may smile, and smile, and be a villain. How sharper than a serpent's tooth it is to have a thankless child. To be or not to be . . ."

He paused, as many of us, half-consciously, murmured the true response.

He smiled.

"See? He is in all of us, whether we want him or not. But perhaps you simply think you are too young to be exposed to him? Then think of this. Shakespeare's Juliet was little older than our Holly Stroud. Her beloved Romeo hardly older than you boys. And think of what those star-crossed lovers knew in their young lives. Love and death, children, before they'd hardly lived at all.

And think of Macduff's poor bairns, gone almost before they came into this troubled world . . ."

He stared at us.

"You do not know the tale?" he said.

He wandered through the aisles between the desks, leaning suddenly down to us at he passed by.

"All my pretty ones? Did you say *all*? O hell-kite! *All*? What, *all* my pretty chickens and their dam *at one fell swoop*?"

The words echoed in the air and in my mind.

I scribbled as he spoke them.

O hell-kite. All my pretty chickens. One fell swoop.

Joyce saw me scribbling. He grinned.

He returned to the front.

"Words," he breathed to us all. "Words words words. Ha! Dismissed!"

That night Dad was cursing, showing me the new marks on his skin. He lamented the bliddy gatekeepers, the fuckin foremen and these soddin scalds and burns.

"Look at the fuckin state of them, Dom. I'm damaged as them ancient tortured fuckin saints. And listen to the inside, to this raspin, wheezin, rattlin, gaspin. Day after bliddy fuckin day, since I was hardly a few years more'n you. Crawlin in the filth and shadows every fuckin day God sends, there inside the bliddy ship, in confined space and dark and filth. It's like I'm the speck o' dirt in me own damn lung, crawlin and crawlin through tubes in search of the way out, and findin the way out, but knowing next day I'll be in there again, fuckin in there yet abliddygain. For what?"

"For all of us," said Mam. "And so you can pay your round at the Iona Club with your good mates. Come on, get washed, get out."

He watched me reading. He saw the book.

"Billy Waggledagger, eh?"

"Aye," I answered.

"Good?" he said.

I shrugged.

"Aye," I said.

I surprised myself by turning my eyes to him, showing the book to him.

"This is what I want to do," I said.

He grunted. "Eh?"

"Be a writer," I said. "Write books."

He laughed. He looked out at the darkening pebbledash.

"What'll you have to write about?"

I shrugged.

"You," I said, for something to say.

"Me? You'd better bliddy not!"

He laughed.

"Or, if ye do, ye'd better tone the bliddy fuckin language down."

I smiled and scribbled it.

Tone the bliddy fuckin language down.

CHAPTER
TWENTY-ONE

I smiled and smiled and was a villain. I started to feel a spite for Holly's singing, her piano playing, for her art, for her family. I cursed like my dad at the music drifting across the street. At school, despite all my supposed talents and skills, I was out of place. I was a caulker's son, a tank cleaner's grandson. Yes, there were others like me from families like mine, but there were also the sons and daughters of draughtsmen, doctors, teachers. I'd been reading Enid Blyton when Holly and her like had been reading Dickens. I'd been listening to Doris Day when she'd been playing Chopin. I'd been to the panto when she'd been watching Chekhov. I'd gone on believing in God and Heaven and Hell and Sin when the Holly Strouds had been calmly discarding the illusions as they grew. I had so much to learn, so much to throw away, and the effort to do it seemed so huge.

I changed, of course. But the boy in the mirror seemed to be turning into a brutish thing, a Vincent McAlinden thing. Hairs on my chin, hairs on my cock-and-balls. I kept pushing my fringe back, scared of finding a new widow's peak there. My muscles thickened. They wrenched me into a copy of my father. Brows thickened, darkened. Lips turned downward. A scowl often took possession of my face. We boys wore shorts as part of our uniform. The sudden growth of dense black hairs on my legs drew much laughter. For a time I was referred to as the Ape Boy and, when we learned about evolution, as the Missing Link.

I worked hard and my marks were good. We were continually tested, graded. To be top of the class must be the bright ones' constant aim. I kept on coming top, or near to top. But as I got to twelve, thirteen, I became ever more uncertain, ever more insecure. Maybe it was the alienation common to all adolescents. But how could I know that when I was in the throes of it? How can anyone know anything true of his life when he is in the throes of the life? All I knew was that I teetered, that there seemed to be a void beneath me, nothing to support me.

I wrote with care at school. I scribbled in secret notebooks at home — violent bloody outbursts of rampant nouns and verbs and blasphemies and curses.

One day Joyce said that we were to read *Macbeth*.

Holly clapped her hands and grinned at me.

"Yes, Miss Stroud?" asked Joyce.

"Eye of newt and toe of frog!" said Holly.

"Indeed!" he said. "And wool of bat and tongue of dog! My favourite of all plays. A thing of blood and guts and sorcery, and gorgeous brutal language."

He curled his lips and bared his teeth.

"In theatrical circles, this play, because of superstition, is often only referred to as . . ."

"The Scottish play," Holly interjected.

"Indeed! And this is to do with fears of doom and disaster and death! Imagine that. A name with such a force, a play with such a force. We neither shall give it its proper terrifying name. But we shall name it something else."

He stared at all the faces.

"We shall turn this into a play for *us*, as all works of art should be. Its language being Scottish is not too far distant from the tongue we use right here. Its setting in the northern wastelands is not too distant from the lands that ring us here. Its action being brutal is not too far distant from the leanings of you boys. We shall call it the Geordie play and we shall speak it in our own dear tongue. And if you do not enjoy it you may . . . what? Hang me in a bottle like a cat and shoot at me!"

In a bottle like a cat and shoot at me!

Holly spoke the lady's part. She ignored the sniggers when she said that she'd given suck and knew how tender 'twas to love the babe that milked her. She glared when I giggled with the others, even though the words were singing in me, even though I knew they'd echo and echo that night in my dreams. I giggled again when I spoke the porter's part and declared that I'd been carousing till the second cock.

She spat at me the words intended for her husband. We fail? Screw your courage to the sticking point and we'll not fail.

The sticking point and we'll not fail.

I giggled again.

"You giggle?" she spat. "You giggle when we are in the throes of killing a king!"

112

Joyce laughed.

"Be kind to him," he said. "Be kind to all the lads. They're only lads, coming up a little way behind the girls."

"Lads!" she said.

"I know. What are we to do with them? Sadly, once I was one of them myself."

He looked at the boys.

"Oh, what it is to be a lad. To wish to be good and be only seen as bad!"

He grinned.

"Who said that? Some minor poet, I fear. Maybe the lads should write the lines about the lads. In the meantime, get practising those proper lines for next time, get them tripping off the tongue. No better words to drum into the brain than those of our great bard! Goodnight, my brutal boys. Goodnight, my sweet sweet girls!"

We still went home together that afternoon, but even though she softened, and though she laughed, and though she praised the lessons of Joyce, there was venom in the lines she practised as she crossed the waste. She softly snarled and pointed to the open McAlinden door.

"O proper stuff!

This is the very painting of your fear.

This is the air-drawn dagger . . ."

Air-drawn dagger!

"Stop it," I said.

"Stop what?"

"Stop bliddy showing off or whatever it is you think you do."

"Oh, Dominic Hall, I shame to wear a heart so white."

A heart so white!

And hurried on, into her house, and left me all alone.

Alone. As the months passed by, I continued to walk the wire with her, and she was at my side, ready to catch me, urging me on. But I told myself that she was false, that she was just indulging me. I imagined her sniggering with her father about me, the clumsy caulker's son. I imagined her dreaming about the other lads, the ones who were becoming more than lads. I told myself that this had always been true. She'd spent time with me only because there'd been no other in the narrow confines of our pebbledashed estate and in the barbaric classrooms of the Miss O'Kanes. Now everything had changed, now that she was at grammar school with children of her ilk, with teachers of her ilk.

One day I snapped that I had other things to do when she came to walk the wire. I stood in the back doorway and rolled my eyes and said it was a stupid childish thing to do.

"You don't mean that," she said.

"I do."

"My God, you think it's beneath you. My God, you think it's *girly*."

I shrugged.

"Or it's just *me?*" she said.

I didn't answer.

114

"My God, you think I've stunted you and held you back."

No answer.

"That's what your dad thinks, isn't it? The silly Stroud lass, the weird woman's daughter stopping his lad from being a lad."

No answer.

"You didn't think that before. Why are you suddenly thinking what your dad wants you to think?"

"I'm not."

"You are."

"And even if I am, what's wrong with thinking like my dad?"

"We're supposed to be moving forward, Dom. We're supposed to be making our own minds up about things."

"Like *you* do?" I said.

"Aye!"

"You think exactly what your dad wants *you* to think."

"No, I don't."

"Going to bliddy plays. Doing bliddy art and bliddy CND. Spoutin fuckin stupid Shakespeare."

"That's not what he wants. It's what all of us should want."

"Is it?"

"Yes! And if you can't see that you're getting even boringer and stupider than I thought."

"Piss off, you freak!" I snapped.

"You piss off too, you boring bliddy git!"

Her mother started belting out "Hernando's Hideaway".

I know a dark secluded place . . .

"That's how *you'll* turn out!" I shouted as she turned from me. "A freak, daughter of a bliddy freak."

She just raised her hands and showed two backward-facing V-signs. She walked to her place across the street a million miles away.

I kicked the outhouse wall. Tiny stones skittered across the concrete. I kicked again. Spat and cursed and spat and cursed. Next day I slung the ship-steel knife at my hip and I went in search of Vincent McAlinden.

CHAPTER
TWENTY-TWO

He was almost a man. He'd soon be leaving school. The death of Bernard had changed him. We all said that. He'd grown quieter. He didn't threaten and scoff. The tale was that he'd become more compliant in school. It was the sadness, of course. The grief. The people of the estate had begun to look upon him with sympathy. Vincent McAlinden? He had gone through purification by fire. Tragedy had enriched him, poor lad. We told ourselves that what we hoped was true: that there was a strain of goodness in each of us, even in this troubling son of the McAlindens.

"Thank God for that," said Mam one evening.

"Aye," said Dad. "Thank God. I knaa what it is to lose mates. I knaa what it can do to you."

We looked at him.

"I went through war," he said.

Mam kissed him.

"And came out safe and sound, thank God," she said.

"As Vincent will. I always said he was just a lad. He'll grow up and find his way. God knaas I was hardly an angel meself. God knaas there's none of us that's angels."

★ ★ ★

It was as if he was expecting me that sunny Saturday morning. He stood leaning in his doorway. I didn't dare to look at him at first, but I slowed down, and hesitated on the path.

"Aye aye," he said.

He repeated it. I stopped, turned. He held an open pack of No. 6.

"Smoke?" he said.

I looked back up the street.

"Nobody'll knaa," he said.

He stepped towards me and I took one. I lit it, tried to inhale, coughed.

"Ye'll learn," he said. "Your throat gets used to it. So what ye wantin?"

"Nothing," I replied. "Nowt."

"That's easy, then."

He was taller than me and had grown leaner. His nose was thickening. He had long sideburns now, dark stubble, and the black widow's peak pointed down towards the space between his grey eyes. The endless fire burned in the house behind.

I felt so young, didn't know what to say, was about to move on.

"I was ganna walk the dog," he said.

He lowered his eyes and I saw the shyness that seemed to be in him, too.

"You could come if you like," he said.

I shrugged.

"Aye," I said. "OK."

118

He got the dog, a black, low-slung thing with bandy legs and wheezing breath. He put a chain on it. It walked between us as we moved down the path alongside the wasteland. Didn't go far. The dog was snorting, straining on its leash.

"Down, Horror!" said Vincent. "I said get down!"

He jerked on the chain. The dog snarled at him.

"It's mental, this one," he said.

Saliva drooled from its open mouth.

"What the hell," said Vincent. "I'll let it run."

He took off the leash and the dog galloped jerkily across the uneven earth. We sat on a pile of stones. Vincent smoked again, said he wouldn't offer me another one just yet. Didn't want to rip my throat apart. I saw a black boat far out on the sea, heading northwards, right on the horizon. The dog barked viciously. It snarled into a hole, then rushed down into it.

"Summat's bit the dust," laughed Vincent. "Horror! Leave it!"

The dog raged for a while, then trotted back to us, with blood on its mouth and peace in its eyes. It sat with us.

"Ye got nae dogs yourself?" said Vincent. "I love mine, the silly sods. They're like me mates."

He let the dog lick his outstretched hand.

I saw that he saw the knife at my hip.

I took it from its sheath and worked the blade into the earth, loosening the close-packed soil, prising out pebbles.

"Ye got plans?" he said.

"Eh?"

"For today. Or are ye fancy free?"

"Dunno."

He watched me for a moment.

"Want to gan shootin?"

I hesitated.

"You don't have to," he said.

"Aye," I said. "I will."

He yelled for the dog, put the chain on it again. We went back to his house. He hauled the dog through the gate, tethered it to the clothes post, went inside. I heard shouting. He came back out with an air rifle angled across his shoulder and a canvas sack hanging at his back.

"We'll gan slaughterin," he said. "Just jokin."

We set off uphill through the estate. Horror howled as we walked away.

"I should tell me parents," I said as we approached our house.

"Aye," he said. "Good idea. Don't want them worryin."

I led him through the gate, past the outhouse, towards the back garden, the back door. Mam was hanging washing on the line.

"Vincent!" she said.

"Howdo, Mrs Hall."

Her eyes were on the gun. I wanted to tell her what she'd told me, that we had to care for Vincent, had to include him in what we did.

"Don't worry, Mrs Hall," said Vincent. "We're not gannin murderin. Thought we might do some target practice on the wastelands. If ye approve of course."

Mam's shoulders slumped.

"A rifle?" she said to me.

"Air gun, Mrs Hall," said Vincent. "Wouldn't hurt a . . . But mebbe it's not the thing, eh? Mam sends her regards by the way."

She thanked him.

"Tell him it's not the thing," I wanted her to say. "Tell him you don't approve. Send the boy and the gun back down again."

Dad came to the door, in his white vest, wiping shaving cream from his face with a white towel.

"Vincent," he said.

"Aye," said Vincent. "Your lad brung us up here."

"Aye?" he asked me.

"Aye," I said.

He lit a cigarette. He eyed the gun.

"I thought we might get some rats, Mr Hall," went on Vincent. "Even some rabbits up on the fields."

"And mebbe a pigeon or two, eh?"

"Aye," said Vincent. "Food for free. Just like in the olden days."

"You'll not get me eating poor little slaughtered beasts," Mam said.

Dad grunted.

"What about the lamb that you'll be chompin on tomorrow?" he said. "What about this mornin's lovely crispy bacon?"

"That's different," she replied.

Dad reached out for the gun. He raised it, looked through the sights, pointed to the sky.

"Everybody likes a gun in their hand," he said.

"Not everybody!" snapped Mam.

She lifted away a shroud of white washing that blew across her from the washing line.

"You OK these days, Vincent?" he said.

"Aye, thanks. Gettin over things, you know."

"That's good. You'll be workin soon, eh?"

"Soon enough."

"That'll help."

"Aye, that'll help."

Dad swung the gun through the air.

"Loaded?" asked Dad.

"No," said Vincent. "D'you want a pellet in it?"

"No, son." He clicked the trigger. "Kapow!" he snapped. He clicked again. "Kapow!"

He weighed the gun between his hands.

"Nice," he said.

"It was me dad's."

"They make them good these days. Back in my time they were as dangerous to the shooter as to the thing to be shot."

He looked at me.

"You ever used one of these afore?"

I shook my head.

He passed it to me. He came close. He moved my hands so that I held the barrel with one hand, had my finger by the trigger with the other. Raised my arms so that the stock rested against my shoulder. Tilted my head so that I could look through the sights.

"How's it feel?" he murmured.

"Feels OK," I said.

"Got to be more than that. Got to feel part of you. Got to feel natural when you pull that trigger. Let the gun ease into your body. Let your body ease into the gun."

"Francis," murmured Mam.

"I was in the army, remember? I was trained. And in me young days there was a ton of these around. Nobody come to no harm."

"To no harm," she scoffed.

"It's natural," he said. "Back then, princes and kings was shooting the tigers. Film stars was blasting at elephants. Us kids on the Tyne got rabbits and rats. We got crows and magpies. A few other things. Nowt wrong with it. Normal boys' stuff, normal men's stuff."

He spoke to me again.

"In the army they said that in the real gunman there's no difference between the gunman and the gun. Not a matter of how to *do* it right, but of how to *feel* it right. And it was the ones that could feel it right become the snipers, the sharpshooters. And even in the jungle they were cold as bliddy ice."

Mam clicked her tongue.

"Such nonsense," she said. "Give the gun back, Dominic."

"If you can't watch this, then get inside," he told her. "What d'you think's going to happen, woman? We're going to start slaughtering ourselves?"

"Don't be stupid," she said.

"Don't call me stupid. Do as you're told and go inside."

She sighed. She went inside.

Dad winked at Vincent, winked at me.

"Women!" he softly said. "They don't get it."

I held the gun. I tried to imagine it being part of me. Tried to imagine being cold as ice and firing it at somebody, like the Japanese, or at Vincent McAlinden.

Kapow! I said inside myself.

"Die!" I breathed aloud.

"Try a couple of shots," said Dad. "Let's see how you get on and then we'll know how safe you'll be. OK, Vincent?"

"OK," he said.

Vincent took the sack from his back, took a box from the pack, took a pellet from the box. A little grey lead thing. He took the gun, snapped it open, placed the pellet into it, closed it again, passed it back.

"There we are," he said.

"Now keep your finger off the trigger," said Dad to me. "And point the barrel away from us. Safety first. It's not exactly lethal, but it'd take an eye out. It'd go deep into your flesh. That's right, Vincent?"

"That's right, Mr Hall."

"Now," said Dad, "what you going to shoot at?"

I looked into the little back garden.

"That half-brick there?" I said.

He came to my back. He held my arms, he raised the gun, he put his head by mine and leaned against me.

"Relax," he said. "Look at the barrel, look at the brick. Stay calm, stay still. Imagine the pellet hitting the brick."

I felt his warm breath on my cheek, smelt the tobacco on him, felt his breathing, his heart.

"Ready?" he whispered.

"Ready."

He stepped away. I squeezed the trigger, the gun recoiled, dust spurted from the earth four feet from the half-brick.

"That's OK," said Dad. "It'll come. Another one, Vincent?"

Vincent picked another pellet from the box.

"Got plenty," he said. He rattled the box. "Dozens of them, Mr Hall."

I fired again. Closer this time.

"Good lad," said Dad. "I think you'll be OK. You think he'll be OK, Vincent?"

Vincent nodded, and they grinned at each other. I imagined Dad's thoughts as they did so: he's just a lad, they're both just lads. Better a lad like Vincent McAlinden with all his faults than the weird draughtsman's daughter from across the street.

He took the gun from me.

"Can I?" he asked Vincent.

"Aye," said Vincent.

Vincent passed Dad a pellet. Dad put it into the gun. He raised the gun.

"That white pebble there," he said.

He fired, missed by inches.

"Out of practice," he said. "Do that in the jungle and it's bliddy curtains. Give us another. Just one more, eh?"

Another pellet. He put it into the gun, held the gun to his shoulder, swivelled so that the barrel pointed into the air. A crow flew over. He followed it, and I watched him, and I watched him pull the trigger, and couldn't breathe. He missed again, but the crow in its flight jerked at the sound of it, veered off in another direction. I breathed.

Dad held the rifle before his eyes, as if it were a thing of great substance, great beauty.

"Them sharpshooters," he said. "They were something. But even they were nowt compared to the bliddy Japs. Made of stone, were they. Still as death, silent as death, dead as death, for hour after bliddy hour till the moment comes. Then a single shot, a single invisible bullet winging through the trees, and one of your mates is gone. Just like that. And it's like nowt at all has happened, but he's dead and gone."

He and Vincent looked at each other again.

"You'll understand something of that, Vincent."

"Aye, Mr Hall."

Dad passed the gun back to him.

"You ever wish there was a war, Vincent?" he said.

Vincent grunted in surprise, as if he'd never thought of such a thing. He put the sack on his back. He angled the gun over his shoulder.

"Aye," he said. "Sometimes I suppose I think I do, Mr Hall."

Dad smiled. He patted me on the back.

"Gan on," he said. "Have a good day with Vincent. Mek sure to bring a rabbit or three for the pot tonight."

Holly was in her garden across the street, before her open front door. She was drawing or painting or writing. Something like that. She looked up from her work as we left the garden.

Vincent groaned.

"That one, eh?" he said. "That little lovely Holly Stroud, eh?"

He walked on.

"But keep your mind on higher things," he said.

CHAPTER
TWENTY-THREE

We went uphill, across the waste, across the fields, to the place of the abandoned pits, to the place of rabbits and rats and rumoured foxes and rumoured ghosts and ghouls. We hid ourselves behind hawthorn hedges. We lay in the long grasses. Vincent saw a single rat and shot and missed. I saw a single rabbit and shot and missed. Weird. Some days this place seemed rampant with rabbits and rats, but not today. We sat at the foot of a hill of pit waste. He'd come prepared. He had a bottle of water and a pair of pork pies in the sack. He swigged from the bottle, then passed it to me. I wiped the rim with my sleeve. He laughed, asked if I was scared I'd catch the McAlinden germ. I felt myself blush. Joking, he said. He gave me a pie: thick crust, then amber jelly surrounding the ball of meat at the centre. I ate. I drank.

He had some cigarettes, cork-tipped Park Drive this time. We smoked. I coughed.

"Just do it like you're breathing," he said. "Divent force it. Just do it natural. You'll learn."

"They kill you," I said. "That's what they're saying now."

"Your dad smokes. My dad smokes. Everybody smokes. And ye got to die of something."

I tried again. My head reeled, again he said I'd learn.

"And anyway," he said. "It's nowt but death."

We lay close together and the sun shone down.

I heard the caulker's din below, the endless tinnitus of this place.

I saw the larks so high high up, and emptiness beyond.

"You and that Holly Stroud," he said. "You done owt with her?"

"Owt?"

"You knaa what I mean."

"No," I murmured.

I thought of just standing up, hurrying home again.

"Get away from him!" said a voice inside me. "Stay with him!"

"You seen her thing?"

I whispered no.

"I would have done if I was you."

He angled the gun into the air, towards the larks, but didn't fire.

"Kapow," he softly said. "Kapow. Kapow."

We lay silent for a while. I played with the knife, slipping the blade into the turf, into the creamy soil beneath.

"She's lovely, she is," he said.

We moved on, seeking more prey. Another rat, shot at and missed. Another rabbit, shot at and missed.

And then he got a rat, which simply scampered to a halt as the pellet hit. Then I got a rabbit, from twenty yards away. I saw its skull in the sights, its twitching ears, I squeezed the trigger and the beast fell. We hurried to it.

It lay in the grass below the brilliant sun. It trembled. Still some life in it.

"Finish it," said Vincent.

But I couldn't move. I just waited for the beast to be still.

"Finish it!"

Vincent grabbed my knife. He brought it down with force into the rabbit's breast and it was motionless at last.

He put his hand on my shoulder, as if to comfort me.

"It's OK," he said.

He picked up the corpse and dropped it into a sack. "The next one'll be easier now."

He suddenly pointed.

"Another one," he said. "Quick!"

I hesitated.

"Don't bliddy think!" he whispered. "Get it done."

I didn't think, I fired, it fell.

"Good lad!" he said.

We hurried to it. Dead. Still.

"Well done," whispered Vincent at my side. "First proper kill."

I picked up the corpse. I held it between my hands. Still warm. Felt the weight of it, the way it draped itself across my fingers, gazed down at the wonder of its fur, perfection of its feet, the smudge of brilliant blood at its throat. Gazed at my trembling hands with the trickles of blood on them.

"It's nowt but a rabbit," said Vincent.

He took it from me and pushed it into the sack.

"Chop off its head and chop off its feet," he said. "Skin it and gut it and give it a wash. Into the pot with a couple of onions. Bliddy lovely."

He lit another cigarette and passed it to me.

I smoked and coughed.

He smiled, and held my shoulder again. There seemed to be tenderness in his fingers, in his voice.

He seemed to be deep in thought for a moment.

"It's nowt but death," he said. "Nowt but bodies. Knaa what I mean?"

"I dunno."

"Bodies. Blood and bones and nowt inside. Even the priests'll tell you the beasts've got no souls."

"They used to try to weigh them," I said.

"Eh?"

"They weighed bodies at the point of death. They said that when a body dies it loses a tiny bit of weight. It proves that there's a soul that leaves at death."

"Humans mebbe. Not poor little bunnies with lead slugs in 'em."

"Mebbe."

"Mebbe! D'you think Bernard had a soul that left him at his death?"

"I dunno, Vincent."

"Me neither. You ever knowed anybody that's died?"

"No."

"Me neither, not till then."

He watched me.

"Must be awful," I said.

"Aye, it is."

We were silent for a time.

"Ah well," he said. "Now kill a bliddy bird."

"Eh?"

"A bird. There's thousands of 'em."

He was right. There was an abundance of them. A hardly visible exultation of them high high above.

And so we started on them.

And unlike the rabbits and rats, the silly birds didn't seem to know that they should stay away, even as we began to kill.

A blackbird landed on a hedge nearby. Vincent raised the gun, I watched him aim and I said nothing. He fired, and the bird dropped from its perch, and there was a sudden fluttering in the hedge and around the hedge as other disturbed birds took frantically to the air, then settled again as silence and peace re-established themselves.

I hardly breathed.

"Kapow!" he whispered.

We went to the hedge. There it was, the dead thing in the grass, the pellet buried somewhere deep inside it, but no sign of the violence that had been worked upon it, as if nothing had happened at all.

"What a bliddy shot!" whispered Vincent. "Kabliddypow!"

He licked his lips. He looked along the hedge. A little flock of sparrows, a family of them maybe. The kind of thing you hardly notice until you begin to see them as something for a kill.

He quickly raised the gun and fired, but nothing fell. The birds scattered into the empty air, and then, the silly things, they came back down again.

He shrugged.

He shot again, he missed again, he shrugged again. Didn't matter. Nothing mattered.

Birds were everywhere, flying over us, fluttering across the grasses, into the hedges.

He passed the gun to me. I think I didn't think. I raised it to my shoulder as my dad had shown me to. Tilted my head and peered through the sights, at nothing first of all. Then hawthorn, grass and weeds and sky. The distant dark sea, the place where the river entered the sea. A river lined with shipyards and half-built ships. All these things in a narrow focus, all these things as targets. I swung the barrel back towards the hedges. Sparrows, maybe the same sparrows, dancing upon the foliage a mere ten yards away. One settled, sang. I calmed. I breathed. Imagined that the gun was part of me, that I was part of the gun. Thought of Japanese snipers, still as death, silent as death, dead as death.

Squeezed the trigger and the sparrow fell.

Stopped breathing and the world stopped turning.

I ceased existing until Vincent thumped me.

"Fucking brilliant!" he said.

We went again to see the new dead thing and there it was, with blood as red as my blood trickling from its throat.

"What a shot!" said Vincent McAlinden. "That shut the bugger up, eh?"

And then we started properly.

We lay in the grass, as if we were at war, as if the birds were the enemy. Vincent became younger, more playful, more enthusiastic. I became older, more careless, more deadly. We passed the gun between us, took turns at loading, firing, missing, killing. I learned the feel of the gun against me, the heft of it in my hands, the sudden snap and whiz of the pellet breaking free and fleeing through the air, the recoil of it against the shoulder, the frustration of the miss, the satisfaction of the kill.

Vincent counted. We got to five, we got to ten, we got sparrows, finches, a wood pigeon that fluttered desperately as it fell, and still the birds kept coming, coming.

"Stupid bliddy things," he said.

We crouched, one knee upon the ground and one foot forward, as I'd seen soldiers do in comics, as I'd seen them pose as toys.

We raised the gun into the air and fired at the flying birds. Much more difficult, much less success, but much more enticing. To catch a bird mid-flight! How skilled would that prove us to be!

We missed, we missed, and then I got one.

A crow, a great slow black thing with widespread wings, a large black target against the everlasting blue. I tracked it for a few seconds and then I fired. And oh the satisfaction when it simply stopped all living movement, when it tumbled through the emptiness towards the earth.

I ran to it and picked it up.

Still warm, dead still.

Vincent hugged me, cursed me, praised my skill.

"What a bliddy killer you are!" he whispered deep into my ear.

He took the gun, he fired, he missed.

And we went on, and yes we killed more birds mid-flight, to go with the ones we'd caught mid-feeding, mid-song.

No larks. They were all too far away, all too tiny, all too unlike birds at all. And though Vincent raised the gun and indeed did aim and fire upon them, I allowed myself to watch him and to say nothing, for I knew there was no way for a little grey lead pellet to reach them up there.

We grew tired as the sun began to fall.

And the joy and satisfaction of it all began to fade.

Just a few pellets left now.

"We've used hundreds!" Vincent gasped. "A few more each and then we're done."

I killed another bird. He killed two.

I loaded one of the final pellets, pointed it towards a sparsely growing hedge. A pigeon perched on a swaying branch there. I took aim. And the foliage parted, and the bird took flight and a face was looking directly back at me, a pale face, fair hair around it, mouth opening as if saying words.

"Jack Law!" I whispered.

"Jack bliddy nosy-parker Law," said Vincent.

Jack started moving forward. He held out his hands, showed the dead birds he held in both of them. He raised them up to show them to us, to show us what we'd done.

His mouth kept opening, closing, as if saying something.

He kept on coming to us.

Vincent grabbed the gun from me. He raised it towards Jack Law.

"Stay back," he said. "I've telt you before, Jack bliddy Law. Go back!"

Jack kept coming. I saw the feathers, wings, beaks, blood in his hands. I saw the horror in his eyes. I saw his mouth opening, closing.

"We wouldn't miss you, Jack Law," said Vincent. "Nobody would fuckin miss you. Nobody would even notice you were fuckin gone."

He stepped forward. He pointed the gun towards Jack's head. Jack kept coming.

"See?" said Vincent. "He's a lunatic. It's likely all a big bliddy dream for him. Stay back. Stay bliddy back!"

Jack stopped only when the gun was six inches from his eyes.

"I'll kill you, Jack," said Vincent. "A pellet through the eye and to your brain. Or what there is of brain."

I couldn't move, was as still as the two of them below the brilliant sun. I watched the two bodies, the handful of dead birds, the gun.

"You know I would," said Vincent very softly, very calm. "You of all others know I would."

A silence lasted minutes more, then Jack backed away at last, into the hedge. He turned his eyes to me before he disappeared. They widened, they were frantic for a moment.

Then he was gone.

"I should have fuckin done it," said Vincent. "Straight into the bliddy eyes. Blinded him at least if not killed him. Then there'd be nowt for him to see as well as nowt to say. What right's a lunatic like that to be here in the same world as us?"

"He's harmless," I said.

"How can you know what he thinks? How can you know what he gets up to? How can you know what he's planning when he's wandering the world alone?"

I shrugged.

"I can't," I said.

"That's right. You can't. And nor can I and nor can nobody."

He fired the final shot into the empty air.

We headed homeward.

"I sometimes want to be him," he said.

"To be Jack Law?"

"Aye. When I'm stuck in school and heading for a lifetime in the yards and he's runnin round the place in freedom. I wonder what it'd be like. Wonder what *I* would be like if I was on the loose like that. No rules. No responsibilities to nobody. You ever wonder that?"

"Aye," I said.

"Aye. You could do anything. Owt you bliddy liked. Mind you, I'd do different bliddy things to him. I'd be bliddy crazier and wilder."

"Is your dad like that?"

"That fucker? Who bliddy knows? But mebbe yes. A bliddy lunatic Jack Law, as mebbe I will be one day. Now slice the heads off?"

"Eh?"

"Off the rabbits. And the feet, and split them open and get the guts. Then skin the buggers."

"Eh?"

"Butchery, Dom. First you kill, then you get yer kill ready for the pot. Use the knife you nicked from the yard."

He took the knife. He sharpened it on a stone. He took the first rabbit and demonstrated. He sawed off the head, snapped the bones that the knife wouldn't saw through. He sliced and wrenched off the feet. Stabbed the point into the soft flesh below the breastbone, sawed up towards the throat and down towards the arse. Upended the beast and moved the blade about inside and let the innards fall. They slithered down on to the grass. I saw what must be heart and lungs among the tubes and blood and slop. He put his fingers in and scooped and tugged out what remained. Then lifted the edge of the beast's pelt and started peeling it away, exposing slick purplish flesh beneath. He tugged and eased and pulled, and it came off in a single coat, and all that remained were bones with flesh on them, smears of blood.

"Needs cleaning proper under a tap or in a stream," he said. "But that'll do for now." He passed the knife. "Now you."

I started on the second one. Cutting, sawing, slicing, trying not to gag. He instructed me. Sometimes he put his hands on mine and guided me. Blood got into my pores, under my fingernails. The knife slipped and nicked me a couple of times. Bone shards nicked me too. I held the rabbit's heart in my palm. I held a lung. I tugged away the world of life that had lain hidden since birth within this bone-protected cavity. I took away the skin. Wrenched open the corpse to the sun and the air. A lovely thing, reduced to scattered body parts, a discarded pelt, a few ounces of food, streaks of slop in the grass.

"Good lad," said Vincent. "Well done. Dominic Hall — killer, butcher. Ha!"

We put the rabbits into their sack. I cleaned the knife by stabbing it into the earth, wiping it on the grass. We moved away and cawing crows quickly fell on the stuff we'd left behind.

Vincent laughed at them.

"Savages," he said. "See how the living is fed by the dead? First the crows, then you and your folks. And you'll be got by worms in the end and the crows'll get the worms and on and on and bliddy on."

We went back down across the fields to our pebbledashed place. He put his arm across my shoulder as we came close to home.

Holly was still in her garden. She raised her eyes to us.

"She telt me I was an animal," he whispered in my ear. "I said I knaa. I telt her she was mental and she said I knaa."

"When? When she painted you?"

"Aye. Must have been."

He waved at her. She didn't move.

"It was a good day, eh?" he said, loud enough for her to hear.

"Aye."

"And we even got to thinkin about souls, which suits you, eh?"

"Aye."

"Lead slugs and souls. Ha! Souls!" He said this loud again. "Mebbe we're all just bodies, eh, despite everythin they try to tell us? Bones and blood and guts and nowt beyond. How can a thing like Jack Law have a soul? How can killers like us have a bliddy soul?"

He pulled me close

"Tek no notice," he breathed. "I'm sure you've got a soul, Dominic Hall. Mebbe not me. What d'you think?"

"Dunno."

"Dunno. Nor me. Mebbe I should weigh you, then kill you, then weigh you quick again. Or you kill me and do the same. Eh?"

I said nothing. Holly went on watching.

"We'll do it again, eh?" said Vincent. "We'll be together again, eh? Me and you, you and me."

I stood straight, looked him in the eye.

"Aye, Vincent."

"Good lad."

I took the sack of rabbits from him and went through the gate. Mam cried to see the dead. She asked me what did I think I was doing. I said they were just rabbits, it was just an air gun, I was just doing what lots of people did. And where did she think her food came from?

"What on earth is happening to you?" she asked.

"Nothing."

"Nothing! Don't you think there's enough death in the world without you adding to it?"

I said nothing.

"Bury the poor beasts. Put them deep in the flower border."

I did so.

She watched me from the door. I got a spade and buried the bodies deep. I crumbled soil on them, then shoved clods of earth on them. As I did so, I relived the thrill of the shot, the thrill of a crow tumbling from the sky. The thrill was in my flesh, my blood, in what might have been my soul.

CHAPTER
TWENTY-FOUR

Does everybody do the things that I did in my adolescence? Does everybody kill and thieve and do other things that they'd never admit to, or that they somehow manage to forget? Or is it just the wayward kids? Or the uncertain kids? Kids like me, drawn to the grace and the beauty of the Holly Strouds of the world, but also drawn to the cruelty and ugliness of the Vincent McAlindens?

Is each of us precarious? Does each of us teeter in the space between the artist and the killer in ourselves? Or do some live a whole life in innocence, and never have the suspicion that somewhere within them lies a Vincent McAlinden to entice, and to be unleashed?

I don't know. I only know of me. I accepted Vincent into my life, he accepted me into his.

It went on for months. We killed not only birds, but other living things. The rabbits and rats that were daft enough to show themselves to us. A black cat that dared to cross our path, that Vincent said was an unlucky event and so the cat deserved to die. A limping dog beside the old mine workings, an ancient mangy collarless thing. I shot this one in the head from ten yards away. We laughed. An act of mercy, I said. An act that put it out of its misery. My mother knew none of these things, of course. I got none of the bodies ready for the pot. I brought home no more murdered beasts. I left unbutchered corpses in the paddocks and hedgerows.

What on earth did we do out there? Mam sometimes asked.

I'd only shrug. Nothing, Mam. Messing about, Mam.

Dad told her to leave me alone. There was a time for lads to be left alone.

We went on killing. And yes, we went a-thieving, too.

Soon after that first day with the birds, I went out seeking him again, found him waiting at his door. He strolled to me, led me away. We went downhill this time, through the lower wasteland, that place of dread that had reverted to a place of play now that the Vincent McAlinden who walked at my side had been tamed. Kids even called out his name along with mine as we walked through, and he called back, and smiled, and they smiled back, for they had forgotten, forgiven, or simply knew nothing of, the earlier terrifying form of Vincent McAlinden. Vincent had been tamed by the loss of his friend. And he was with Dominic Hall, a new and better friend for him.

We passed the endless leaping girls with their endless elemental skipping song as they spun the rope around each other's heads and feet and leapt and leapt in order to avoid the whirring edge of night.

January, February, March, April, Ma-ay . . .

Away from the place of play and down the rocky path and into town. To the little town square with the fountain at its heart where old men in dark caps sat with dogs and leaned on sticks and murmured of the old days to each other. Past the scents of beer outside the Blue Bell, the scents of lotions at Lough's Barber shop, the scents of saveloy and gravy outside Myer's pork shop, the scents of cigarette smoke and pipe smoke everywhere. Kids everywhere, dogs running everywhere, women in headscarves with shopping bags. A priest, Father Boyle, hurrying somewhere with his hand held to his chest, where the Host must be hidden and secure, waiting to be pressed on to the tongue of one in sickness or one in grief or one about to die. The sounds of sparrows and traffic, of playing children, of gossiping women, of laughing women, of coughing men, of wheezing men.

Vincent paused for a moment as we crossed the square.

"Sometimes," he said.

"Sometimes what?"

"I think I see him."

"Who?"

"Him that's bliddy gone."

"Bernard?"

"No, not him. Me bliddy father, Dom. Think I see him on one of the benches or sitting behind the glass in the pub. Like he's come back or like he's a bliddy ghost or something or like he's never even gone away. Then I look more close and of course it isn't him, the bastard."

"Do you want to see him?"

144

"You must be bliddy jokin. But mebbe yes. Mebbe if I did, I'd murder him. Kapow!"

"Do you remember him?"

"Don't want to, but aye, I sometimes do. And I see him in me dreams. Nightmares, more like."

He spat, he cursed.

"He won't come back. We're free of him, the bliddy get."

He spat again.

"I'm in his place now," he said.

We passed a fruit shop. I smiled at a neighbour inside and then a few yards further on I felt an apple in my hand, placed there by Vincent.

"Didn't see a thing, did you?" he said. "And neither did they."

We bit and chewed and the juice ran down our chins, and beyond the sudden dread I felt at the eating of the fruit I found a place in me in which I could smile at this, in which I could laugh, in which I could delight at the taste of fruit and friendship and crime together.

"It's nowt," said Vincent. "And it's bliddy easy, and it's done by everybody, and naebody gets harmed."

Further on we shared our coins and Vincent bought a pack of five Park Drive and we crouched and smoked, in an alley between the fishmonger's and Lang's Betting Shop, and goggled at the great North Sea cod, almost as big as we were, that lay on the fishmonger's slab with herrings and crabs all open to the outside air.

And when we'd smoked he handed a packet of fruit gums to me, and a packet of chewing gum, and he snorted at my astonishment, and said again that it was easy, oh so easy, and that everybody did it. Bliddy everybody, man.

On we went, down the High Street.

"Now you," he said as we approached another fruit shop, Connor's, whose boxes lay open on a table outside.

I shuddered, my footsteps faltered, and he knew it.

"Just lift one out," he said, so matter-of-fact, "and keep it by your side and keep on walking on."

I hesitated.

"Just do it. Learn from me. Nobody will see."

Again my heart was stopped, and then it started thumping and my brain was filled with agitation.

"Believe that you can do it and you will," whispered my friend. "Hand straight in and hand straight out and keep on walking. Easy."

We were almost upon it. I looked towards the sky, the drifting clouds. Beyond the fruit shop roof, the steeple of the church appeared about to topple over us.

I was cold as ice, as hot as fire.

We walked. I put my hand inside the box, I lifted out a fruit, I walked. It was as if it wasn't me, as if another boy had done this thing. We walked together, Vincent, the different me and me.

"Well done!" he whispered.

He grasped my wrist and squeezed it fast, a touch of reassurance, of respect.

We came to the foot of the street. We leaned against the wall of the Beeswing pub, below its green dome.

I showed the hard pear in my hand.

I bit, I passed it to him and he bit, too.

146

He grinned. He swiped his hand across his lips to catch the juice.

"See?" he said. "And after all it's just a pear. It's just a piece of bliddy fruit. And now you've done it once it all gets easier."

And on we walked, and continued all morning to thieve more childish things, just sweets, just fruit, just things that were hardly noticed, things that hardly mattered to anyone at all.

CHAPTER
TWENTY-FIVE

And on we went beyond the Beeswing pub and passed the railway station and crossed the railway line, hesitating on the footbridge to feel the power of the Newcastle train as it thundered beneath, and then on again, chewing our stolen Beech-Nut gum, following the ancient terraced streets, the ones that hadn't been swept away along with the hovels in which so many of us had spent the first years of our lives. And the scent of the river was coming to us now, and the sound of gulls from above the water, and the din of the yards was closer, more intense. We walked down through old paddocks in which squat black and black-and-white ponies chewed the grass or lifted their heads and regarded us with questioning tender eyes. And other lads and other girls were wandering, and all of us were glancing at each other and wondering should we be interested, should we be friendly, should we be wary or suspicious or scared? Vincent strutted, he held his head high, he was Vincent McAlinden after all, many of these must surely know him, or know of his old reputation.

He lit a Park Drive and blew wild plumes of smoke into the air and said, "Sod 'em," apparently to nothing, to no one. "Sod 'em all, eh, Dominic?"

"Aye," I answered, though I knew not why.

"Aye," I answered. "Sod 'em all."

And then to the river itself, to a place where the paddocks petered to a pebbly rubbly muddy slope with the water slopping at its foot. We sat on the final patch of green, on stones, with grass about us drifting upon the downriver breeze, and Vincent told me this was the life, wasn't this just the best of bliddy lives?

I laughed. I muttered that yes, it probably bliddy was. I looked down at the jetsam on the shore, the bones of beasts and the boughs of trees, and the condoms and the broken timbers and the stones and boxes and bottles that had settled upon the silt, and saw the logs and the trees and the litter being carried upon the water, and I smelt the stench of the dark and filthy Tyne, and I saw the ancientness of the stonework beneath the jetties on the opposite bank, and I looked along the shore, and saw the shipyards and their great cranes and their great ships stretching to the sea, and I saw the distant sky above the distant invisible sea, and I took all these things into me. This is where I had come from, this place. The buildings in which I'd been raised were gone, but they lived on inside me.

"That's where I'll end up," he said. "Down here in the bliddy yard. Soon, before too long. Going each morning to the noise and the filth. Not like you. You'll be up and off and fancy free."

I felt his hand upon me, upon my shoulder, and I felt his face against mine, and felt his breath upon me, and heard that breath carrying his words into my ear.

"Won't you?" he said. "Won't you be free as a bird while I'm crawling round in a filthy tank?"

"I will," I said.

"That's right. Let's fight," he said.

"What?"

"Fight. It's what we should do. Let's do it all and bliddy fight."

I didn't understand but somehow my body did understand, and I rolled my head and turned my eyes towards the sky, and it was as if my soul recoiled inside myself, rebalanced itself and then turned again, and found a different and very new way of being, and I looked upon this new friend, Vincent McAlinden, who had terrified me since childhood, who sought me out to take me killing and thieving and who now was close to me and about to fight me, and I turned back to him again and muttered yes to him. I grunted bliddy yes.

We rolled away from the river and the stones. He rolled on top of me and knelt on my shoulders and held my wrists to the earth and snarled down at me.

"Howay, then," he said. "Don't hold back. Do bliddy something."

I squirmed, I struggled beneath him, I shoved him off.

"Well done," he snarled. He grabbed me, and we wrestled. "Hurt us!" he said. "Bliddy hurt us, man!"

I gripped him tight, I stamped the earth, I felt the power in my new squat muscles and the desire to struggle in my blood. I got him round the chest and squeezed him hard. I was shorter than him, but I had my father's caulker's body and my father's caulker's strength. I was astonished by the effort we needed to stay upright, the effort I needed to try to make him fall, the effort I needed just to breathe, to keep on doing this. Snot and tears came from me. Blood came from me. I saw these things on Vincent McAlinden too and didn't know if they had come from him or come from me. I spun him round and at last he fell.

"Good lad," he snarled. "Now the knife!"

"Eh?"

"Get your knife and bliddy stab us now!"

"What?"

Suddenly his own knife was in his hand, pointing towards me. He got to his feet. He grinned.

"Or are ye just goin to be defenceless?"

I took out my ship-steel knife. He crouched low and circled me. I crouched low as well. He beckoned me with his free hand.

"Howay," he said. "Stab us, Dom."

He lunged at me. I backed away.

"Cos I'm tellin you — if you don't do me, I fuckin will do you."

He lunged again. Again.

I gasped in terror, and in greater terror as I lunged at him and stabbed my knife towards him.

"That's the way," he hissed. "Again! Do it like ye bliddy mean it, man."

I stabbed the air again. Suddenly he grabbed my wrist and pulled me close. He raised his knife. I grabbed his wrist.

"That's right," he groaned.

151

Linked together like that, we struggled. We resisted each other, we pressed our blades towards each other. I knew the torment of resisting and attacking in the same moment, the terror of a sharp steel blade just inches from my flesh. We gasped and grunted. Vincent grinned, he urged me on. We rocked each other back and forth. Suddenly he was down again and I was squatting over him and my snot and blood dangled down in a long gluey string upon his face.

"Divent stop," he hissed. "This is yer chance, Dom. Do it now. Now!"

The image of my knife in his throat flashed within me.

I blinked my eyes to make it go.

"Submit," I said, as we boys used to say to each other in St Lawrence's Infants when we gave each other Chinese burns or played our innocent fighting games in the schoolyard. "Give in, Vincent McAlinden!"

He laughed.

"Aye," he said. "I submit. And that'll dae."

We rolled apart.

"Who'd've thought ye had that in ye, young Dom?" he said.

I licked my fingers and cleaned the snot and blood away from myself, and Vincent did the same. I tried to clean away the grass stains and mud stains, and Vincent did the same.

"I'll get ye next time," Vincent said.

"Naa," I answered. "You never will."

"Ha. Give us your blood."

He made a small cut with his knife in the ball of his thumb, held it towards me. I did the same with my knife in my thumb. We pressed the wounds together.

"Now I'm in you and you're in me," he said. "Brothers in blood."

He sighed and closed his eyes. We lay in the grass.

"Linked forever," he murmured.

It became strangely peaceful as we lay there by the river, as our hearts and breathing calmed. The sky was beautiful, the blue of the day beginning to be streaked with red and gold and black. Black marks of birds moved beautifully across it. There was an aching inside me that seemed as great as the sky above, as great as the world itself. And Vincent, in his matter-of-fact daring, came close to me again and breathed his breath on me, then pressed his lips to mine, and for the first time I got the weird harsh taste of him.

He breathed his harsh-sweet words into me.

"Let us see you," he whispered.

I glanced into his eyes.

"You knaa what I mean, Dominic," he whispered.

I let him see me. He let me see him.

"Good lad," he said. "Now let's touch."

CHAPTER
TWENTY-SIX

We fought many times after that. We came to expect it after a day of slaughtering or of thieving, or of simply roaming these streets and fields and riverbanks. I saw him differently. He wasn't just a brute in a brutish form. He fought, but he also laughed and played with me, as if he was a child. Maybe in those months, he experienced something of a childhood that he'd never had, or that he'd left behind. And maybe I experienced what it might be to be a certain kind of man. And we had friendship, the kind of friendship I'd never known with Holly Stroud, the kind of friendship he'd never had with Bernard.

Sometimes it seemed that we were preparing for war. We did press-ups and squats. We raised rocks above our heads. We challenged each other to lift boulders. We fought with jagged stones in our hands, slavering as we feigned attempts to break each other's skull. We continued to fight with our knives, gripping each other's wrists, forcing the blade closer closer to the other's throat. We cursed and spat. We called each other the blackest of names. We cursed each other's family, each other's ancestors. We called each other animal names: rat, pig, ape, dog. We named each other after genitalia and human waste. We bled and drooled. Our muscles tightened, strengthened. Our minds seethed, bodies ached, souls coarsened. We went home at the end of such days drained of energy, drained of thought. Bruises and wounds on me, marks of grass and earth on me. Wildness in my eyes.

Early on, after one of the first scary ecstatic afternoons with Vincent, I returned home as night was coming on. I lowered myself painfully down on to the sofa.

"Dominic?" Mam gasped. "What on earth?"

"Eh?" I grunted.

"What you been getting up to out there? Who on earth . . ."

I groaned a meaningless answer.

"Dominic?" said Dad.

He stroked his cheek in contemplation for a moment.

"Leave him," he said softly.

He continued to regard me, my hooded eyes, my hunched body.

"He's got the beast in him," he said.

"The what?" said Mam.

He laughed.

"Haven't you, my son?" he said.

"Don't talk such nonsense," whispered Mam.

I turned and groaned at her again, a kind of growl.

"See?" Dad said.

"See what?"

"It'll run right through him, then out it'll run again."

He smoked his cigarette.

"Down, boy!" he laughed.

I turned from them both, went to the table, did my homework. The subject was biology, the contents of the blood. Haemoglobin, oxygen, metabolic waste. I named them all, and within myself I named the other matter rushing through me: excitement, yearning, wildness, dread, and the blood and breath of Vincent McAlinden.

Mam came to me, put her arm across my shoulder. I leaned back, became a child again for a few short moments and let myself be held by her.

"My lovely child," she sighed.

Then I leaned forward again and wrote on, with my neat hand writing, my fluent sentences, my clear diagrams, my accurate naming of parts.

Later, when I was in bed, Dad came to me. I felt his coarse hand on my brow. I thought he'd speak, but he said nothing. He only sat there as the darkness deepened, his coarse hand on my brow.

"Be careful," he whispered at last. "Don't go too far."

Next day I wrestled with Vincent McAlinden again, by a brook that ran down towards the Tyne. We struggled in the flowing water, bodies bruised by stones. I forced his face down into the water, as if to drown him, as if to kill, then hauled him out again.

"Submit?" I snarled. "Submit?"

"Yes." He smiled through tears. "Well done. I submit. Come here."

CHAPTER
TWENTY-SEVEN

At school, nobody saw beyond the mask. My marks were good. I stayed near the top of the class. I put words in an order and shape that pleased my teachers. I could write a sentence, a paragraph, a page. My words came fluently step by step by step. I could change a page of tangled text to a few sentences of rhythm and meaning. Could precis and comprehend, could analyse and parse, could charm and move and convince. The Ape Boy had a flow, a grace, an imagination. Who was this alien graceful boy, I wondered, as my muscles continued to thicken, and my hairs to grow, as I continued to thieve and kill, as I continued to fight and kiss with Vincent McAlinden?

Holly seemed a world away, a being from a distant age, a distant past. I hardly acknowledged her. She became a gymnast, a dancer, a trampolinist. She was celebrated for it. She was in her element, using springboards, bars and beams, horses, rings and ropes. Leaping, climbing, cartwheeling and spiralling, she seemed at times, they said, about to fly. And though she grew older, her body remained small, a thing of great delicacy and great strength, a lovely thing, a bird-like thing. Often I caught her watching me as I watched her, but I couldn't go to her. When I heard her voice or her piano playing drifting through the air, I tilted my head and listened. I knew that I could easily be entranced. Part of me wanted to reach out to her, to hold tight to her, as if I could be somehow rescued by her, as if her bird-like strength could lift me up and leave behind the boy who fought and loved with Vincent McAlinden. But I turned away, told myself that I was finished with her, that she was finished with me. Holly and her family would leave the estate and I'd be left alone at last to be the boy that I was bound to be.

My mam would ask, "No time for Holly Stroud these days?"

I'd tell her that we'd grown apart.

I'd laugh and tell her, "She's a lass, Mam!"

And Dad would shrug and say that this was bound to happen, this was just the way of the world. No point in fighting it.

"And he's got plenty time for girls," he said.

Bill Stroud kept a kindly eye on me. He smiled. He waved. I knew that he might be the only one to see through the mask towards the boy inside. I knew he'd make no judgements, no demands, he'd ask no difficult questions of me.

What if Bill had been my father? What if I'd been born as Dominic Stroud? What if Holly'd been born as Holly Hall? I tried to imagine drawings flowing easily from my fingers, songs drifting easily upon my breath. I imagined being at ease in the world, no need to struggle with it and with myself. How would it be to be such a graceful thing?

And how would it be to be Vincent McAlinden, to be formed like that, born like that, raised like that, to have desires and habits like that? What if I'd been Dominic McAlinden?

No answers to questions like that. But they pestered me and pestered me. Did they pester everyone? How would it be to be anyone? Why am I *me*? Why? Why am I not someone else?

CHAPTER
TWENTY-EIGHT

That last day started with a fight about smoking. I was hooked by now. I woke up, lit up, breathed the smoke out through the bedroom window. I washed, fiercely brushed my teeth.

"You think I can't smell it?" said Mam when I went downstairs. "You think it doesn't bother us?"

Dad laughed. He lit a cigarette of his own.

"Stunts your growth," he said. "Just look at me."

She waved his smoke away from her face.

"You should stop as well," she said. "It'll kill the two of you."

"Kill!" mocked Dad.

"Yes! Kill! Do you not *care*?"

He relented.

"Mebbe too late for me," he said. "But your mother's right. Stop before it gets its hooks in you."

She put her hand on my shoulder. She stared into my eyes. I stared back at her. Her eyes so clear, so bright. Her touch so vividly alive.

"Please, Dominic," she said.

Dad breathed his smoke towards me.

Mam tried to blow it away. She coughed. She coughed again.

"See?" she said. "It'll damage us all."

"Everybody tries it once," he said to her. "He'll see how daft it is."

She coughed again.

Again.

"Stop it!" she said.

She went into the kitchen.

"She'll get over it," Dad said. He winked. He drew on his cigarette. "But she's right. Pack it in."

He went into the garden.

I took a cigarette from Dad's packet on the hearth. I took some coins from her purse on the kitchen table. I went downhill. I bought five No. 6 and stole two Milky Ways. I met Vincent behind the Blue Bell pub. We walked down to the little park on Holly Hill. Sixth-form girls were playing tennis in short skirts and T-shirts. They saw us, giggled at us.

"Bliddy gorgeous!" he snarled.

He bared his teeth at me.

"Aren't they?" he snapped.

"Yes," I said.

"Bliddy yes! But they wouldn't want me, would they? *Would* they?"

"I . . ."

"Bliddy no."

He turned away. We left the park.

"Bliddy sun!" he said, holding his hand against it.

"Bliddy you!" he said as our shoulders touched.

"You ever want to get it over with?" he said. "Get everything you want?"

"Everything?" I said.

"Yes, bliddy everything right bliddy now."

He smoked and spat.

"And d'you ever want to do damage? I mean proper bliddy damage."

He moved fast. I almost ran to keep up with him.

"Course you've got the time to wait," he said. "You'll not be dropped into a tank in a few months' time. You'll be Dominic Goody Two-Shoes for ages more." He grabbed me, tugged me to his side. "One day we'll just start smashing things up, the likes of me, and takin what we want. Good job we've got no bombs. Cos we'd be using them and dropping them and blasting everything to bliddy bits. You understand?"

I said nothing.

"Of course you divent understand. Keep up, will you! That's why you shove us into tanks and hulls, to keep us down. But we're bliddy seethin and all we want is to do damage damage bliddy damage. Move! Keep up!"

I held out the packet of No. 6 and a Milky Way.

"Look how hard you are!" he snorted. "You smoke, you slaughter ickle dicky birds, you pinch sweeties, you fight, you pretend to nearly kill, you look at bouncing tits and naked legs."

He lit a cigarette, he bit the Milky Way.

"Look at them!" he said.

"Look at who?"

"At all of them. At everybliddybody. Look how bliddy tame they are."

I looked. Familiar faces, familiar bodies, doing familiar things in familiar places.

162

"I'd do the whole damn bliddy lot. Bliddy wallop. Bliddy bang!"

He made a fist.

"That's what war is, isn't it?" he said. "Bomb the boring bliddy world to mek it jump."

He turned to me.

"I'd drop a bomb on you as well, you dozy prat."

He laughed.

"Mebbe the Holly Strouds should be marching and chanting against me! CMD. Campaign for McAlinden Disarmament! Ha!"

We walked on.

"Why's it all so bliddy ordinary? Why?"

"Because it is," I said.

"What kind of answer's that? I thought you had some bliddy brains in you! Move! Keep up, will ye!"

We walked, we smoked.

"I dream of killing me own dad," he said. "Huntin him down and splittin his head with a rock. Sometimes it's God I'm after to pay him back for all the crap down here, but when he turns around I see me father standing there. Then I get him with a knife, a bayonet, a gun." He raised his hand high and brought it down quick. "Kapow! Die, you dog!"

He tugged me to his side.

"You must dream like that," he said.

"I don't," I told him.

"You must," he said.

"I don't."

"Huh!"

He snarled a laugh. We hurried on. We stole some fruit. Stole an egg from a tray outside Walter Willson's. There was nothing we could do with this, so Vincent flung it down an ancient alleyway between a butcher's and a bank.

"To hell with it all," Vincent muttered. "To hell with this, to hell with that, to hell with him, to hell with her!"

We walked the road towards Newcastle, entered the fringes of Gateshead. Hidden river on our right beyond a labyrinth of terraced houses.

Kids watched us walk, suspicious. Vincent glared.

"To hell with you! And with you, and you!"

Young kids scattered from him. Older kids backed off, turned their eyes away, moved on.

We came to the unfamiliar alleyways and shops of Gateshead town. Nobody smiling at us, nobody greeting us. Took a lane that turned to a track that passed by a line of old pigeon crees. A man rattling a tin of food and calling into the sky. A sudden rush and clatter of wings above our heads as his birds returned to him. Then a little park with children swinging on creaking swings. Then tree-lined streets, grassy verges, cultivated gardens, a sense of peace. Stone houses with stained-glass windows, little turreted towers, driveways. We wandered more slowly now, breathing this different oh-so-unfamiliar air. We moved through the heavy shade of roadside trees. No sounds of caulkers here, no scent of the Tyne, no underlying engine din. Vincent snapped off the heads of red roses overhanging the path. Threw a stone at a squirrel in a treetop. Cursed a dog, a golden Labrador, threw another stone at that. Pointed to gleaming cars, to furnishings, paintings, bookcases seen through high windows.

"Look. Rich gits," he muttered. "To hell with 'em."

Then there it was, the familiar place, like something from a previous dream. The driveway, the car, the heavy wooden front door wide open, letting air and light into a polished hallway. Who said we should go through the gate? Neither of us. We didn't even speak. The open door seemed open just for us. We walked the driveway to it. Shadow beneath the trees then bright sunlight, shadows then light. The earth felt paper-thin, felt hardly there at all. Seemed to be nobody around. Kids in a distant garden. Dog in a distant street. I see us now, two boys before an open door. See us both lean sideways to look in. See us edge together into that hallway. There's no sound in the house. Scents of polish and flowers, everything so clean. And a narrow table against a wall below a painting of Tyneside as it used to be: sail-boats on the river, quaint houses on an old stone bridge, fields between the streets.

Another open door, into a room of books. I know where I am now, of course.

Vincent's curse brings me back to the here and now.

"Treasure, Dom," he whispers.

A five-pound note on the hall table, held there by a chunk of marble. Vincent lifts the marble, I take the note, close my hand around it, slide it into my pocket. Tiptoe further in, to the door of the room where my words are. Peep into it. Silent, empty, books stacked high on all the walls. Armchairs, a sofa, a great white

165

marble fireplace. No heartbeat, no breath. I think of my childish words in my childish script in here, my treasure story, lying in this room with all these books. It'll have been long ripped up. It'll have been long ago thrown away, the childish thing. A bit of scribble by the cleaner's son, scrawl by a brat from the pebbledash. I think of my mother, working here, polishing the furniture, dusting the shelves, washing the windows, telling the lady of the house about her son. Does she talk about her son? And if she does, is it in order to praise him as it used to be? Or does she whisper doubts and troubles about her changing boy? Does she sing as she works? Is there any evidence of her here? Not a sound, not a smell. Just the cleanliness, the orderliness. I take a little silver spoon from a little table and put it in my pocket. Vincent grins. He upends a vase of roses on to the floor. He crushes a little statue of a farmer beneath his feet. He takes a silver ashtray. I reach up to the books on the shelves, start to get them down, to rip them apart, to scatter them around us on the floor. And then Vincent opens his zip and pisses down on to them. Giggles savagely. Whispers for me to join him, and I do, and I grin with him at what we're up to, and a roar of terror fills my brain. What am I doing? And how will my mother clean this? And then we're out again, hurrying down the hall, and out through the door, and Vincent gasps with savage delight.

"A gift from bliddy God above!" he says.

And now he's at a rabbit hutch, murmuring to the little black rabbit there, stroking his thumb and fingers together. And poor silly thing, it comes to him and poor silly me says nowt. And now Vincent opens its door and takes his knife and cuts its poor throat. And I'm so weirdly excited that I go to him and I'm the one that bliddy butchers it, the one that saws off its still-warm head with my ship-steel knife and rolls it across the earth before the hutch.

And I put my knife in its sheath again and we retrace slow steps along the precarious drive, and enter the peaceful street again and continue walking and continue to try to stay calm, and Vincent sighs a curse, sighs praise of me, of both of us.

"We're cool as cats," he says.

He turns his face to the bounteous sky.

"We're bliddy brilliant!" he sighs.

We turn the corner of the street, then run like little scampering kids again, back through the park, back past the crees, back below the rushing pigeons, back through a dusty shadowed lane towards the world we know.

"We're free!" he says.

"The thing you done with the bliddy books!" he says.

"Bliddy fantastic!" he says.

"But, Christ, the rabbit?" I say.

"Poor ickle thing."

He shows the blood still on his fingers. I look at the blood on my own and want to scream.

"Why did we do the rabbit?" I say.

He grabs me and kisses me full on the lips. I try to pull away but he just laughs. Wipes his bloody fingers on my throat.

"Cos we wanted to. Cos you wanted to." He giggles. "You got its bliddy head off fast enough."

Then his knife's in his hand again. He has me by the scruff of the neck and he's holding the knife to my throat and he's suddenly so strong, stronger than he's ever been, and I can't get free of him.

"Do ye not *understand*?" he says.

"It's nowt to do with bliddy *why*," he snarls.

"And there'll be no *why* if I do you," he says.

He thrusts forward and kisses again.

"Don't worry," he says.

"I'm just jokin," he says.

He puts the knife away into its sheath.

"We're pals," he says. "And more than pals, eh? Pals that kill and pals that kiss and pals that . . . Ha!"

His eyes are bloodshot. His teeth are bared. He licks his lips.

We walk again. He tells me to walk natural and normal.

"I'm your guide," he says.

"Nobody else'd get you doing the things I get you to do," he says.

"You know that, don't you?" he says.

"And you like it, don't you?" he says.

We walk.

I try to shake the rabbit and the knife from my brain. Try to shake everything we've done from my brain.

"Ye'll remember this for evermore," he says.

I try not to scream.

We show each other our bounty and we laugh.

And walk.

And think it's over, and think we've got away with it.

168

CHAPTER
TWENTY-NINE

The car moved slowly at our side. A small blue Ford Anglia, an amber light spinning slowly on its roof, with a policeman and a woman in it.

"Now then, lads!" called the policeman.

We didn't turn.

"Just stop where you are and I'll have a little word with you. Just gimme a second, eh?"

Vincent laughed, he breathed his bitter words into my face.

"Payback time."

The car stopped, the policeman stepped out.

"Ready to run?" said Vincent.

He laughed.

"No, course you aren't."

He laughed.

"I'll soon be in the tanks. I wonder will I ever see you there. Ha!"

Then he walked quickly away.

The policeman came to my side. We watched Vincent diminish in the distance, become absorbed into the familiar streets close to home.

"Farewell!" the policeman called.

"You'll give me his details, of course. Won't you, son?"

I couldn't answer.

"Course you will. I'm PC Romero."

He tilted his head.

"Dominic Hall," I whispered.

"So, Dominic. Is it you that's got the fiver, or is it your disappeared pal?"

I took out the note. I took out the silver spoon, held them out towards him.

"Nowt else?"

"No."

"Just the urination, of course," he said. "And the books. And the rabbit." He sighed. "Ah yes, the rabbit!"

He leaned close to me, shook his head, widened his eyes in astonishment.

"*Why* the rabbit?"

I put my bloody hand to my bloody throat.

It was like somebody else was speaking my words.

"It wasn't me."

He reached down and took my bloodied knife from its sheath. He grinned.

"Make that stand up in court, son. But enough of all this chat. Say hello to Mrs Charlton."

The woman came out of the car. Brown woollen coat, brown shoes, brown glossy hair. All neat, all clean.

"This is the lady whose house you burgled," said PC Romero. "The lady whose house you defiled. The lady whose rabbit you slaughtered."

I held out the fiver and the spoon to her.

"Whoa," said Romero. "That's evidence, son."

He took the note and wrapped a handkerchief around the spoon.

"There'll be fingerprints," he said, "and character checks and school checks and chats with Mam and Dad and then . . . Ah, Dominic, who can know what then?"

"Why did you do it, you filthy boy?" said Mrs Charlton.

I answer like a trembling child.

"You're Mrs Charlton. I sent you a story once. You said it was lovely. You said I must be a very clever little boy."

CHAPTER
THIRTY

I cried like that boy as we headed home. I sat in the back of the car. What did this woman make of this place: this small square with the fountain at its heart; Dragone's coffee shop with condensation on its windows and steam seeping from its door; Bamling's fruit shop with the tempting apples in boxes outside; Myer's pork shop with the pig's head grinning through the glass; the great codfish on the fishmonger's slab? These scampering children, these head-scarved women, these old men with their dogs, these working men in boiler suits heading wearily homeward after half-shifts in the yards?

Her head was still, her eyes were cold.

We entered the estate. Through her cold eyes I saw the crumbling pebbledash, the cracks in the pavements, the potholes in the roads, the sinking garden walls. Kids in filthy vests made dens in little gardens. Faces at the windows watching this police car bringing Dominic Hall home.

We pulled up outside the house.

Mrs Stroud was singing.

Once I had a secret love . . .

Girls were singing too, their never-ending skipping song.

A pony whinnied, a cockerel called.

My parents stood at the front window.

And I looked through the cold eyes again: this tiny house in a pale narrow street. This creaking gate, this concrete earth, this outhouse, this washing line with sheets on it, these hooks for a childish tightrope. And this little neat living room with flowery curtains, cheap workaday furniture. This squat muscular man, this caulker with damaged hands and damaged lungs, this father sucking in smoke, breathing it out, this lovely little shocked mother.

And I saw through their eyes too. I saw their boy, the boy who was supposed to walk away from all of this towards the sky.

The tale of the tawdry boy was told to them. The plunder and the knife were shown to them.

Mrs Charlton touched the lamp that she had given us those few short years ago, the one that Mam had cared for as a precious thing.

She sighed.

"I do not wish to stay long," she said. "I just wish this to be over with."

She ran her fingers across the towers and minarets upon the lamp.

"I will not press charges," she said.

"Are you certain of that, Mrs Charlton?" said the policeman.

"I wish to be sullied no further. I will show mercy." She looked Mam in the eye. "Only for your sake, Elaine."

Mam caught her breath. She sobbed. Mrs Charlton turned her face away.

"What about the other boy?" asked Romero.

"Oh yes, the other brute." She shuddered. "To think that there are two of them with the same leanings. Scare him, officer, but leave him to his filth."

Romero shrugged.

"I loved your little story," Mrs Charlton said. "I kept it on my bookshelves for a year or more. I showed it to my guests. I knew from your mother that there were such high hopes for you. I thought you were such a credit to her . . ."

Her voice trailed off.

"Who'd have thought there was such a . . . *thing* beneath?"

She pushed the lamp away with extended fingertip.

"I wish never to see you again, Dominic," she said. "And I'm afraid that I do not wish to see you again either, Elaine."

She shrugged.

"I am sorry about that. But what else could you expect?"

She stood in the living-room doorway as the policeman took details of me, my school, my father and his place of work, my mother and her places of work. He said that he must pass on some details of this to my school. Of course he bliddy should, my father said. He asked for details of Vincent McAlinden. I hesitated.

"Dominic," said Dad, "the officer asked for details of Vincent McAlinden."

I said who Vincent was, where he lived, where he went to school.

"Hardly peas in a pod, then," he said. "But who can ever tell?"

He wrote in his notebook.

"You're a grammar school boy," he said to me. "One of the privileged. So what ambitions do you have?"

No answers.

"How will you grasp the opportunities that are offered to you?"

"He's very clever," said Mam.

"Clever enough to do the things he did today. And to do the other things that he must do."

"Oh, Dominic," whispered Mam. "What else is it you do?"

I could not answer.

"Were you not like this?" I wanted to ask the stupid policeman. "Do you not have memories of this beneath your stupid uniform?"

"Whatever it is," said Romero, "you'd better stop it now. It gets to be a habit. The first time's hard, the second's easier. And then the third . . . And we know you now. We'll see you. We'll find you out."

He scanned us all.

"You're on a knife edge," he said.

Then he shrugged.

"I hope we don't have to meet again."

Dad held his hand out to him. He didn't take it. He put my knife on to the table. He turned away.

Mrs Charlton gave a final shudder of disgust. They went away.

Holly and her father watched from the house across the street.

"Why did it have to be Mrs Charlton?" whispered Mam.

"She should be asking for the bloody birch," Dad said.

"You do it, then!" I said to him.

He came at me. I tried to hold him off but I let myself fall like a child. I wanted to cry out, Daddy! Daddy! Mammy! Mammy! He raised his fist and I got ready for the pain, but Mam pulled him away from me.

"Don't, Francis," she groaned. "Not that."

"What else you been up to?" he said. "What crimes, what filth?"

"Nothing. I don't know. I don't remember!"

"Was it Vincent that made you do such things?" said Mam.

"Don't you bloody dare say yes to that!" said Dad.

He raised his fist again. I cowered.

He lit a cigarette. Bared his teeth at me. He took the knife, pressed the point to the hearth and stamped on it viciously until it snapped in two. Flung the pieces into the bin.

Glared at me, glared at me, seethed with contempt for me.

"Mebbe I need to be drunk to do it right," he groaned.

He got his jacket, went out to the Iona Club.

I wanted to collapse in Mam's arms.

"Is this what you were brought up for?" she said.

No answer.

"And to do it to me as well."

"You?"

"Like you did to Mrs Charlton."

I couldn't look at her.

"I told myself it wasn't true. I wouldn't believe the evidence of my eyes. You took money from my purse, Dominic. Didn't you? *Didn't* you?"

No answer.

"O sweet Jesus," she whispered. "I do believe you've forgotten it."

Her eyes remained upon me.

"Do you see the damage you've done today?" she said.

No answer.

"Oh, how you've wounded me."

It was late at night when Dad came home. Mam and I had gone to our beds. I didn't sleep. Heard him, his footsteps on the pavement. Then the click of the gate, the click of the door, the groan of his breath, his feet on the stairs, my mother's call: "Francis? That you?"

No answer. My door opened, and he was at me.

He stank of beer, of cigarettes. His words were slurred, his actions slovenly. He punched me hard on my cheek. He pressed his hands around my throat. He beat my head against the pillow.

"My dad would have bliddy killed you," he slurred.

"So kill me, then," I grunted.

We writhed together on the bed.

"You must have done it!" I yelled at him. "You must have done the kind of things I've done!"

177

"Burgled? Pissed like a pig in somebody's house? Killed an innocent beast? Who do you think you're bliddy talkin to?"

We writhed and fought, our snot and spit and tears and blood upon us. Mam came in, begging him to stop. He took no notice of her. He seemed to want to beat me to death.

He just groaned at last and collapsed on me.

"Oh, Dominic," he whispered. "What you done, my stupid boy?"

We slept together on my bed for a while.

When I woke up he was sitting on the bed's edge. The moon shone through the thin curtains. His silhouetted face was turned from me.

"I'll tell you what I did," he said.

CHAPTER
THIRTY-ONE

"There was two of us," he said, "me and Mickey Carr, a Westgate lad. We were bairns, hardly older than you are, Dom. Who had the sense to send lads like us to fight a war? Who had the sense to send us to the jungle? Monkeys in the trees, and birds as bright as fire, and snakes and spiders. I was used to the banks of the Tyne, Mickey was used to the coalfields of County Durham. Jesus, it was hot. It was steaming bliddy hot. Sweat ran across your eyes and got to rot your feet if you weren't careful. We stuck together, Mickey Carr and me, like good pals do. It was up to the likes of us to save the world, they said. We used to laugh, used to say that we were bliddy heroes. We didn't go far that day. We never went far. Too damn dangerous to go too deep into the trees. The sarge told us what to do. Just have a little reconnoitre, lads. Stay where it's familiar. Keep in sight. Keep looking back to check you ain't gone too far. We only went a few short yards, and there he was, down in a little hole. Weird. We thought he was dead but turned out he was fast asleep. Kicked him. He shifted. Weird. A sleeping Jap. Didn't know they had such weakness in them. He was just a kid as well. A kid like me, like you. Only difference was that smooth skin

179

they have. Them clear eyes. Them slender bodies. Couldn't tell if he was scared or not. He lay there looking up, then raised his hands. We didn't believe him. Japs don't do things like that."

He paused. He lit another cigarette.

"And?" said Mam.

"We didn't even look at each other, Mickey and me. We were on him before we thought, before we knew what we were doing, though we knew not to use guns, too loud. We stuck our knives in him. We just jumped on him and stuck our knives in him. Stabbed him. Like that. Stabbed him. Stabbed him."

He smoked. He shook.

"We told the sergeant he was reaching for his gun," he said. "Course he was, he said. Good lads. Good brave bonny lads. Now get that blood off you."

He stared out at the moon.

"We killed him," he whispered.

"You were scared," said Mam.

"Terrified. And it was in a war. A bliddy war! Imagine what happens all around the world in bliddy war."

"And think what he might have done to you, Francis."

"Ha. Me son stole a fiver from the hallway of a house. He killed a pet rabbit. I killed a lad in cold blood that might have been myself and might have been my son."

"It was war," said Mam again.

"Aye, war. And the sergeant said that now we'd done it once, the next time would be easier."

"And was it?" she said.

No answer.

"Was it, Francis?"

"You don't want to know. You don't know what you'll do till you come to it. There's lads walking round the streets today with tales to tell that they'll never bliddy tell."

Mam stroked his back. He lit another cigarette.

"Make sure such tales don't enter your life, Dominic," he said.

He drew deep, breathed out. Mam coughed.

"We buried him in a shallow grave," he said. "Hard to dig in the jungle with so many tangled roots around. Next night we hear somethin growlin, snortin, diggin the lad back up again. Last I heard, Mickey was panel-beating, out Consett way. Listen to them bliddy howlin dogs. Let's gan to sleep now, eh?"

We didn't move.

"Who *are* you both?" sighed Mam at last.

"Your husband," he whispered.

"Your son," I said.

We sat like that in my little room as the sun rose over our pale and fragile estate.

CHAPTER
THIRTY-TWO

"You never know with boys," said Creel. "Such talent for disguise, for misdirection . . ."

I was with my parents in his office. He had a police report on his desk. He had my books, my recent marks, my school report.

"None of this seems to have affected his work," he said.

He peered at me.

"How can that be?" he asked me. "But of course you do not know. Of course there *is* no answer."

My parents sat awkwardly in hard upright chairs. I stood at their side.

"We are subject to great mysteries," he said. "Are we not?"

"Yes, sir," whispered Mam.

"Yes indeed. As I prepared for this meeting, Dominic, your English teacher talked of you with unbridled admiration — of an old essay on 'The Secret Sharer', for instance. He even quoted you to me. 'The sharer is a hidden element of the narrator's self.' That, from one who was so young. From one who has, to all appearances, continued to flourish under our care. One who is even the linchpin of our football team. But a strange deception has occurred. We have been prey to an illusion. And what are we to do with you?"

"I don't know, sir."

"And nor do I."

He turned to Dad.

"We were once boys, Mr Hall. What would have been done with us had our indiscretions been discovered? And Mrs Hall, you who are of the more transparent section of humanity, what do you think should be done?"

"I don't know, sir. I don't think he knew what he was doing."

"Can that — such an *extraordinary* that — be so? But what would that say of our morality? And we must ask, in this place with crucifixes nailed to the walls and priests roaming in the corridors, what would that say of sin? What would that say of goodness and of our intention to avoid all evil?"

"I don't know, sir."

"And nor do I, Mrs Hall. This is a place of education. Our purpose is to bring knowledge to the children in our care. Perhaps it would be better to tell them all day long about the things we do not know." He stared at us across his arched fingertips. "But enough. Were we to ponder that, there would be no end to our pondering. Dominic, had charges been pressed, we would have had to cast you into the wilderness. But you received mercy. This must be a turning point. You must not do again the things that we know that you have done. And you must not do again the things which we do not know you have done."

He smiled.

"There must be a punishment, I suppose. Do you approve of punishments, Mr Hall, Mrs Hall?"

"Mebbe there should be a lot more punishment," said Dad. "He's been let off by Mrs Charlton. He's been let off by the police . . ."

"And by you?" said Creel.

"My first thought was to thrash him, like my dad would have thrashed me, to within an inch of my life."

"But you did not."

Dad looked down.

"No, sir."

Creel turned his eyes to Mam.

"What good would it do?" she whispered.

"Spare the rod, spoil the child. You don't believe that, Mrs Hall?"

"I know there's enough pain in the world without inflicting more on our children."

"And you," said Creel to me. "What punishment would pay you back for your wrongdoings? What punishment would ensure that you do not transgress again?"

"I don't know, sir."

He reached below his desk and lifted a cane. It was three feet long, hooked at one end. He flexed it between his hands and peered over it into my eyes. He swished it through the air. He bared his teeth, he grimaced, he raised the cane and held it in the air above my head, as if about to strike.

He laughed.

"How easy it is," he said, "for we teachers to strike dread into those in our care."

He put the cane away again.

"I should like the boy," he said, "to write for me. What say you to that, Mr Hall?"

"I'd say he's a lucky bugger. Sorry, sir."

"Perhaps he is. Perhaps we could ask if that is a punishment at all. But maybe it is the best of all punishments — one that makes use of the sinner's gifts, and that helps him to truly change. What do you think, Mrs Hall?"

"I don't mind, sir."

"Well, then, Dominic Hall. I should like you to write an answer to the question which must engage us all: Is it possible for one human being to know and to understand another? Will you do that for me?"

"Yes, sir."

"Good lad. And don't just write, 'I don't know', though that indeed may be the only honest answer that any of us could give."

CHAPTER
THIRTY-THREE

I wrote about the mysteries of Jack Law and Mrs Stroud. I told tales to explain the causes of Jack's silence and Mrs Stroud's seclusion. I changed their names to protect them, wrote about them as if they were inventions. I wrote of wordlessness and singing and angels, of curtained bedrooms and bird-filled hawthorn hedges. And I wrote stories that rose from riverside hovels and pebbledashed estates, stories of poltergeists and ponies and bleeding statues, of children endlessly bombing Berlin and bayoneting the Japanese. In the midst of my writing one day, I looked up and saw Holly in the cracked and dusty street, looking up at me.

I put down the pen and went out.

"Hello, Dominic," she said, so easily.

"Hello, Holly."

We walked the crooked pavements.

She said she'd heard about what I'd done. I told her there was a lot more than she'd heard.

"I killed things," I said.

She kept on walking.

"Birds," I said. "Sparrows and robins and finches and crows."

"Poor things."

"And other things. A cat. A dog."

"And how did it feel?"

"It felt OK."

We walked rapidly towards the sunlit fields.

"It did," I said. "It felt weirdly OK."

"Exciting?"

"Yes. We stole things, too."

"And was that exciting, too?"

"Yes. But not so much."

We walked.

"We did other things, Holly."

I took a long deep breath. I slowed my steps.

"Holly," I said. "We kissed each other."

She sighed, walked on, with sunlight burning in her hair, grass swishing underneath her feet.

"And we did other things," I said.

"I don't really want to know, not now. Mam says the music has been sweeter than ever in these past few weeks. She says the angels seem closer to the earth somehow."

I said nothing.

"She really does believe these things," she said.

"Maybe because they're true."

"No, they're not. And how did *that* feel, kissing Vincent McAlinden?"

"I don't know."

"She says that we live in ancient days, no matter what the world and all the things within it say. She says the heart of time stands still and that present, past and future are illusions. But maybe she's just mad. Maybe she should be locked away. Lots of people say that. Do you say that?"

"I don't know, Holly."

"You don't know much. She's frightened of walking."

"Of walking?"

"That's how it started, says my dad. She became frightened of walking, then of seeing others walk. He says she's frightened of seeing one step then another, one thing then another."

She sighed and hesitated, and then lay down on the turf and let the sunlight fall on her.

"When I was little," she said, "I never thought about how strange she was. The strange seems normal when you live with it."

"We're all strange in some way."

"I think of growing up and going to university. I think of all the places in the world I want to travel to, but I'm scared."

"Of what?"

"That I'll end up just like her, lying in the darkness and listening to the bloody music of the bloody spheres."

"You've got too much life for that."

"So did she, or so she says. She used to say she was a scamp that skipped along the banks of the Tyne. She used to say that she'd been an ordinary kid. So kissing Vincent McAlinden and other things are over now?"

"Yes. They are."

She lay back in the grass and her shirt lifted and exposed the flesh above her jeans. There was a dark circle there. She lifted the shirt higher to show an uneven CND symbol, etched into the skin, a clumsy home-made tattoo. The skin around it was pink with inflammation. She touched it tenderly with her fingertips.

"Vincent did it," she said. "With ink, and the point of a compass sterilized in flames."

I couldn't speak. Vincent McAlinden. Holly Stroud.

"When?"

"Not long ago. Probably when you were up to what you were up to with him." She shrugged. "I wanted to paint him again. Mam wanted to see how he's been changing as he grows, or if he'd stayed the same."

"Have your parents seen?"

"Mam hasn't seen me naked since I was a little girl. Dad will never see, of course. It's just for me, and for the others that I allow to see."

She ran her fingertips across the marks.

"I'll regret it, of course. It's not the most beautiful thing."

"It goes with this," I said, and I raised my hair to show the half-forgotten but still extant mark caused years ago by Vincent McAlinden's spinning stone.

"He said he's marked me on the inside, too."

"Ha! So he got both of us. Now I sometimes dream that my whole body's covered with words and patterns and pictures. Like a book, or a work of art. It'd be weird and beautiful."

"Can I touch?" I said.

"Yes."

I touched gently. Smooth warm skin, a slight roughness where the marks were.

"Did it hurt?" I said.

"Yes. But he said I'd be able to stand it. He was right."

She held my fingers against her.

"I was stupid, wasn't I?" she said.

I shrugged.

"We both were. And we both weren't."

"What would *you* write on my skin?" she said.

I shrugged.

"Stories. Stories where you don't end up in dark rooms being weird."

"That's good. Vincent's in the yard now. A working man."

"I know."

"In my last painting he was climbing through a trapdoor on a deck. His head's hanging down like a beast's, his arms hang down like fallen wings."

"Did you do other things with him?" I said.

She looked away.

"Not much."

"Kissed him?"

"Yes."

We lay side by side and stared into the sky.

"Was it exciting?"

"Ha. Yes. I wanted to hate him, but it was no good. It was exciting and strange."

"There was a strange taste on him."

"Yes. I tasted that, too."

"It's over. He's a working man. We'll all move on. Do you feel grown up, Dom?"

"Grown up?"

"Now you've killed and thieved and kissed your friend."

"Dunno what it means, to be grown up. Mebbe we keep on growing up until we die."

"And then we die."

"And never get to be grown up."

"And we're all kids, no matter how old we are."

"Kids disguised by adult bodies."

"Masked by adult faces."

"And we understand nothing."

"That's right, Dom. Absolutely bliddy nowt at all!"

We laughed. Then we kissed each other hard, there on the warm grass of the wide playing fields below the abundant sky, and it was wonderful and strange and very new.

CHAPTER
THIRTY-FOUR

I gave my writing to Creel. He passed it to Joyce.

"I could hate this," he told me. "It tells me what I'm not."

It was lunchtime and we were on the school field. Some kids nearby were climbing on each other to make a pyramid. Three stood in a line at the base. Two climbed on to their shoulders and stood there giggling and swaying.

"I'm a novelist manqué, Dominic. I see stories all around, but my pen makes nothing but sketches, images, useless starts and paltry endings."

A boy tried to scramble up to stand at the top, but the pyramid tottered and he fell again.

We laughed. Joyce called to him to try again.

"Maybe the greatness of my namesake holds me back," he said.

He opened a notebook and showed me a scribbled page with the title at the top.

"I have the idea for a novel called *The Singing of Angels*. I know I'll never finish it."

He laughed.

"It'll come to nothing," he said.

"You should just write it," I said.

"It's so simple, isn't it? You want to write it, so write it. You want to live, so live! Ha!"

He read some of my pages, and sighed.

"It's so good, Dominic."

"Can I ask you something, sir?"

He looked up in surprise.

"Yes."

"Did you do the kind of things that I did, when you were young?"

"That's quite a question to ask a teacher."

"I know, sir."

"If I did say yes, imagine what the governors and the priests and the villains of the classrooms would make of it. Oh, look at those youngsters!"

The kids were starting again, three at the bottom, two climbing up, the smallest one urging them on and waiting his turn.

"And if I just said no, you'd suspect that it was a lie. Stand firm, boys! And truth is everything, or so we're told. I stole fruit, as perhaps we all do. I had the chance to do other things."

"Did you do them?"

He shrugged, looked away, looked back again.

"No. Yes. Not many of them. The weird thing is, I don't really remember, Dominic."

The small boy reached upwards, and his friends took his hands.

"We grow in order to discover ourselves. But maybe we just discover ways of hiding our selves from ourselves."

We watched the boy clambering upwards.

"Climb, lad!" called Joyce. "Maybe I had your talent when I was your age, Dom. But I didn't have the other thing."

"What other thing?" I said.

"I wasn't cold enough. I wasn't wild enough. Go on, lad! Ha! I was always too correct, Dom."

He ran his finger along a line of my work.

"Maybe it's why I became a teacher — to teach about the things I wasn't brave enough to do myself. This has such great rhythm, Dom. Hold him! And I've tried to be a good teacher."

"You are," I said.

"Thank you. Be careful with your talent. Don't let it damage you. Don't let it take you too far from the people you love."

The kids teetered on each other's shoulders. The pyramid stood almost-firm for a short moment, the kids all roared in triumph, then the whole thing fell.

Joyce ran to the children. He lifted the small boy to his feet and stood before him, laughing in delight.

CHAPTER
THIRTY-FIVE

Dad wheezed. She coughed. Dad wheezed. She coughed. Noises in the night that came through the thin walls of our little house to me. He wheezed. She coughed. It went on for nights. I heard them whispering. I heard them wondering.

One morning I came down and she was slumped head forward at the kitchen table. She smiled weakly at me. Was that blood at the corner of her mouth?

Dad was in his working clothes. It was late. He should have been gone an hour ago.

"You got to stay with her today," he said. "Go to the Strouds and call the doctor for her."

"I'm fine," she whispered. "He has school to go to."

"Do as I say," said Dad. "The both of you. Get the doctor, Dominic."

He left. We heard his running feet on the pavement outside.

"He'll get docked," she said. "They might even send him home. I told him to go an hour ago."

Yes. Blood. A tiny pale smudge of it at the corner of her mouth.

"We don't want you missing stuff as well," she said.

She wiped the smudge away with her wrist.

"He's fussing," she said. "You go to school now, Dominic."

She retched, began to cough again.

I went to the Strouds. Holly stood behind me as I called the doctor, who said she'd come mid-morning.

"Shall I stay with you?" asked Holly.

I shook my head.

"What is it?" she said.

"A cough. A cold."

I listened. Holly's mother sweetly sang.

"Where are the angels now?" I asked.

I shivered. Did I want them to be close or to be far away?

I went back home. I led Mam to her bed. She leaned on me as we ascended the stairs. She sighed as she lay down again.

"It's nothing, Dominic," she whispered. "It's just a cold."

She stroked my head.

"Silly boy," she said. "Stop your worrying, will you?"

She coughed. More blood, little spatters of it on her handkerchief.

The doctor came at eleven, in her black Rover car. Dr Molly, in a fur-collared green coat with the familiar scent of dog on her. Dogs in the car: two black-eyed white bull terriers that stared out as she closed the car door and walked through the gate. Black leather bag in her hand with buckled straps around it.

"Good morning, Dominic. Goodness, how grown up you've become." She smiled. "And where is our patient?"

I let her in, heard the low muffled single bark of her dogs, guided her up.

"Good morning, Mrs Hall. And what appears to be the problem?"

"Just a cold, Dr Molly, a cough. They're fussing, Doctor."

The doctor took out a stethoscope, asked Mam to sit up, to lower her nightgown, asked me to turn away. I turned, heard the murmured words: *Breathe in. And now breathe out. Hold it. Yes. Again, please. And now again. And how long have you been coughing, my dear? Not long, Doctor. A week or so, Doctor. A little longer, perhaps. And how long has there been blood? Not long, just a few days, Doctor. A bit longer, perhaps. Your husband? At work, Doctor. He's a caulker in the yards. And is there pain? Not much, thank you, Doctor. You're sleeping? A little, thank you, Doctor. There is just your son with you? Yes, Doctor. Turn back again, Dominic, if you would.*

She rolled up her stethoscope.

She took out a prescription pad from her bag.

"Will you be able to get this for your mother this morning?"

"Yes, Doctor."

"Good lad."

She scribbled some notes, fast and hard.

Mam coughed, coughed again.

"We'll see about getting a check-up for you, Mrs Hall. Get you up to the hospital for that, I think."

Mam didn't speak. I didn't speak.

"A little X-ray or two, I think. That kind of thing."

197

We didn't speak.

"I'll sort it out. You have a telephone?"

"No, Doctor," I answered.

"We'll send a card."

She closed her bag. She tugged at her fur collar.

"It's probably nothing," she said. "Lie back, Mrs Hall. Rest is important."

I led her down to the door. She smiled on the threshold.

"Oh, how quickly you children grow," she said. "You'll stay with her today?"

"Yes, Doctor."

"Good lad. Quickly down to get her prescription, then back up home to her."

She smiled sadly.

"It's likely nothing. We'll sort her out, Dominic, and you'll all be right as rain again."

She tousled my hair and went on smiling.

"Yes, how very quickly," she said.

Then turned back to her barking dogs.

I ran down through the waste for her prescription. I got it at Sisterson's. The smell of disinfectant in there, of bleach, of cleanliness. I stood at the counter, waiting, found myself slipping my hand into a box of lozenges that lay open there. Watched my hand take one tube, then another, and put them in my pocket.

"Three times a day," said the pharmacist. He handed me a box with a bottle in it. "No more than that."

I looked at him, waited for him to find me out.

"And this one is for sleeping," he said, handing me another box. "One at bedtime. No more than that."

I nodded, waited a moment more.

"Off you go, then. The quicker it's started, the quicker she's well."

I turned and ran.

At home, she lay half sleeping. She sat up as I entered, tilted her head.

"Do you hear?" she said.

I tilted my own head.

"So beautiful," she said.

"It's only Mrs Stroud again," I said.

"Is it?"

"Yes." I opened the bottle, poured out a spoonful, held it to her lips.

"Are you certain? Only Mrs Stroud?"

"Yes, Mam. Yes. Now take this."

"The bastards docked me half a bloody day," said Dad as he came through the door at dusk. "I said, what would you do if your lass weren't well? We'd make arrangements, they said. I'll arrange your bloody face, I wanted to say. Don't worry. I didn't get the words out. How is she?"

"OK. The doctor came. There's stuff for her. They're sorting X-rays out."

"Hell's teeth."

"She said it's nothing."

"Nowt. Good. What'll we eat?"

"Dunno."

"You could get some chips, eh? I'll give you some cash, you'll get some chips."

"Aye."

"Mebbe a little bit later, eh?"

"Aye."

He tilted his head, listened to silence.

"Dan Liver's lass has got a cough. Billy Wells's lass and all. It's going round, Dominic. The time of year. Or something in the air. And lots of it down there in the bliddy yard, of course. It's brung on by the filth, the cold, the filthy bloody river. It's us that works down there that brings it home. Germs. Coughs and colds. Sneezes. No wonder the lasses is all getting ill. I'll gan up and see her, eh?"

"Aye, Dad."

"You OK? You been OK?"

"Aye."

"You're a good lad. I'll gan up, then, eh?"

"Aye. Go on."

He turned away and then turned back again.

"I'm frightened, Dominic. Ha. Can you credit that?"

"It's mebbe nothing, Dad."

"The blood, though. On your lass's mouth, on your wife's mouth. There's been blood today?"

"Just a bit. Go and see her, Dad."

"Aye. Then I'll give you cash, you'll get some grub, it'll all be fine. We'll laugh about it in a week or so."

"Aye, Dad. Aye."

"That's right. Haha! Bloody bliddy aye."

I went down for the chips. The sky darkened, reddened, intensified. Vincent McAlinden sat silhouetted in his doorway as I passed by. I didn't pause.

"Silent as Jack Law, eh?" he said.

"Me mam's not well," I blurted.

"That's a pity."

He held out a cigarette.

I hesitated. A sudden urge to go to him, to be with him.

"I'm going for some chips," I said.

"Tek a quick drag. Pass the time of night."

He came to the fence. I took the cigarette from him, put it to my lips.

"It came to nowt, then, eh?" he said. "They could have done us but they didn't."

"They didn't."

"You're the lucky one. Nothin they did would have mattered to me, but they could have truly buggered you."

"I know," I said.

"You been saved," he said. "Allelujah!"

I sucked the smoke into my lungs, breathed it out again, felt the pleasant harshness in my throat.

"I'm workin now," he said. "I'm in the tanks."

I caught the scent of the yard on him, the sourness I knew from Dad but with an extra edge to it. The filth of the tanks, I guessed.

I inhaled the smoke again.

"Me mam's not well," I blurted out again.

"Poor diddums. D'you remember all that ballocks about Hell?"

"Hell?"

"Aye, all them stories. About the noise, the never-ending din, the screeching and the grinding? That's what it's like down there inside the tanks. Like the noise of bliddy Hell. And them fuckin gates, creakin every morning to let you in, slammin shut behind you, creakin open every night to let you out."

He laughed again.

"The money's nice. I get me smokes. I get some pints down at the Angel in Bill Quay, where they divent give a toss how old you are. And lasses. Bliddy hell. Them lasses in the yard, Dom. Them little office cleaners and them canteen girls. The things they'll do for a coin or two." He laughed. He winked. "Not like that little Holly Stroud. She's comin along very nicely, eh . . ."

He laughed as I backed away and headed down the rocky path.

"Get your chips for your mammy," he said. "Hahahaha!"

I stood in the queue in the chip shop, in the steam, in the sound of the bubbling fat. I wanted to tug somebody's arm, to blurt out to them me mam's not well. Did nothing. Said nothing. Took home three portions of chips, wrapped in the *News of the World*. Peeled the paper from the chips, put them on plates, put salt and vinegar on, HP Sauce, made some mugs of tea, took it all up to her room.

She was asleep.

He was on a chair at her side, looking down at her.

"She took a pill, it knocked her out," he said. "Best thing for her, eh? A good night's sleep. That's what she needs."

"That's right, Dad."

We ate the chips, drank the tea. He wheezed, like always. Her breath was gentle, long breaths in and long breaths out and not a cough.

"What we worrying for?" he said.

"We're daft," I said. "It's nowt."

"Eat up," he said. "It's nowt."

CHAPTER
THIRTY-SIX

Late Sunday afternoon, a few days later. Bells were ringing in a distant church. Holly had a brand-new wire, a long cable that her dad had brought out from the yard. It was a lovely thing, with interweaving filaments and a dark grey glossy gleam.

She curled it across her shoulder and led me up towards the larks.

She asked about my mam. I said there seemed to be no more blood.

"It should be the other one," she said.

"The other one?"

"*My* mother, Dominic."

She took me to the top beyond the pits, to where the landscape of the west was visible, the pitheads and winding gear on the Durham moors, the purple-headed moors beyond, and the Cheviots far off in the hazy north. Hardly a breath of wind up here for once, and the late sunlight was warm.

She took me to two hawthorn trees that stood at the very top, twelve feet apart. One was white and one was red. The blossoms were already falling and the buds of berries were already showing at their hearts.

"That's them," she said.

"Them?"

The trees were old: gnarled trunks, a mass of tangled branches, a hundred thousand thorns. They stood on a stony ridge, with roots reaching down into the cracks and openings in the stone itself.

She told me to crouch with her and to look up into them.

"Imagine walking from one tree to another," she said. "Imagine our silhouettes against the sky. Against a blazing sunset, Dominic!"

Too many branches, too many thorns, I told her.

"We'll cut them and prune them to make a space for us."

"We can't do that to the poor trees."

"The Killer Hall is saying *that*?"

She showed me the place on each tree where the wire should be fixed. She showed me that the wire was long enough to reach.

Then took a knife from her pocket, clicked a switch and a long thin pointed blade snapped out.

"A gift from our friend Vincent," she said.

She held the blade against a stem that grew out from the trunk.

"Not the right kind of knife for this," she said. "We need an axe or a saw or just a bigger knife or something. We'll clear the clutter away. There'll be space for the wire and for us. And the branches left behind will be a canopy."

She held the knife against a thin bough with blue-grey lichen on it, with the remnants of white blossom on it, with the new berry already becoming exposed.

She started to cut. And then we saw Jack Law, his head just visible over the ridge.

"Don't look," said Holly. "Maybe he'll come closer."

She started to cut.

"Vincent said I might need the knife to protect myself," she said.

"From who?"

"That's what I said." She laughed. "Maybe from you, the murderer! Hush. Jack's very close."

I saw him from the corner of my eye, moving forward step by tentative step. He moved faster. I couldn't not turn to him. I turned and he stopped. He reached out his hands towards Holly and her knife. Then dropped to his knees and focused his eyes on the tree and joined his hands as if in prayer. He moved his lips.

"He's praying to the tree," Holly whispered.

"To the tree?"

Now she dropped to her knees.

"You as well," she said.

"What?"

"We pray to the tree before we cut it," she said. "Like ancient hunters apologized to the spirits of their prey. Put your hands together, Dominic. Pray."

"Pray what?"

"Do it for Jack Law."

I shrugged, knelt down, joined my hands together.

"Pray to what?" I said.

"To the tree. To nothingness."

I prayed into the nothingness.

"Make my mother better," I murmured. "Keep her safe."

Minutes passed. Jack Law stood up and started to back away.

"Don't go," said Holly. "We won't harm you, Jack."

But he just turned and walked his smooth and rapid walk. He turned his face to us, then walked again. We followed him down the slope on the far side.

CHAPTER
THIRTY-SEVEN

Here were ancient paddocks and hawthorn lanes and the humps of old earthworks and old mine workings. Jack moved smoothly as he always did. There were long evening shadows now and we kept losing sight of him, then seeing him again. He led us through a low opening in a hedge and we found ourselves in a small field with blue and yellow flowers growing in the tangled grass. Now he did stop, and he did turn. The sun shone on his flaxen hair. His eyes gleamed. Was he looking directly at us? Beyond him was another opening in another hedge. He paused, looked back, went on again. He moved through the opening.

"We should go back now," I said.

"No, Dom," she said. "Let's go on."

The sun was almost at the horizon. The sky to the west was burning. Against it were the dark etchings of the coalfield. I thought of men tunnelling deep down inside the earth while we were up here in the late light. I thought of the bones of men who had died down there, turning the whole earth to their grave.

"We'll get lost," I said.

"Of course we won't!" she said, but I heard the shudder in her voice.

She moved towards the second opening and I followed her. So dark in there beneath the hedge. She held my hand as we went through and came into a paddock, all tussocks and unearthed stones and a broken fence at the far side. And another rocky out-crop like the one with the hawthorns on it. This time there was an ancient oak tree whose twisted roots gripped the rock. There was a gap in the roots, an opening two feet or so high with a gleam of light burning in it.

We went towards it slowly.

"Is this *it*?" she whispered. "Is *this* where Jack Law lives?"

We crawled to the opening in the rock.

We whispered Jack's name.

No answer.

We looked inside. There was a cavity there, not big enough for a home. Just big enough for a body or two to lie down in. There were candles burning on more cracks in the rock inside. The candlelight showed the pictures on the walls and roof.

"There's God!" whispered Holly.

He was high up on the wall. A sentimental hackneyed God in white robes with white beard. The rock around him and above him was painted in flaking crackling sky-blue. Angels flew there on widespread wings. There were awkward figures that must have been saints in prayer. There was a white bird, there was a tiny tongue of white fire. This was the childish sentimental Heaven we'd been told about in junior school, but here, inside this rock upon the hill, smudged by the soot of

209

the candles, it was a thing of beauty. It quickened our hearts, it made us catch our breath.

We stared for minutes. We didn't crawl in. Maybe we were scared. Maybe we felt it would be a kind of trespass if we did go in. We lay close to the opening. Such silence in there, such light. We gazed for minutes and then we left. The world seemed much darker now. We heard a low murmuring sound — like weird singing, or maybe just the breeze moving through the grass and across the rocks.

We hurried back through the paddocks, the hedges, past the earthworks. A flock of crows cawed as they scattered from some trees and took erratic flight above our heads. We caught sight of each other's golden face. Holly laughed, and suddenly kissed me on the cheek. "Phew!" she whispered. "Bloody hell!" And then we ran to the top and to the hawthorn trees. I snapped off the blossomed fruiting lichen-laden bough to carry home for Mam. We headed past the spawn ponds and the mines and the gorse. We ran down through the fields and as we ran we heard the voices of parents ringing out across the roofs and across the darkened sky as they called their playing children home.

CHAPTER
THIRTY-EIGHT

She was already half asleep.

I sat on the bed beside her.

"I brought you this," I whispered.

She stirred.

I already had it in a glass vase. It angled upwards through the clear water, the white falling blossom and the new red fruit exposed.

"I'll put it here," I whispered.

I put it on her bedside table beside her clock, her box of white handkerchiefs.

She came round, opened her eyes.

"Hawthorn," she said.

"Yes."

She closed her eyes again.

"It's lovely, Dominic," she whispered.

She put her hand on mine as if to comfort me.

"It's beautiful, my son."

CHAPTER
THIRTY-NINE

The cough abated. No more blood. But pains in her back, pains in her legs, pains in her head. She said it was nothing, it was all the lying around and sitting around she'd been doing. She just needed to get back to normal. One night her screaming woke me up.

An ambulance came to take her to hospital for X-rays. Dad took a day off work and went with her. The ambulance brought them home again. They said the radiologist had been so kind, so sweet, was a girl they knew, in fact, the daughter of a nice lass from down Stoneygate way. Nothing happened. She went on coughing a little. She got out of bed each morning, made breakfast. I saw her wincing as she moved, I saw her losing weight.

I took to leaving the house early, calling into church on my way to school. I'd kneel beneath the cross that hung suspended above the front pews. How did it stay up there? The cords that held it were so thin, hardly visible. As I had when I was a child, I waited for the cross to fall, for Christ's body to crash to earth and shatter. But he hung there as he always had, with his arms spread wide, making the shapes of pain, making the shape of an angel with outstretched wings against the dark brown roof above. At first I stupidly tried to pray, but soon I took to cursing his silence, his changelessness. He'd hung there all my life without affecting anything, without changing anything, despite all the fervent bodies below him, despite all the eyes on him, despite the endless prayers. I cursed the creamy shining bloody body of him, the blood fixed in mid-trickle on his skin, the suffering eyes that looked upon nothing and nobody. And I cursed his mother as well. There she was, like always, high up in her niche in the wall, in her sky-blue clothes, with the serpents crushed beneath her feet, with her eyes turned down towards us.

"What are you going to do?" I yelled from deep inside myself. "What the fuck? *What?*"

Nothing, was the answer.

Silence, was the answer.

She stood there like he hung there, two jokes, two massive lies.

CHAPTER
FORTY

Holly came to me with a saw, with a long-bladed knife, with some pruning shears, with the wire.

We went quickly to our trees. The blossom was nearly gone by now.

"First cut away the old dead stuff," she said.

Some of it was so old, so sapless, it could be just snapped off. Thin boughs cut easily. They tumbled down on to the grass. We sawed off the bigger boughs. We snagged our skin on thorns. Bulbs of blood and trickles of blood appeared on our skin. We kept moving in with the cutting tools, moving back again, assessing, revising, editing, changing. We trimmed tiny single growths, snapped off single thorns. The boughs that remained reached up towards the sky to form an interleaving arch. They appeared to form an upturned nest with the sky as ground, the ground as sky.

We pulled away the cuttings so that the earth under the trees was clear, just tangled grass with flowers in it.

We watched for Jack Law, but there was no sign of him.

We attached the wire between the trees. We attached it to branching boughs and tightened it with the tightening winch. It was almost as high as my shoulder.

Holly went up first. She shinned up into the red tree, stood with one foot on the wire, one foot on a bough, back pressed against the boughs behind, and then stepped out and walked the wire against the sky. So secure in her walking, in her balance, in just being herself up there. She leapt down and rolled across the grass to my feet.

Then me, squat me with the muscles and the hair and the thickening chest. Me, the chimpanzee. I climbed up into the white tree. I walked on the wire. I stepped, slithered, teetered, but I got across. I crossed again. Paused at the centre, stood there swaying high above the river and the town, against the sky.

I dropped to the earth, caught the scent of decay.

I sniffed, I looked around.

"It's the hawthorn," said Holly Stroud.

She lifted a cut stem to her face.

"It's known for it," she said.

We kept on walking, improving. We untied the wire.

We walked away from our trees, our beautiful damaged pruned trees.

CHAPTER
FORTY-ONE

They took Mam away the very next day. An ambulance again, so garish, so massive-looking in our little street. She walked out with Dad. She lay down on a stretcher inside. I stood at the ambulance doorway.

"All this fuss," she said to me as we said goodbye. "You make sure you get to school now. Work hard, be good. I'll soon be back. This fuss!"

Her lips trembled as she kissed me, and I saw how pleased she was, to be taken away from having to be so strong. I watched the ambulance drive away. Its orange light began to flash and spin. I didn't go to school. I went down to steal fruit from Bamling's. I stole Beech-Nut and a Mars Bar. I bought five Park Drive and smoked them one after the other by the railway line and sickened myself with them. I eyed up flying birds and thought *Kapow!* I thought how puny my transgressions were. How puny I was to have allowed them to affect me so much. Stealing a fiver from an open doorway! What was that? What a child I was! I walked back and forward through the familiar streets. I thought of Mrs Charlton, her contempt for us as she travelled through our estate, as she stood in our little house. She shouldn't have got that far. Instead of pissing on her carpet, I should have found her, and murdered her in her home. I thought of God, of non-existent useless absent God. "Save my mother and I will be good," I said into the nothingness. "Let her die and I'll start to kill!"

I gathered some stones and put them in my pocket. I went into the church. It was silent and empty.

I started to fling the stones at Christ, trying to bring him down, to break his stillness, his stupid silence.

"Fall!" I said, in savage whispers. "Fucking fall."

He rocked and swung and creaked as the stones struck. I saw the marks I made on his body. Flakes of his skin and tiny fragments of his flesh drifted to the floor. The stones that missed scattered down on to the altar, littered the white cloth there and the red carpet around it.

"Fall. Fall! Fall!"

I aimed for the cords that held the cross, but even when I hit them I didn't bring him down, his cross didn't fall.

He just hung there, swayed and shuddered there.

I heard doors opening beyond the altar. Heard running feet. Maybe I should have stood my ground. But I ran out again. The great church door groaned open and groaned shut behind me.

I ran across the wasteland.

I knew that she would surely die.

It only took two weeks. I saw her a few times more. I was with her when she died. A Tuesday afternoon. A message had been sent to Dad, but there was no way of knowing if it would get to him, and no way of knowing if he'd be set free. Through the window of her little room I could see the river and the yard, the dark and distant sea. I knelt at the bedside. I held her hand and whispered that everything would be OK, that Dad would be with us soon.

"Yes, it is," she whispered. "Yes, he will."

She was stunned by pain and morphine. Her breath diminished to a whistle but her lips still moved. Boats were important, she whispered. She said that she could see them on the shore.

"Will you wave?" she gasped.

"Yes, Mam."

Her body jerked and her breath came to an end.

I kissed her brow.

A nurse came in.

I should have called her, she said.

There would have been nothing she could do, she whispered.

"She died knowing that she was loved," she said.

Then Dad arrived. He had the smell of the yard on him. Sweat trickled down over the dust and oil on his face.

"The gates were locked," he said. "They wouldn't let me out."

He wiped his filthy hands on a towel.

"They said wait till shift's end. It's just a few minutes' time. I could see the hospital through the locked gates. I climbed over them. Somebody even tried to pull me down as I was climbing them."

He groaned.

"I saw her go," he said. "I saw her soul."

218

I listened.

"I was running. I was still right down on the High Street. I kept my eyes on the hospital. And I saw her, Dominic. I saw her soul rising from the roof of the hospital and disappearing into the sky. Her! Yes! Don't go! Not yet!"

He leaned to her now.

"Oh, love. Oh, how I ran. Where are you now?"

CHAPTER
FORTY-TWO

She came back home. A hearse drew up. A top-hatted undertaker led her in. She was carried by men in shiny black suits and grubby black shoes and white nylon shirts and slipshod black ties. They closed the front-room curtains, laid her on trestles, opened the coffin lid. Mascara on her lashes, foundation on her face. Neighbours and relatives came to drink tea and to eat ham sandwiches. They brought cards and flowers. They said she was just as lovely as she'd been in life. They said she was out of pain now, it was a blessing it'd been so quick. Father Caffrey came. He drank whisky and smoked cigarettes with Dad. He said it was impossible to always understand the ways of God but there was always a purpose to events in this world. He said she'd gone to a better place. He said we'd all be with her there one day. Dad said that was a load of crap. He said God must be a fucking cunt to do a thing like this. The priest said he understood our pain, our confusion. Dad told him no, he didn't. He said if he was going to drink his whisky he should just shut the fuck up and fucking drink.

I left the house when the Brothers arrived, as they always did when a Catholic died. They gathered in the garden, whispering, wearing black ties and pompous faces, carrying rolled-up rosary beads in their pockets. I slipped past them, shrugged off their attempts at comforting words and comforting touches, and went to Holly. We watched from her window as the Brothers went in, so many of them I wondered how they'd fit into the room around her. Even through the window we heard the ghastly beat and drone of their chants, their *Thy will be done*, their *Pray for us sinners*, their *Deliver us from evil*. I imagined our little house vibrating with it, humming with it. The estate shone pale beneath a sickle moon. The gardens darkened.

"Let's go," I said.

We walked the ring of the estate, then went through the alleyway that led to the upper wasteland. Kids had a fire burning there. We sat on stones beside it. There was a white tent nearby.

A boy came to us.

"We're campin oot," he said. "We're never gannin yem again."

"There's been a war," said another. "Everythin's gone. Everybody's deed. We're the last of the survivors."

"But we're ready to kill," said the first. "I'm Dan and he's Stan."

They lifted black potatoes from the edge of the fire and gave them to us. We cracked the hard scorched skins and nibbled at the steaming creamy flesh inside.

"We seen three shooting stars," said Dan. "And we think there's a fox in that hedge there."

"And the ghosts of the slaughtered'll be comin at midnight," said Stan.

"It's true," said Dan. "You ever seen the ghosts? There's always been a load of them roond here, ever since I was a little bairn. I could see them, I could hear them groanin and stuff."

"The ghosts of what?" said Holly Stroud.

"Ghosts of the deed. Ghosts of them from the past that's still aroond."

"They can find nae peace," said Stan. "They roam the earth for evermore and evermore."

We fell silent for a time. We listened to the hissing and the crackle of the fire. Holly hummed something hymn-like. I scraped at the ashes with my feet.

"You could tek your lass in the tent and shag her if you like," said Stan.

"Aye," said Dan. "We got to get mankind started up again."

We laughed and ate the delicious potatoes. We saw a shooting star, and another.

"That might be nothing but a bit of dust," I said.

"Are you the one that's mam just died?" said Stan.

"Aye."

"Ye'll get over it. Me dad died last year. Me mam says the best thing to do is pretend I never loved him and he never loved me. Then I won't feel so bad."

"So are you doing that?" I said.

"Aye."

"And is it working?"

"I think so. You want another spud?"

"No."

"She says I got to pretend he was never even here. She says I got to think that what I think I remember aboot him is really just a dream."

"And is that working?"

"I think it is. Sometimes I'm not sure if what I remember is real. You should try it."

"I will," I said.

"Good. Now we got to gan and get ready for the comin of the ghosts."

We stayed a while and then we left.

In the shadows between the fire and the estate we kissed each other hard. I held Holly tight, and wanted to disappear into her.

Then Dad's yells echoed over the rooftops.

The Brothers were leaving the estate. We pushed our way through a group of them.

One pushed back.

"Stop your shoving," he snarled.

"Son of the bloody father," said another.

Another caught me for a moment by the arm.

"Keep an eye on him," he murmured.

Dad was at Holly's door, yelling at Bill Stroud. His fists were flailing. The priest was trying to haul him back.

"Howay, then, Mr Bliddy Conchie Draughtsman!" Dad yelled. "Let's see some fight! Let's have it out at bliddy last."

I put my arms around him.

"Please, Dad!" I called.

He writhed, snorted, grunted, swung his fists.

"Why wasn't it yours?" he snarled at Bill. "Why wasn't it the bliddy maniac upstairs?"

Bill stepped forward and held him, too.

"Oh, Francis," he said.

"Daddy!" I begged. "Daddy, please!"

He slumped at last. He let us pull him back. He leaned upon me as we shuffled across the street.

"Would you like me to stay?" said the priest at the door.

"No, Father," Dad sighed. "Just fuck off back to your God."

We went inside. He went to her one more time. I helped him up the stairs and into his bed and then went down again.

There was a scent of hawthorn in the coffin room.

I touched her icy brow. I kissed her icy cheek.

They laid her in the earth next day.

CHAPTER
FORTY-THREE

Dad drank. He drank in the Iona Club and tottered home to drink again. He drank cans of McEwan's Export and bottles of Bell's whisky. He chain-smoked Player's No. 6. I smoked along with him, and he didn't care, and we flicked our fag ends into cinders and ashes that slid out from the grate. We ate Heinz Baked Beans, Heinz Spaghetti, sausages, fried eggs, tinned tomatoes, Ambrosia Creamed Rice. Loaf after loaf of white sliced bread. Bags of chips smothered in HP Sauce. We hardly washed the dishes, we hardly changed the sheets. Light bulbs flickered out and weren't replaced. We wore pants for days and shirts for weeks. The house smelt, we smelt. We watched *The Outer Limits* and *The Twilight Zone*. We lay awake at four a.m. and listened to the howling dogs and the night-shift caulkers and we stared into the horrors of the night. I'd hear him weeping, hear him cursing, hear him wrestling with himself within his tangled sheets. I'd hear him rising with a groan to go downhill to his detested work. I'd get up and follow him an hour later.

At school, Creel and Joyce tried to comfort me. Joyce tried to give me poems for grieving. The poems told of veils, of separation, of lights in darkness, of a coming-together again. They tried to tell me that death itself would die.

I ripped them up, dropped them into bins, burned them in my heart. I scribbled my own words of hate, yowls of rage and snarls of spite. I cursed, blasphemed and howled on to page after empty page. I wrote of monstrous murders, of knives, guns, hatchets, of broken bones and severed flesh and pouring blood and seeping gore.

I wrote that every missile should be launched right now and all bombs dropped. I dreamed of the whole world blazing bright.

Holly stayed at my side. She went down to school with me. She sought me out after lessons and at break times.

She said there was meaning in nothing, and that was the only meaning we could know.

She painted me and painted me: against the pebbledash, against fierce flames, against abundant never-ending stars, against the hawthorn trees, upon the wire against the foliage and the sky. In each of them I had a different face, a different shape. I was old, I was young, I was a tender innocent, I was a brute.

When I questioned the variety, she laughed.

"We have everything inside us," she said.

"Each of us is everybody," she said.

We hardly knew what we were saying but we said such things and thought such things. We were young. We were testing ourselves out against the pebbledash and against the future and the past.

She painted my mother for me, as she had been in my first memory, reaching up to a clothes line with bright blue sky beyond and with bright translucent fabrics dancing around her head.

I hung these paintings in my room. Dad hated them.

"Fucking art," he said. "What's the use of fucking art?"

I tried to lift myself. I worked hard. The time of O levels was approaching. I read, I revised, I committed great chunks of history and geography to heart. I memorized list after list of French vocabulary. I learned Archimedes' principle and SOHCAHTOA and Euclid's *Elements*. I drew the human lungs and the human brain and named their parts. I learned the speeches of King Lear.

But to the girdle do the gods inherit,
Beneath is all the fiends';
There's hell, there's darkness, there's the sulphurous pit,
Burning, scalding, stench, consumption;
fie, fie, fie! pah, pah!

I sat by the hearth cramming information into my brain and Dad wavered between pride, astonishment and scorn. One day, *Oh, I'm so proud of you, Dominic. You are what it's all been for.* And on another, *What's the bliddy point of it? There's nae place for the likes of us. You'd be better getting a trade, learnin a skill. What's the point of all this learnin and all these bliddy books?* And then tears would be falling from his eyes. *Oh, she was so proud of you. Wasn't she so proud.*

And then again, *What is the point? What's the point of this of that of anybliddything at all?*

I got on with it. I felt like I was face down to an icy deck, that I slithered all alone through a dark and filthy double hull.

CHAPTER
FORTY-FOUR

One day I ran uphill alone in search of what? In search of skylarks, of light, of disappearance? In order to run and not stop running till I'd run into a new life that wasn't me, in which there was not a me at all? I ran past the hawthorn trees upon their crag and ran to the rock with the heavenly space in it. Could see it nowhere, told myself it had just been an illusion, a kind of dream. Then there it was. Gnarled shrubs and the ancient oak, the jagged stone beneath, the narrow opening between the roots. It was as if it had been prepared for me. I crouched and saw that new candles had been recently lit, illuminating Heaven. I slithered in, the knee-high opening just wide enough to let me through. I lay facing upwards. The air was warm and scented by the candles. The only sound seemed to be the tiny hiss of the candles burning, the tiny crackle of the paper shifting. The floor was soft. I ran my fingertips across the sky, across the saints and angels, God in glory, Christ at his side, the dove and the tongues of fire to the Holy Ghost. I tried to pray. *Our Father, who art in Heaven.* Knew I could not. As I looked close, I saw that Heaven was painted upon other images, earlier shapes. There was graffiti visible just beneath the blue: cocks and balls and blasphemy and scrawled black curses. Jack's Heaven was painted over coarseness, mischief, violence, grief, confusion. Maybe it had been repainted many times. I closed my eyes. I wept for a while. After what could have been a thousand years the tears stopped and I grew still and calm.

Took a pen from my pocket. Looked into Heaven again. Found an empty space, edged with a pair of angels, not too far from God. I drew my mother there: a clumsy drawing on the uneven rock, but as beautiful as those Jack Law had drawn. She stood straight, and she looked down towards me, smiling. I breathed easily. I lay and smiled back at her. I was with her, inside some vast and comforting open space inside this little slab of rock. Began to disappear, perhaps began to sleep.

And then I felt the touch upon my cheek.

And opened my eyes.

And Jack Law was there.

He lay looking in through the opening, his hand stretched out to me. His eyes so gentle, as was his touch.

"Jack," I breathed.

He moved his lips in reply, and though no sound came out I felt his breath on me.

"I drew her," I said. "I put her in here, in your Heaven."

I pointed to the rock.

"Look. There she is."

He looked. He nodded. He touched me again, upon my cheek. His face relaxed, almost a smile.

"Can you speak?" I whispered.

He just looked back at me.

"Can you?" I said. "Can you understand me?"

He tenderly touched my lips. Then pointed to his own. He touched his lips with his index finger, a row of three touches along his top lip, a row of three touches upon the bottom lip. Then pursed his lips together and made a little grunting sound, and relaxed them again. And then I saw the ancient marks at the edge of his beard, and I think I understood.

The marks were stitch marks, three tiny marks on his top lip visible through his beard, three tiny marks on the bottom lip.

"Oh, Jack," I whispered.

I imagined black thread tying the marks together.

"Who stitched you, Jack?" I said.

He sighed. Did he understand the question? Did he understand anything?

"A teacher?" I said. "A priest? Your parents?"

His mouth opened, closed.

"Did it happen in the war?"

A groan escaped from him.

"Tell me, Jack," I whispered. "Can you say anything?"

He spoke two syllables. Two vowels.

"E — U."

"Again," I breathed.

"E — U."

It could have been "Hello". It could have been "Heaven". It could have been meaningless. Just a sound, just a grunt. No way to tell.

"E — U," I whispered in reply.

His face softened, he smiled.

I didn't ask him to try again.

We gazed at each other through the narrow opening in the rock, two shy creatures encountering each other for the very first time, and recognizing each other.

I pointed to Mam, there in the heavenly rock.

"She's there," I said.

He smiled. We looked at her together, in the space that seemed to have been prepared for her.

And he opened his mouth and he sang, a single pure wordless high-pitched note. He paused, took a breath, and sang the same long note again. And touched my cheek again.

And then he stopped. There were no words. Just, "E-u. E-u."

"E-u, Jack Law," I breathed.

CHAPTER
FORTY-FIVE

A knock at the door and Bill Stroud was there, a white cloth folded across his arm, carnation in his buttonhole and a great smile on his face.

"Greetings, *mes amis*!" he said. "We should like to invite you to a celebration."

"What celebration?" said Dad.

"A celebration to mark the great achievements of these two fine *enfants* of ours."

I laughed.

"For the O-level results," I said.

I'd passed them all, as Holly had. Dad and I had celebrated in a way: cans of beer on the sofa, a couple of cream cakes, tears for Mam. He'd fallen asleep on the sofa. I had to shake him awake, tell him to go to bed, it would soon be time for him to get up.

He was in his vest. He had a cigarette burning between his fingers.

"I'm not dressed for it," he said.

"It is an informal gathering, Francis. A little *pique-nique*. Come as you are!"

Dad shrugged, was about to step out.

"Put a shirt on, Dad," I said.

"We'll be two minutes," I said to Bill.

"We shall be ready for you. Red or white?"

We both hesitated.

"Wine," said Bill. "White or red? Could I recommend the Côtes du Rhône?"

"Aye," said Dad. "That."

"What kind of bliddy crap is this?" he said as Bill walked back.

"A party," I said.

"The kind of thing Mam would have put on to celebrate," I said.

"Shove off," he said.

He put a shirt on. He put a packet of Embassy and some Swan Vestas into its pocket.

"Fuckin wine," he said as we walked across.

Holly kissed me twice on the cheek, as she said the French would have done. There was a long French stick, a bottle of sparkling water, black olives, a box of Camembert, slices of ham, tomatoes from Bill's allotment.

Bill poured the Côtes du Rhône. He held up his glass to the sky to show the beauty of it.

"To our *enfants magnifiques!*" he announced.

We chinked our glasses and we drank.

"To our *funambules!*" he said, and we drank again.

He was already tipsy.

"That means tightrope walkers," he said to Dad. "For these children, *absolument* anything is possible! To the *ciel!* Now drink it down, *mes amis*. There's plenty more where that came from. We have made a very successful visit this very *matin* to Fenwicks' *merveilleux delicatessen*. Aven't we, *ma petite?*"

"We 'ave, *mon papa!*" said Holly.

He wiped his lips with the white cloth, topped up Dad's glass.

"A bit different from Federation Ale, eh, Francis?" he said. "Now 'ave one of these cigarettes."

They were Gitanes. Dad slid one out. He sniffed it before letting Bill light it. He cursed as he drew in the smoke. He coughed and cursed again.

"Ah, *oui,*" said Bill. "They like their cigarettes to have a kick, those funny French! Some *fromage,* Francis! Some ham and bread! We bring the Mediterranean to the pebbledash. We bring sunshine to the North! *Mangez! Buvez!* Hoy it doon! *Relaxez-vous! Enjoyezvous!*"

Holly cut the Camembert into triangles, cut the bread into sections.

"This is *la vie!*" said Bill.

Dad threw the Gitane away and lit an Embassy. He sliced open some bread and put a slice of ham into it. He ate, he swigged more wine. Bill brought another bottle.

I slooshed Côtes du Rhône around my mouth. I tried a Gitane and found it unsmokably harsh. Bill laughed. I leaned back in my chair, leaned against the pebbledash, and its tiny points pressed into my back.

Soon Mrs Stroud upstairs started singing.

Non, rien de rien,
Non, je ne regrette rien.
Ni le bien qu'on m'a fait
Ni le mal tout ça m'est bien égal . . .

"Ah, she's in *l'esprit* of it all!" said Bill.

"*Chantez, ma chérie!*" he called.

A distant dog started howling, as if to sing along.

"Hell's bliddy teeth!" said Dad.

We ate, we drank, all of us got tipsy.

We went home soon afterwards.

When I got there he groaned.

"What kind of world we livin in?"

"A lovely one," I slurred.

"Lovely! Mebbe you should move across the street and live with them bliddy nutcases!"

Ultima Thule

CHAPTER
FORTY-SIX

We cleaned the house. We ate fruit and vegetables. Dad strengthened, but he said I was turning into the father and he was turning into the child and how could that be right? What kind of man was a man like that?

"A good man," I said.

"Not till I pull meself up from the pit."

It was a northern spring. We had the fire blazing. He cupped my chin in his hand and regarded me.

"I don't know you, my own son," he said. "How can that be right?"

"I don't know you," I said.

"There's nowt to know. A miserable caulker. But you, you're different, and you'll be grown and gone afore I know."

He stared from the window. Sleet splashed down on to the pebbledash outside.

"And this is hardly a place that'll draw you back," he said.

That Sunday all the sleet was gone. The sun began its peaceful relentless archway through a clear sky. It was a northern spring. The air was warm in the light. We walked together out of the estate and then downhill towards our little railway station. We took a train through Gateshead and Newcastle and along the Tyne Valley. He wanted to take me to the country, to a special place.

I remember the sparkle of the river as we crossed it at Newcastle, the sooty stone of the buildings, the astounding green arch of the town's main bridge, the cranes and warehouses, the boats and the seagulls swooping over them. I remember the nap of the red railway seats and the shiny patches where it had worn away. I remember how long my hair was, how short was his, how he had slicked it back with Brylcreem. He wore a white collar spread out over the lapels of his black jacket. I wore scrubbed-pale Levi's jeans, striped cheesecloth shirt, Levi's jacket and Kicker shoes. I remember the reflection of his face against the outside in the glass, how the window framed him within the places that we passed through.

I said nothing today about his smoking, his wheezing, about my fears that he'd be taken from me, too.

As we rattled alongside the river, he gently sang an ancient song, the song of lovers separated by the Tyne.

"I cannot get tae my love if I would dee
For the waters of Tyne run between her and me . . ."

I told him that it was lovely, that I hadn't heard him sing since I was a little boy.

"There's some would say that that's a blessin. Now it's you."

"Eh?"

"I do one, you do one. That's how it was in the good owld bad owld days."

I shrugged and watched the water flowing. I had a notebook with me — words of mine, words of others.

"Sweet Tyne," I read, "Run softly till I end my song. Sweet Tyne, run softly, cos I speak not loud nor long. But at me back in a blast I hear. The din of caulkers and the skylark's song."

"What's that?" he said.

"Poetry, Dad," I answered.

"Ha! See me meanin? How'd you end up doin bliddy poetry?"

"It's mebbe not so different from your songs," I said. I watched the water.

"Mebbe it was your songs that got me started on it."

"Aye? Then here's another."

And he set off on "Felton Lonnen", closing his eyes as he breathed the beautiful song of hope and loss.

"He's always oot roamin the lang summer's day through,

He's always oot roamin away from the farm.

Through hedges and ditches and valleys and hillsides,

Aa hope that me hinny will come to nae harm."

We were sunlit, suddenly brilliant in the gaps between fast-flickering shadows. We glanced easily at each other. I took in his scars and blemishes, the sadness in his eyes. I kept pushing my hair back, thinking of ways to express the fact of sitting here with him, being carried through the world with him, and thinking ahead to the time when I must leave him.

"Used to come out this way when we were courtin," he said.

He kept on humming softly.

"She liked the country, did me bonny lass. She used to say we'd come out to the country when me work was done. Ha. As if we ever could."

We went through Dunston, left the edges of the city, passed through Blaydon.

"You should've seen her back in them days, boy," he said. "She was a looker. How'd she ever end up choosin me?"

There were fields of cows and sheep now. The first lambs were gambolling. Men stood in the water fishing. A bunch of kids walked on the riverbank with a crowd of scampering dogs. The moors of the west were closer, brighter.

We got out at Wylam. We walked through the woods above the station. We drank pints of bitter on a wooden bench outside the Dr Syntax Inn. We ate the cheese sandwiches we'd brought. He said they'd sat exactly here on such a day as this. Said he could taste the hard-boiled eggs they'd had. And the beer tasted just the same as it did back then. He raised his glass to the sky. He laughed.

"Praise be," he said. "I love this stuff, ye knaa."

"I know."

He shook his head, he shrugged.

"So lovely," he said. "The taste of it, that bitterness and sweetness, the feelin of it gannin doon, the feelin of it settlin in you, spreadin through you."

The sunlight streamed through the liquid and the glass, illuminating the brilliant amber of it.

"Is it daft to say it's beautiful?" he said.

"No."

"It is," he said. "It truly bliddy is."

He swigged.

"And the same sun shines," he said. "And the same trees grow. And the same pub sign still swings in the breeze. And I close me eyes and it's her I see that's sittin there, not you." He swigged his beer. He touched my hand. "Divent worry, son. I'm not descendin. It's just I sometimes wonder, how come everything didn't die that day?"

We walked again through fields. There was still dew in the grass. He named the tiny blue flowers as speedwell. I played, walking in circles and spirals, kept looking back to see where we'd come from, the lovely patterns of our footsteps in the grass. He led me through a copse of birch trees to a place of ancient sandpits and quarries. He told me that all of this was like walking back into the past. A path led us right into one of the sandpits and he pointed up and showed me the line of holes that had been burrowed by birds into the sandy soil at the top.

"Sand martins," he said. "We done this as well."

He started to climb, on all fours, the sand falling away in waves and clumps around and below him. He told me to follow. Climbing was slow and difficult. The sand so soft, so dense, warm at the surface but cold within. We kept sliding backwards, but then the earth became more solid where it became more steep. Almost at the top, he said we should pause. We gathered our breath. The brown-and-white fork-tailed creatures whirled around us, singing their alarms, beating their wings within inches of our faces.

"Just the same as then," he said.

Poor troubled things, who were we to be here in their place?

"We'll just stay a moment," he whispered. "They won't remember nowt."

He shinned a little higher.

"And mebbe that's the way to be," he said.

He put his hand into one of the holes. He reached deep until almost his whole arm had disappeared. He sighed, drew his hand out again, opened it and showed the small white egg on his palm.

"They won't know," he said. "They cannot count. There was five of them in there. You do it now. Another nest."

I didn't dare at first, but knew I must. I shoved with my feet in the sand and climbed higher. I fearfully put my hand into one of the holes. Slow as slow I reached inside. I remember the grit, the cold sand against my skin, the rising thrill and fear. I recall how my hand and arm seemed to fit so well in there. And then I touched it, the bird that hadn't left its nest. It shivered and vibrated and quaked against my fingers. I felt its feathers, its beak, its claws. I gaped and gasped in terror and wonder. I told myself do not recoil. I touched the stunning terrified frantic life within and then let go at last, and tumbled down the quarry slope and yelped.

He slithered down and lay with me. I told him what I'd felt.

As I told it, it intensified in me.

He opened his mouth, raised his hand to it, and allowed the egg he was holding there to drop out on to his palm.

"Safest place of aal," he said.

He showed it, the lovely impossible fragile thing.

"Think what this is," he said, and his brow furrowed as he had that thought. He pointed to the sky, where the birds were less frantic now. "And think what it'll turn to. How can such a thing occur?"

I gazed at his blemished nicotine-stained fingers and the beautiful white creation that they held.

"I don't know," I said. "Nobody knows. That's the amazing thing about it all."

He kept on staring at the egg.

"Is that the way to think about it? To think that naebody knaas?" he said. "Is that a better way than thinking that there must be a God and there must be a truth and there must be a bliddy answer to it all?"

"I think so," I said.

"Good. I never really had much time for God and I never knew much truth." He pondered. "But I guess that meks us lonely, eh?"

I shrugged.

"Mebbe."

"So what? Couldn't be much lonelier than I am."

He reached out and held my arm.

"Unless ye were took from me, of course."

Then took a thin penknife from his pocket, made tiny holes in each end of the egg, put the egg to his lips and blew and the yolk and white spattered down on to the sand. He wiped away the salty dribble of yolk from the corner of his lips. He spat. The yolk and the white were just a mess on the earth. The creature that would have grown from them was gone before it lived. The song it would have sung was silent.

"Used to have a hundred of these," he said. "All boys did. All of us were collectors and admirers, back in them old days."

He wrapped the egg in a handkerchief, put it in his jacket pocket.

"So she was alive in there?" he said.

I nodded. Yes.

"That's the kind of thing you'll remember for evermore."

After a time we followed our tracks through the grass back towards the woods. This time the marks of our footsteps intertwined more closely, made two curving interlinking pathways, our elegant drawing upon the earth.

We drank again outside the Dr Syntax. He sang a brighter song now, "The Blaydon Races".

"I went to Blaydon Races, 'twas on the ninth of June

Eighteen hundred and sixty-two on a summer's afternoon . . ."

I read to him again.

"Hope is the thing with feathers

That perches in the soul,

And sings the tune without the words,

And never stops at all."

He grinned. He swigged his beautiful beer. His white shirt collar gleamed in the afternoon light. I had a sudden vision of a bird hatching in his mouth, flying

246

free into the air above the fields and woods and sandpits. I told him and he laughed and he tipped his head back and opened his mouth and we both saw the bird flying free from him again.

"We can imagine anything," I said.

"Anythin," he answered. "Anythin at aal."

We drank some more. We felt the birds fluttering inside us.

We dozed against each other on the red seats as the train headed along the valley and through the darkening city. We walked towards the pale estate. We paused on the wasteland. I held him tight, and I felt the tender fluttering of my poor lovely father's heart.

CHAPTER
FORTY-SEVEN

I grew my hair so that it hung across my ears and curled across my collar. I practised yoga in my bedroom. I stood on my head and contemplated nothingness. While Dad snored and grunted in his sleep, I tried to travel in the astral plane. I lay flat on my bed, closed my eyes, breathed deeply, slowly. Tried to empty my mind of all unnecessary thoughts, all distractions. Pictured my spirit breaking free, leaving my body behind. Imagined looking down upon myself from above. Imagined going higher, rising through the roof of the house, away from the estate, away from Tyneside, moving eastwards across the North Sea towards India, Nepal, the mysterious palaces and peaks and valleys of Tibet, and towards the unknown unseen worlds beyond. I never made it.

I worked at Dixon's newsagent's, delivering *Chronicles* in the evenings and the Sundays at weekends. I stole Beech-Nut and Mars Bars and packets of Park Drive. I slipped my hand into the till a few times. I saved up to buy my jeans and shirts and books. I got a Saturday job at the Co-op in Newcastle. I sold boiler suits and anoraks and slacks and blazers. Customers would raise their arms as I measured their chests and I'd catch the scent of sweat on them. I measured their inside legs using a tape with a three-inch-long steel end to make sure I didn't touch their balls.

One Saturday during my lunchtime from the Co-op, I wandered into Handysides, a little run-down Victorian arcade off Percy Street, and discovered Ultima Thule. A sign on the door said that the shop lay beyond the limits of the known world. It was next door to Vercelli's Coffee Bar and just across the alley from Psychic Giftes.

It was run by a poet, Tom Pickard, and a novelist, Tony Jackson. It smelt of joss sticks, tobacco, dust. I found pamphlets of concrete poetry and fractured prose. And little magazines — *Grunt, Stand, Steel, Lighthouse, Black Middens Review* — that invited writers to send in stories and poems. I dreamed of seeing my own work in such pages, but would I ever dare to send in my adolescent words? They seemed so forceful as they rushed down my arm and through my pen and on to paper, but within an hour or so they seemed as useless as the graffiti beneath Jack Law's covering of heavenly blue. I saw little posses of real writers in that shop, men with haggard faces, goatee beards and intense eyes, women in floral frocks smoking roll-ups. I dreamed of going up to them and saying, "I am Dominic Hall and I am like you." I didn't dare. I was silent, and too small, too young and far too shy beside them. Then one day I was with Holly in there and she nudged me.

"Go on," she said. "Be brave."

Took a deep breath, clenched my fists, went up to Pickard.

"Hello," I said.

"Aye."

I didn't know how to go on. I wanted to turn around.

"I seen you in here before," he said.

"It's a brilliant p-place."

He laughed.

"Aa knaa that," he said. "Tell us something new. What ye writin?"

"Eh?" I said.

"It's obvious. What ye writin?"

I took a breath. I hardly dared.

"Poems," I said. "And a tale about a cruel kid and a silent tramp."

"He's brilliant," said Holly.

"You sent them anywhere?"

"Not yet. I will."

"Do it. Shy bairns get nowt."

"I know."

He laughed, came closer.

"Do I smell the yards on you?" he said.

"My dad's a caulker."

"Smoothin the lines that the welder makes. Good background for a writer. And you?" he said to Holly.

"I paint," she said. "I draw. My dad's a draughtsman."

Pickard laughed again.

"Seems we got the future in the shop today," he said.

"Shy bairns get *nowt*!" I whispered inside myself.

"I wondered," I said, "if there's any jobs in here."

250

"This is Newcassel, ye knaa. This is a bliddy *book* shop, ye knaa."

"A few hours sometimes. You wouldn't have to pay me much."

"Wouldn't be *able* to pay ye much. Give us a line of poetry."

"Eh?"

"A line of poetry. If we're ganna employ a poet we'd better knaa we're employin a poet. Give us a line."

"Go *on*, Dominic," said Holly.

"I touched the stitch marks on his lips," I said.

"Another."

"I heard the crackle of the rods and the thunder of the hammers. I saw men bending to the deck as if in prayer."

"How old are ye?"

"Sixteen. Nearly seventeen."

He called across the little shop to Jackson.

"Tony! Howay over and meet the new member of staff. We'll pay ye in books and tickets to the Tower. That's aal reet? It should be for a bliddy poet."

A few hours, here and there. Sometimes I went straight from school to do half an hour before closing time. Served poets and novelists and students and teachers and seekers after arcane paranormal truths. Served kids like myself with the shy and yearning eyes of would-be writers. Blushed along with blokes who spotted *Oz* and Henry Miller in the window and came to scan the shelves of underground magazines in search of porn. I read *Steel* and *Black Middens Review* and *Bullocks* and *Grunt*. Kept the joss sticks burning. Kept

251

the shelves in order. Cleared the ashtrays. Made coffee for Pickard and Jackson and tried to stay cool and calm as I tried to chat with them. Gaped at the famous poets passing through for their readings at Morden Tower: Patten, Corso, Bunting, Dunn, McGough, Mitchell, Heaney. Loved the sensations of being in the same room as them, touching the same books as them, drinking from the same cups as them. I read William Burroughs with thrill and confusion and didn't have a clue what he was on about. I read Kerouac and rode with him from my pebbledashed house across the rails and roads of the USA and across the border into Mexico. I read Paul Klee's words about taking a line for a walk, and I tried to make sense of John Cage's explorations of silence. I found Hemingway, read his stories aloud to myself, and fell in love with such syntax that worked so fluently on a northern tongue. I read Pickard and McGough, poets of the North who dared to write in northern rhythms and words. Pickard was right. Writing was like welding and caulking, spattering ink on to the sheets, then hammering it to make it neat and smooth and watertight. And writing books must be like making ships, welding words and pages in pursuit of an elusive image of the finished perfect thing.

"Mebbe we'll get you to read sometime," Pickard said.

"Eh?"

"At the Tower. A poem or two. Get ye started."

Shy bairns get nowt.

"Great," I said.

We saw Ginsberg and Ferlinghetti at the Tower. We sat in that dark candlelit room in the ancient city walls and sipped red wine and let the rhythms of New York and California sing in our northern brains. We shivered as Ferlinghetti read to us. We clutched each other, as we had in the circus on the playing fields so long ago, when the poet stood up on his chair and spread his arms like wings and teetered over us as if about to fall and called out:

> Constantly risking absurdity
> > and death
> whenever he performs
> > above the heads
> > > of his audience
> the poet like an acrobat
> > climbs on rime
> > to a high wire of his own making
> and balancing on eyebeams
> > above a sea of faces
> paces his way
> > to the other side of day.

I started to send poems and stories to magazines. The editor of *Bullocks* wrote back that a story called "Pebbledash Poltergeist" was too way out even for them. *Black Middens* said that the same story was far too English, far too staid. I sent again, was rejected again. I didn't tell my dad about this, but I told Bill Stroud.

253

"Rejection is nowt," he said. "The world's brimful of folk who'll say you cannot do what you can do. Be brave, press on. You're hardly more than a child and a lifetime of wonders lies in wait."

We went to the Oxford Ballroom on Mondays and danced to Motown. At weekends we went to the A'Gogo and saw the Junco Partners, the Animals, Pink Floyd and Cream.

I bought an old second-hand record player. I went to Windows Music in Newcastle and bought Jefferson Airplane and the Deviants, and stole the Grateful Dead. I dreamed of finding sources of marijuana and LSD to accompany the music, but this was the pebbledashed North, this was Tyneside, and I didn't have a clue where to go to, who to talk to. So I bought cans of McEwan's Export and drank instead.

I drank them in my room with Holly lying at my side. We listened to the sounds from the sunlit West Coast and she sang and hummed along as we dreamed of being free. We kissed, and slipped our hands inside each other's clothes, and wondered if this was what was meant by love. We sang, we kissed, we began to penetrate each other more and more deeply, seeking the Ultima Thule that lay inside ourselves and beyond ourselves.

CHAPTER
FORTY-EIGHT

What are the roots that clutch? What branches grow out of the stony rubbish? Joyce read *The Waste Land* at the beginning of lunchtime each Friday. We could just turn up and listen. Didn't have to ask any questions, didn't have to say anything unless we wanted to.

He said that silence was maybe the only proper response to something so amazing. Even when we thought we understood, we'd find out that we didn't.

"What does it mean?" he asked.

"Shantih shantih shantih," he answered. "Jug jug jug."

He said that Eliot himself probably didn't know how he'd done what he had done. And why should he? Like all true creators, he was astonished by his own creation.

"Weialala leia," he said. "Waly waly waly." He laughed. "It's nearly Geordie. Why aye, man. Why aye!"

I loved the way the words moved in the air, the way they set up such rhythms and disturbances in my body and brain. And I loved the silence afterwards, in which the words continued. You cannot say, or guess, for you know only A heap of broken images, where the sun beats, And the dead tree gives no shelter. I knew nothing, Looking into the heart of light, the silence.

One Friday I left the reading with Holly.

"I'm going to perform," I said. "You can announce it."

It was something people had started to do, performances in the sixth-form common room. Last week Bella Carr had read a poem called "Scream" in a high-pitched frantic voice. It was a Geordie homage to Ginsberg's "Howl".

"What'll I say you're going to do?" asked Holly.

"I'm playing the piano."

"The piano? You?"

"Aye. For four minutes thirty-three seconds."

"Oh, that!"

The Zombies were on the record player as we went in. She switched it off.

"Dominic will now perform," she said.

I was already at the piano.

"He will play a piece by an American composer called John Cage. It is called 4′33″."

I held my watch in my hand. I lifted the piano lid, hesitated and immediately closed it again.

"Howay, Dom!" Ricky Eckart yelled. "Get on with it!"

There was the noise of the road outside, the howling of younger kids in the yard outside.

I lifted the lid again, hesitated, took a deep breath and closed it again.

I watched the watch.

Heather Milford whispered, "Poor soul. He's gannin daft, ye knaa."

256

Somewhere far off a desperate teacher yelled. Minutes passed. I checked the watch, lifted the lid, held it poised above the keys, then closed it again. I didn't look at the kids gathering around me. I watched the watch. A couple of minutes passed: voices, laughter, curses, shifting chairs. I suddenly lifted the lid again, straightened my back, breathed deeply, then stood up and bowed.

"Nice one, Dominic!" Ricky yelled.

Much applause.

"That," said Holly, "was four minutes thirty-three seconds."

"Four minutes thirty-three seconds of nowt!" laughed Willie Cook.

"There's no such thing as nowt," said Holly. "There's no such thing as silence."

"Each something," I said, "is a celebration of the nothing that supports it."

"Very true," said Willie. "So very very true, Dominic."

I grinned, took Holly's hand and walked away from the piano.

"That was bliddy brilliant!" she whispered.

Everybody had kind of heard about the silent composition. The music with no music. Just as we'd heard of the play without actors and without any words, and the paintings that were plain white or totally black. We'd all laughed at the idea of such stuff. We maybe doubted its very existence. But now here it was in this ordinary Tyneside place. And I'd never thought it could be so weird, so disconcerting.

"Did you hear that little bird outside?" said Holly. "Did you hear that teacher yelling far away?"

"Aye."

I'd also heard *The Waste Land* in me, and my mother's final breaths and her final silence, and my father's wheezing, and the sound of McAlinden pissing down on to a rug, and the voice of Mrs Stroud, and Jack Law's grunts and Jack Law's song. And my own heart, and my own yearnings. And I heard the silence of the world that was not silence but was filled with traffic and factory and shipyard din and the cries of children and the songs of birds. All the sounds that made the song of this part of the earth, all the sounds that made our local music of the spheres. And I heard the laughter of my friends and of the lovely Holly Stroud, and I knew I'd hear the silent piece for evermore, even when there was no piano anywhere to be seen.

There was much laughter. I knew that I'd begin a tradition, that John Cage would be played in this place many times.

"Now!" shouted Bella Carr. "After that, I think it's time for 'Scream' again!"

She jumped on to a chair and started yelling.

"I seen the best of the Geordies gannin mad and getting pissed and stuffin chips and broon into themsels

and starin doon into the Tyne from broken yards and yellin at the stars from shattered factories

and rippin their heeds wide open on the bridges and runnin naked on the moors and drawin doon the wind and sky

258

and smokin No. 6 and electric bananas and gritty little lumps of Moroccan black

and dancin to Motown at the Oxford and to Hendrix at the A'Gogo

and staggerin from council estates to colleges and universities

and hallucinatin Seaton Sluice and Plessey Woods and Jackie Milburn and St Bede

and taalkin ballocks to Classics scholars and kickin in the heeds of aal the tossers from the public schools

and headin for the lovely bitter beaches on the lovely bitter summer days . . ."

CHAPTER
FORTY-NINE

Which is what Holly and I did, that early August Saturday, which was not bitter at all, when we first made proper love. We took a blanket each, something to swim in, a little money. I had a tin of luncheon meat, a tin of tomatoes, a loaf of white bread. She had ham and apples. She carried a rucksack, I rolled my things into the blanket and tied it around my shoulders with a belt. I had *The Mersey Sound*, she had Plath's *Ariel*. We both wore faded jeans and faded shirts.

Dad was on a half-shift at the yard.

Bill stood at his gate and watched us leave.

"Wish I could come," he said.

"Dad," said Holly.

"But I watch the shadow of the travellers' backs as they disappear."

He gave us a bottle of Hirondelle wine.

We took the train to Newcastle, walked northwards through the city. Arrived at the beginning of the Great North Road. There were others there, a line of young people heading for the sea. Those at the front held out their arms and raised their thumbs. The line diminished. Soon we came to the front. Lifts were easy then, before we became suspicious, and the roads were slow, before the bypasses were built.

We were picked up by a lawyer in a Rover. He told us that he'd travelled all the way from Wolverhampton to find the woman who had left him for another.

"Where is she now?" asked Holly.

He didn't know. In a village beyond Morpeth, he thought. She was called Chantelle and she was from the South. He loved her desperately. He'd drive through the villages, ask questions about a woman with an unfamiliar accent.

"It's a wild-goose chase," he said. "But it's a journey I have to make." He laughed. "I'm a lawyer. I thought I was a sensible man. But where's the sense in this?"

He bought us lunch in a roadside pub, the Fox.

"Why am I telling *you* all this?" he said. "Because I'll never see you again, I guess. Because you're young. I missed all that. I grew up in the war. Is it good to be young today?"

We told him that it was. Before he dropped us off he said, "Maybe I'll never go back again. Maybe it's not too late to be the me I might have been."

We bounced towards Alnwick with a pair of terrified sheep in the open-backed pickup truck of a wizened farmer who told us as we left him that he would nivver have let his kids dae what we were daeing. Ower much freedom these days, he told us. That's the top 'n' bliddy borrom of it. What if he let his sheep just wander where they wished? What'd happen to them then? Tek care, he said. There's alwiz a villain or three hangin aboot roond here. He gave us a pound note. Divent hoy it away it on rubbish, he said.

We were picked up by a gentle German named Hans in an old green van. There were ancient stone-cutting tools in an enamel bowl on the back seat. He told us they were everywhere in these parts, knives and axes just below the grass.

"I'm a remnant of war," he said, "discovering other remnants of other wars."

He'd been a prisoner of war during World War Two.

"I was travelling," he said. "A student, a young man on my own seeing the wonders of Northumberland. My plan was to be a historian, an archaeologist. But war impeded me."

He drove slowly. He pointed to a kestrel that hovered above the roadside, a pair of swans that flew seaward high above. He'd been detained in a tin shack in the Cheviots with another German and an Austrian.

"War seemed far away," he said, "for all of us. The farmers let us till their fields, which is where I first began to find these things. They even let us drink with them in their country bars. People were so kind, even on the nights we heard the bombs, even as we stood at the village's edge as the sky darkened and we saw the fires of Tyneside shining bright in the sky to the south. It is not you, they said. We know it is not you."

He lived in his own shack now, a stone and timber place with two rooms and without electricity. He lived alone. He had only once been home to Germany. He collected stone artefacts. He kept a pair of goats. Sometimes he served at a bar and in spring he helped farmers with their lambs. He was happy. People were very kind. He did not understand the world. Did we? He told us to visit him sometime. We would find his shack in the Simonside Hills, next to a sheet of black rock upon which mysterious circles and spirals had been carved many thousands of years ago.

"You must live in peace," he told us. "We are only in this world for a short period of vivid and wonderful waking in an eternity of dreamless dark."

We walked the final mile towards the sea. Fishing boats moved on it, the homeward-heading ones surrounded by white storms of dancing birds. The islands, the Farnes, reached towards the horizon. The red-and-white hooped Longstone Lighthouse stood on the rocks of Outer Farne.

We kept pausing, staring.

"It's just so beautiful," said Holly. "And it's where we're from, and it's like Heaven."

We walked by the sea into Beadnell. In the harbour there were little fishing boats and sailing boats. Families picnicked on the beach. Kids splashed and screamed in the water. A fire burned at the far end of the long curved bay. We took off our shoes and waded ankle-high through the icy water towards it.

Someone was singing Joni Mitchell.

Out of the city
And down to the seaside
To sun on my shoulders
And wind in my hair . . .

We paused by the rock pools and saw scuttling crabs, limpets, barnacles, grey little fish, dark rubbery anemones. Foot-long jellyfish were stranded on the sand. The rocks were black. Brown seaweed swayed in the surf. Strips of it lay dead and pungent on the tideline and flies buzzed on it. There was a line of great concrete cubes below the dunes, tank traps left over from the war. It was all so northern, so un-Californian, but Joni Mitchell's words mingled with the crying of the dainty terns that danced above the water. A flight of our exotic-looking bird, the puffin, dashed by above our heads. A pair of seals raised their whiskery heads from the water and watched as we waved and hooted at them.

The kids at the fire were sixteen, seventeen, eighteen, poised at the end of schooldays. We hailed the ones we knew, and the ones we didn't know. All of us were friends. Some of the boys wore necklaces of stones and seeds. Some who could manage it had scrawny beards. There were bottles of Newcastle Brown Ale, cans of Younger's Tartan, bottles of wine like ours.

The sun was warm all afternoon. High-up gannets headed further north towards invisible Bass Rock. There was talk of where we'd come from, where we were and where we'd go. We talked about those we knew who were following the trail to Afghanistan or had gone to Athens on the Magic Bus.

"That'll be us soon," we said.

A blond boy on a rock burned a lump of dope and rolled a joint and passed it round. I hardly dared to touch it, but I took a shallow drag and passed it on.

The boys started playing Fally the Best in the dunes. It was a game that all boys played on these beaches. You imagined that war was going on. You took turns to tiptoe through the dunes. You kept crouching, tense, watchful, apprehensive. You knew that the silent enemy was somewhere close by. They waited, hidden, with their weapons poised — their rifles, their grenades, their knives. You came to the crest of the dunes. You never survived. You screamed in agony as the machine-gun bullets thudded into you, as the grenades burst open and shrapnel ripped its way into your flesh, as the sniper hiding still as death in the marram grass hit you with a single deadly shot, as the silent spinning knife struck deep into the heart.

"Die!" called the killers. "Die!"

"Aaaagh!" you screamed. "Ayeeee!"

And you fell, in ostentatious agony, and tumbled down the dune, and lay dead still in distorted shapes upon the sand. And you were given a score out of ten, and you laughed, and rose, and brushed the sand away, and started again, and killed again and died again, and started again, again, again.

The sun went down over the Cheviots and dunes behind. The air cooled, the game ended. We hung our blankets across our shoulders. We searched the jetsam for more fuel.

We cooked potatoes in the fire. We ate bread and tins of meat, tomatoes and beans. We drank beer and wine. The fire glowed more brightly. The sky burned red and orange behind and all continued darkening. The sea moved gently, gleamed metallic. The Longstone

265

Lighthouse light began to turn, just distant flashes at first, but soon the cone-shaped beam was visible, sweeping across the sea, the islands, the beach and us. The dope smokers sighed more deeply than the rest of us, but we all sighed, we all muttered and murmured. The cone of light intensified and we moved from darkness to light, darkness to light. We saw the lights of boats like stars beneath the stars. I sat with my arm around Holly. We sang along to the guitars, to the tambourine that someone gently swung. We kissed, and then we slipped away from the fire, walked hand-in-hand to the dunes. We found a hollow edged with marram grass, a kind of nest from which we could see the fire and the lighthouse light, the boats, the stars, the darkness of the sky to the north, the glow of the city to the south. The sand was still warm from the day's sun. We kissed, and undressed each other. Do you have anything? we asked each other. No. We laughed. Oh, God, to be so unprepared after so much preparation. We made love and told each other that what would be would be. We told each other we had loved each other since that first moment we saw each other from the windows of our opposite houses. We made love again, and then lay silent and naked, as the light swept across us and away from us and back to us again.

She ran her fingers across the sand upon my skin.

She smiled.

"Pebbledashed Dominic," she whispered.

How strange to think of that.

"On Beadnell Beach," I said, "I can connect nothing with nothing."

A boy sang "The Times They Are A-Changin'".

The voice moved on, and back into time, into the strains of "Felton Lonnen".

"The kye's come hyem, but Aa see not me hinny;
The kye's come hyem, but Aa see not me bairn;
Aa'd rather loss aall the kye than loss me bairn."

Then silence, just the turning of the sea, beating of our hearts, soft sighing of our breath. We pulled the blankets close around us and we slept.

CHAPTER
FIFTY

"Dominic. Dom!"

She was shaking me awake.

"Look!" she whispered.

She held the marram grass aside. The tide was out, the sea was still, the red edge of the sun rose over the Farnes. An ambulance slithered and swerved its way along the beach. A police car stood by the smouldering fire. Gulls called. Girls cried. Kids held each other tight. They stood around in nervous little groups. They knelt in depression and dejection. A policeman moved among them, scribbling in a notebook. Another policeman crouched by the body lying on the sand.

We didn't move. Just watched as the ambulance came closer, as the stretcher was brought out, as the body was laid on it, lifted into the ambulance and carried away. The policemen stayed as the kids collected their belongings. Two boys got into the car and were driven away. The others trudged afterwards, carrying their sacks and blankets and guitars, leaving a trail of scattered footprints in the glistening wet sand. We stayed till they'd all gone, till the beach was cleared, till the sun was huge and orange and round and the sea shivered as it turned and started to come back in again.

Then we went down. Stood among the litter — the smouldering timbers, the ash, the cans and bottles, the bread crusts, the cigarette ends. Still early. Nobody around except a single dog walker along by the harbour. A black low-flying jet roared by above our heads, then another.

We headed back towards the village through the dunes. We stood at the roadside and hitched. A red car swerved to a halt.

"Get in."

He drove us quickly away. A middle-aged man with a long scar on his cheek.

"You're the third lot I've picked up already," he said. "I'm doing my duty to get rid of you all."

He turned to glare at Holly in the back seat, swerved towards a ditch, swerved back into the middle of the road.

"Who do you think you are?" he said. "Coming up here with your guitars and drink and drugs and sex."

"Did he die?" I said.

"It was the same last year, the same the year before. Wailing all the night, drowning in your own damn sick, leaving the place like a midden."

"Did he?"

"How old are you? Seventeen? Eighteen? What are your parents thinking of?"

He roared through the silent villages towards the A1. Another pair of long-haired hitchers stood in a lay-by at Chathill. He blared his horn at them. He flung a V-sign at them. He put his foot down.

"Layabouts!" he snarled.

269

We leaned back in our seats. We clung on to door handles.

"What effect do you think you have on our children?"

"*Did* he die?" said Holly.

"It'd be a lesson for you all if he did. Is this what we fought a war for? No, he didn't. Get ready to get out."

He shuddered to a halt at Felton.

"Get away from here and back to your Tyneside hovels. And don't come back."

CHAPTER
FIFTY-ONE

"There's bin a death," said Dad.

We were in the kitchen. I was frying chops and chips.

"One of the tank lads," he said. "Straight overboard. Straight doon to the bliddy dock. With not a bliddy hope."

Nothing I could say.

"End of the shift. He was steppin down on to the shipside ladder. Mebbe it was loose or slippy, mebbe he just took a wrong step. Who knows?" He sighed. "They're not too clever, that lot. Mebbe he was showin off or something. Mebbe anything."

"Who was he?"

"Miller, he was called. A young'n, not been there too long. A bit of a clot by all accounts, but a canny lad, they say. You wouldn't know him, son."

"One of McAlinden's lot?"

"Eh?"

"Vincent. He's in the tanks, isn't he?"

"He's been took out. He's just a bliddy skiver now, one of them that wanders about pretendin they're goin somewhere special and doin something useful."

"And they keep him on?"

"There's always a few like that. Nobody knows quite what they do. They're usually ones that's soft in the head or hard as bliddy nails. The talk is that McAlinden's got some kind of pull with Blister."

"Blister?"

"Ye'll find out. He's always had his bliddy favourites."

I put the food on the plates. We sat together at the table.

"What do you mean, I'll find out?"

"It's awful, but it made us think of you."

"Of me?"

He poured HP Sauce across the chips.

"They've been takin students on for the holidays. Usin them as cleaners and gofers and stuff."

"Aye?"

"So I thought we could mebbe get you something for a couple of weeks afore school starts again."

"In the tank?"

"Aye." He shrugged. "They're a man short, after all." He laughed. "A job, eh? An amazin thought, eh?"

I dunked HP on to my plate.

"The wage'll be canny enough."

I chewed a chip.

"Or is it beneath you?" he said.

"Course it's not."

"Good. It's your roots, you know. Your heritage. I'll put in a word, see what's what."

He laughed.

"I already have, to tell the truth," he said.

He lifted a forkful of pork to his mouth.

272

"Long ago," he said, "I telt you I'd find a way to let you see." He rolled his eyes and grinned. "Mebbe the time has come."

CHAPTER
FIFTY-TWO

Holly and I made love in the hills now. We'd make our way across the fields towards the top. We'd go beyond the hawthorn trees, to the copses and meadows and paddocks on the opposite slope. We found beautiful places, where only the birds could see us. An ancient grassy clearing in a birch wood. A mossy bank at the edge of a flowered meadow. We heard groups of kids playing nearby. We saw distant couples walking hand-in-hand, maybe heading for their own sanctuaries. No one came to disturb us. We took precautions now, of course. Once a little black dog appeared, rushing at us to lick us and leap across our feet, before pelting back to its unseen hidden master. We heard bleating sheep and lowing cows. Once there was an hour when we heard the regular twang of an air rifle and regular yells of triumph. And as always there were the traffic and the factories and the insects in the air and singing birds.

We looked down to the streets of Gateshead, the bridges across the shining river to Newcastle, the city itself and Northumberland beyond, all of it shimmering in the heat of the warmest days.

The world was changing, as it always is. The land was being scraped clean of the past. Rows of terraced streets were being demolished. There were immense cranes, bulldozers, earth-shifters. New towers of flats were rising all across Tyneside, so that families could be lifted from the earth into the sky.

We looked down upon it from our sanctuaries and enclaves. We were happy. We were in love.

Once, heading homeward, we saw Jack Law. He was sitting on the lowest almost-horizontal branch of a chestnut tree. We waved and he returned our wave. We saw him again, another day, sitting cross-legged in long grass facing the sun.

"Is he *watching* us?" we asked each other.

"No," said Holly. "He's watching over us."

CHAPTER
FIFTY-THREE

Bright morning. Sun shining through the thin curtains. Dad shook me awake.

"Out of your pit," he said. "On with your stuff, get tea and grub in you, bait in your sack, sack on your back, then off we gan to the river. This is work. We can't be late. You hear me?"

Down we went. I ate cold toast as we walked. Feet rang out on the pavements. Sun rose over the distant sea. The river gleamed. Men walked from all directions, from alleyways between houses, from back lanes behind tight-packed terraced streets, from distant pebbledashed estates. They walked or rode black squeaky bikes. Sometimes a Honda 50 or a Lambretta puttered past. The crowd increased as we came closer to the river. Down through the streets towards the high steel gates, the great cranes, the gantries. Men were gathering at the other side of the gates, night shift finished, waiting to be set free. Dad showed me the entrances for the draughtsmen and office staff. He showed me the car parks for their cars.

"Them," he said, "and us. And never the twain shall bliddy meet."

A siren wailed and the gates creaked open. The night-shift workers were released. We shuffled forward.

"We won't see each other," said Dad. "Just do what you're telt and watch for the holes. We'll have a pint in the Iona after."

He took me to the door of a wooden shed.

"This is him," he said. "Me lad. Dominic. Treat him good. If you cannot manage that, at least keep him alive."

Then was gone, hurrying to clock in on time.

There were three men there, smoking cigarettes, draining mugs of tea. Men, but they seemed no older than me. They wore overalls, shabby boots. Face masks hung about their necks. Each had a bucket with a dustpan and hand brush in it. There was a pile of dustpans, brushes and buckets at their feet.

"That's yer weapons," said one of them. "Here's a mask if you like your lungs. Name's Norman."

He held out a cheap metal face mask and a white gauze mouth pad.

"You put the pad in them clips like this," said Norman. "Hurry up, or Blister'll be at us."

I took the mask, worked out how to get the pad on it, hung it around my neck. Got a bucket, a pan, a brush.

"You're the bliddy boffin, eh?" said Norman.

"Boffin?"

"This is Jakey. The handsome one's called Silversleeve. You'll knaa why when he's got a cold."

Silversleeve and Jakey nodded.

"Ye heard aboot our mate?" said Norman. "Poor owld Windy?"

"My dad told me."

"He was a good lad. This place is full of peril. Keep your eyes and lugs wide open and tek care."

"And watch who ye waalk with," said Silversleeve.

"Where's that bliddy cleanin gang?" yelled somebody from outside.

"Nick off, Blister!" Norman shouted back. "We're training the new lad."

"Training? Get out of that shed and in that tank!"

Norman grinned. I knew him now: Norman Dobson. Miss O'Kane's class, just along the river from here. Did Norman remember? No sign of it. I recalled the catechism test: *What will Christ say to the wicked, put your hand out, Norman Dobson, we will help you to be saved.*

And then the hiss and crack of the cane of Miss O'Kane as it whipped in rhythm on to Norman's outstretched obedient hand: "Go *away* from me, with your curse upon *you*, to the eternal *fire* . . ."

"Norman Dobson, you lazy prat!" yelled Blister's voice again.

Norman flicked a V-sign towards the door.

"Coming, Blister!" he called. "Watch!"

And he led us out, and we walked towards the ship that waited, half formed in its dock, casting a huge dark shadow over everything below. We walked through great heaps of steel sheets, men working with acetylene burners, men crouching to the earth with welding masks and welding rods flickering. There were scaffolding and ladders against the ship. The din of riveting and caulking was intense. The air was filled with fumes, the smell of oil and drains and piss. We paused at the foot of a ladder and Norman pointed down to the hard earth. He had to yell against the din. "This is where it happened!" Then looked upwards to the monstrous curved steel wall. He spat, wiped a tear from his eye, then led us up a series of steep ladders to the deck. On the deck itself there were curls of cables, heaps of curving pipes, more piles of sheet steel. There were pools of oil, splinters of metal, spatters of bird shit, cigarette ends everywhere.

"Watch yer bliddy feet!" yelled somebody as I stumbled on a cable.

"He's right," said Norman. "Watch your feet, Boff."

I thought I saw Dad far away, or what seemed to be the shape of Dad. He leaned down to the deck as if in prayer, pressing down his caulking hammer to the steel. I paused to watch.

"Hell's teeth, Dominic!" Norman snapped. "This ain't a place for dreamin in!"

He pointed down. There was a rectangular hole in the deck just in front of my feet.

"We want to get at least one damn day from you afore you're gone. Don't want you endin up like Windy, do we? Or like our Jakey."

Jakey grinned, toothlessly. He lifted his cap, swept his hair back, showed a great pale gash across his skull. He rolled back his sleeve to show the weird angle of his forearm. He put his hand across the bottom of his spine and groaned as if in massive pain. Then yelped like a dog and flapped his tongue and winked.

"Bottom is a b-bloody long way down," he said.

279

Silversleeve laughed. Wiped his nose noisily on his sleeve. Slung the bucket across his arm.

"So in we go," said Norman. He widened his eyes at me. "Ready? Follow me."

I quaked. Norman crouched and backed his way down into the opening. Stepped on to the top of a steel ladder that descended into the dark. Went down, looked up, his face illuminated by the sky above.

"Howay," he said. He laughed. "Not feared of heights, are you? If you are, they've sent you to the wrong damn place."

Still I couldn't move.

"Divent be scared," he said. "I'll guide you doon."

I looked back, saw Dad, or the man in the shape of Dad, watching from afar.

"Just do it," said Silversleeve. "Do it and you'll quick get used to it. Do it for as long as us and ye'll know it's nowt at aal."

I crouched as Norman had, I edged backwards until my reaching foot slipped beyond the steel and felt nothingness. Shuffled backwards, reached down with the foot until I felt the ladder's rungs. Kept shuffling and sliding backwards.

"That's the way," said Silversleeve.

"B-bottom is a 1-long way down," said Jakey.

I kept on going. Stepped properly on to the ladder, gripped the first rung and went in.

"Good lad," said Norman. "Keep on comin. I'll give you space. Step down, step down. Let Silversleeve and Jakey follow. We're with you. Divent worry. You won't faal."

You won't faal. It was what I had told myself as I walked the rope between the drainpipe and the outhouse, as I walked the wire between the hawthorn trees. But I had fallen, many times, but just four feet or so, and I had been prepared for it, had turned every fall into a leap. Here, in this place, I couldn't look down, couldn't see how many four feets of emptiness were beneath. How prepare for that, how leap into the littered darkness? I told myself I didn't have to do this at all. Told myself I could just turn away and leave the place. The place had no claim on me. I had no responsibility to it. And what was Dad doing sending me, his son, to this? And then I told myself how stupid I was. Men came down here day after day and day after day and had done for ten thousand days before. Yes, Windy Miller had fallen, but that was rare, and Windy was a clot. And this was my heritage. I kept on staring at the wall of steel behind the ladder, six inches from my face. Gripped the cold rungs tight, kept stepping down, stepping down. Riveters and caulkers attacked the metal from outside. There were tiny explosions somewhere. The ladder and the walls continually trembled.

"OK!" yelled Norman. "Tek a break. Nae need to rush now. Blister knaas we're in."

Now I clung to the ladder and dared to look. Spotlights dangled down on cables. The lights were garish, narrow-focused. Great gulfs of dimness lay between them. The tank was as deep as the ship itself and broad as a church. Dark-shadowed rubbish was cluttered and heaped up in the bottom.

"Looks like the net's in tight today!" yelled Norman.

I saw it, the dark meshed lines that stretched from wall to wall.

"Mind you," continued Norman, "didn't we say that on Jakey's big day!"

Jakey guffawed, Silversleeve sniffed, the ladder trembled. I yelped as something fluttered past my head. The others laughed again.

"The deadly spuggies of the tank!" said Silversleeve.

"Blister!" hissed Norman. He leaned right back, shouted up at the silhouetted face that had appeared in the hole above.

"Blister man! Bugger off and chase some proper skivers!"

Blister didn't move.

"We're doin it, Blister! Look!"

And Norman stepped from the ladder on to one of the strengthening ledges that were arranged all around the walls of the tank. He swept his brush across the ledge and a cloud of dust and debris scattered away.

"See!" he yelled.

"I want it done tobliddyday!" came the answering voice. "Or there'll be bliddy hell to pay!"

Norman laughed.

"It needs wetting doon!" he yelled.

The face disappeared, returned again. Blister sprayed water from a hosepipe down into the tank and on to us.

"Keeps the dust down, Dom," shouted Norman. "But meks things slippery. Tek care."

Blister kept on spraying.

"Enough?" he yelled.

"Enough!" answered Norman. "You'll start a bliddy flood."

Blister laughed and disappeared.

"Bye-bye, Blister!" shouted Norman. He spoke to me again. "Mask on now. You can dae this one with me."

"Do what?" I said.

"This. Which ain't too hard to learn. I'll show you."

He knelt on the ledge. He bowed forward, brushed again. He crawled away from the ladder, brushing the ledge in front of him, and a cloud rose around him and tumbled down through the light of the spotlights into the gloom below.

I quaked again. The ledge was less than three feet wide. It ran all around the walls of the tank. There were other ledges further down.

"We do *that*?" I said.

"Aye," said Silversleeve. "Brush it doon, then crane it up."

"Piece of p-piss for a boff like you," said Jakey.

"Ship's getting near to finish," said Norman. "Our job's to brush it doon and get the shite oot. Then come back in to wash it doon. Then a final spit 'n' polish and the lid gans on the hatch and it's ready for the oil."

He crawled away, brushing as he went.

"This is the mucky stage! I gan this way, you gan that. Meet up in the middle. Then we gan to the one below."

He paused.

"Gan on," he said. "Divent worry. Just get on the shelf."

"It'll b-be aal reet!" said Jakey.

I couldn't answer.

"Just divent look doon," said Norman.

"Keep your mind on higher things!" laughed Silversleeve.

I did it at last. Took a deep breath. Knew that I wouldn't fall, that a three-foot ledge of metal was a different thing from a half-inch of rope. I put on the mask. Crept out from the ladder, crept around the ledge, swept trash to the depths, crawled forward, swept again, swept again. In places the ledge was wet. The knees of my jeans were soon damp and caked with filth. The mask was useless. I breathed in dust and grit. Found all kinds of stuff. The dried-out withered body of an ancient bird. Another. And another. Over the ledge they went. I tried not to look down. Imagined falling so very far. Would the net be strong enough to hold me? Or was it just for show? I knew that Windy wasn't the only one to fall. Men went overboard into the dock or into the river, men stepped out on to a duckboard that wasn't there, they simply took a wrong turn and tumbled down into the murk, men walked from open decks into the river itself. Many injuries, lots of frights and yes, an occasional death. I crawled and swept, met Norman at the centre, on the opposite wall of the tank. Norman shook my hand, then we turned and went our separate ways back to the ladder again. Jakey and Silversleeve swept the ledge below. Then I went with Norman to the ledge below that, where we swept again, where dust from the ledge above cascaded down upon us. The tank was a cloud of dust dancing in the spotlights. Sometimes an obscure sparrow fluttered through it. The caulkers and riveters dinned. After the second ledge, we came to the net. We clambered through, further down into the murk. We swept the ledge below. Then came to the bottom of the tank at last and rested, sitting on the great metal struts that rose from the floor. Norman was black in the spotlights. Red shining lips when he lifted his blackened mask away.

"Havin fun?" he asked.

I lifted my own mask, rolled my eyes.

"See, you didn't tumble," he said.

The others finished and came to join us. We all sat together on a strut.

"Tek five, eh?" said Norman.

Silversleeve rolled a cigarette and lit it and breathed smoke and dust into himself and out into the dust again.

"That's better," he sighed. "That's just lovely."

He coughed, retched, smoked again.

There was a stench of urine and rot. A shaft of widening light shone down from the distant rectangular hole. It illuminated the dancing dust, the fluttering trapped birds, the quartet of filthy workers in the depths. It framed far-off sunlight and bright blue sky. I turned my face towards it and let the light and the image of the light pour into me.

A siren wailed.

"Break time," said Norman. "Up we gan, then back we'll come."

We climbed the ladder towards the light. Climbed out.

Up there, men sprawled upon the deck, smoking, drinking mugs of tea.

I saw the shape of Dad far away. I waved, got no response.

"Look out!" called somebody nearby. "It's the beasts of the deep come back to the earth!"

CHAPTER
FIFTY-FOUR

We sat at the edge of the deck and let our legs dangle over the river far below. The others smoked. Silversleeve indicated the sewage on the water, the floating dead birds and passing condoms.

"Just like the inside of your mind, Norm," he said.

"No, it is not," said Norman. "Me head is empty as an oil tank. Just rubbish and crap heaped up in it and loonies like you and me and Jakey crawlin roond inside." He leaned towards Silversleeve. "Gan on, tap it, Silver. Thump it hard. Nowt but emptiness."

Silversleeve gently rapped Norman's skull with his knuckles. He grinned.

"Enj-joyin it, B-boff?" said Jakey.

"Aye," I said, and said it again, for it was strangely true.

I looked at Norman, remembered him at the desk alongside me, remembered the shock of seeing his exercise book for the first time, seeing that nothing of what he saw made sense. It was just scrawl, random assortments of roaming letters and empty spaces with full stops stabbed down at the end of each line. The boy couldn't hold the pencil properly, but gripped it in his fist like a knife and dragged it clumsily back and forth across the page. His lip would curl and his tongue hang out as he tried to write. His breath would slurp and snort in his throat.

One day Miss O'Kane appeared above us, massive in her faded green tweed jacket and brown feathered hat. She lifted Norman's book between her thumb and finger, and let it dangle in the air.

"What should we do with a thing like this?" she said to the class.

No one spoke. The cane of Miss O'Kane lay still and silent on her desk.

"And what should we do with a *boy* like this?"

No one spoke.

"What do *you* think, Dominic?" she continued.

No reply.

"Come along, Dominic, what do you *think*?"

"Nothing, Miss," I muttered at last.

She laughed bitterly.

"Nothing indeed," she said. She sighed. "Then I will do your thinking for you. Norman Dobson," she said, "have you looked at Dominic's work? Have you seen what diligence and care and attention can produce? Have you seen what a *good* boy can do?"

Norman slumped. Miss O'Kane licked a silver star and pressed it down on to my book. Norman turned his head to look. The teacher laughed out in delight.

"Are you trying to *copy*, boy?" she snapped. "Are you trying to reap the benefits of another's virtue?"

He didn't speak. None of the others dared to speak. She took Norman by his ear, led him to her desk, bent him over it and thrashed him with the cane of Miss O'Kane.

I remembered that. And I remembered the catechism test, but little more. We must have continued at St Lawrence's together, but maybe in different classes. Maybe he was one of the crowd that gathered to play in the great football games that streamed back and forward on the playing fields above the pebbledashed estate. Maybe we'd knelt together at the altar rail in church, waiting for the Host to be pressed like silver stars on to our tongues.

"Do you remember Miss O'Kane?" I asked him now.

Norman twisted his face and laughed.

"Aye," he said. "And I remember you. And I remember Miss O'Bliddykane and all the other Miss O'Bliddykanes."

He spat towards the river.

"You passed, eh?"

I shrugged and nodded. The eleven-plus, he meant.

"Course you did," said Norman.

The siren wailed. We all stood up and headed back towards the tank.

"I used to dream of stabbin her, killin her, stringin her up," said Norman. "Hated her, and all the rest of them. What a waste of hate. They divent deserve it." He smoked. "She'd say I'm in the right place now, eh, squirmin roond in muck?"

He pulled up his mask from where it dangled around his throat.

"And I remember your mother," he said quickly.

I caught my breath.

"Aye," said Norman. "I remember she was nice to me. Outside the school one day. She must've been waitin for you. She tapped us on the shoulder. 'Hello, Norman,' she said. She put a fruit gum in me hand. She was a good woman. She was kind to us. I remember her."

He put the filthy mask upon his filthy face, told us to pick up our buckets and he led us down again.

CHAPTER
FIFTY-FIVE

Months-old sandwiches and pies. Discarded welding rods and broken glass. Wedges of steel, holey buckets, ruined boots, *Evening Chronicles* from six months back. Sodden copies of *Parade* and *Playboy* and *Daily Mirrors*. Paint brushes and half-empty tins of paint. Broken timbers, lengths of pipe, scrambles of wire and cables. Ripped overalls and shirts and torn tarpaulins, socks, snapped knives, hammers, twisted chisels. A scent of piss, of waste and rot. Dust and grit that'd been swept down and layered over everything. And dead sparrows. And a dead herring gull.

"D-disgusting," said Jakey.

"They hoy it in cos they knaa there's us to bring it oot," said Norman.

"K-keeps us in work," said Jakey.

"So let's give thanks to them above. Thanks to yez aal in the sunny world above!"

"Get on with it!" boomed Blister through the caulkers' din.

"We're doin it, Blister!" called Norman. "What do you think we're doin? Sunbathin?"

He groaned.

"I hate it is the bliddy truth of it. I dae it aal day long and I dae it in me dreams at neet and I dae it when I'm waking up. Is this what lads is bliddy born for? Is it?"

"Yes, it is," said Silversleeve, "if you're the ones that's born to be us and turn oot to be us."

"Nae other w-way," said Jakey.

Norman laughed.

"And that is bliddy dreadful and it's bliddy true. Haha! So mebbe it's time to do a Joe Nelson."

"Joe Nelson?" I said.

"Suicide Joe. A welder come to the end of his time. The ship's aal ready to be launched. He checks the net has been took out and in he jumps headbliddyfirst. Wallop and blam and broken bones and squirtin blood and there's an end to it. Bang. Why wait that lang?"

Jakey laughed.

"Cos you're a ch-chicken."

"Squawk squawk!" went Norman, shuffling his non-existent feathers.

He turned his eyes to me.

"Different for you, of course," he said. "What've you been born to be?"

I shrugged.

"Dunno."

"What d'you *want* to be?"

"Myself." It sounded pathetic down here in the tank. "Nothing." I thought of feathers and I looked up at the distant square of sky and I laughed. "A skylark!" I drew on the flamboyant part of myself. "A tightrope walker!"

"Aye?" said Jakey.

"Aye."

"You m-mean it?"

"Aye!"

"I seen a tightrope walker once," said Norman. "Years ago."

"The circus on the playing fields!" I said.

"Aye, that one. You were there an aal?"

"Aye," I said. "I loved it."

"And me. I liked the clowns. Liked the donkeys. And there was a strongman, I think I remember."

"Aye," I said. "Rudolfo."

"See?" said Norman to the others. "He even remembers the names."

He pondered the darkness at his feet.

"Thought them like you would want to be an office worker. Or a teacher or something."

"Naah," I said. "Far too boring."

He lowered his eyes.

"I remember your books. I remember aal the ticks on your sums and how you could write and write and read and read. Bit different from me."

"Ye could be a wr-writer, then," said Jakey.

"Aye!" said Silversleeve. "And write aboot us!"

"Now that would be a f-fascinatin tale!"

"One day they went d-doon in the tank, they crawled in the muck, that neet they come b-back oot again, they done the same for many years and then they died. The End."

Blister's voice: "Get on with it! Get on with it!"

"You used to help us sometimes," said Norman. "You remember that?"

He laughed gently.

"Ye showed us how to hold the pen. 'Stay on the line, Norman,' you whispered."

"GET ON WITH IT!"

"Who'd've thought we'd meet again doon here?"

"Who'd've thought it, eh?" I said.

We smiled at each other. The others looked away.

"GET BLIDDY ON WITH IT!"

We got on with it. Silversleeve went to the top and passed down a rope with a hook on the end of it. We started at one edge of the tank and worked across. We tied the bigger objects to the rope and Silversleeve hauled them up. The rope kept coming down and going up.

We moved across the floor of the tank, clambering over the struts. The oldest deep-down waste was slimy. We swept it into buckets, tied the buckets to the rope. I kept tightening my mask against the intensifying stench. Norman laughed.

"Be glad," he said, "they give us dirty rates for this."

"D-double bottoms are even b-better," said Jakey.

"Aye," laughed Norman, "confined space as well as filth."

"If y-you're up to it," said Jakey. "If you don't pass out like Silversleeve that b-bliddy day."

We lifted, hauled, yanked, pulled, pushed, swept, bucketed, yelled, groaned and laughed and retched. The afternoon wore on. Jakey sighed to find a nest of mice within an ancient battered cloth cap.

"Oh, b-babies!" he said in amazement.

We all looked down to see the tiny naked creatures squirming there.

294

"They grow from filth," said Norman. "That's one good thing about the filth. New life."

I laughed.

"They can't!" I said. "It can't happen like that."

"Well, how else do they get here, Boff?" said Norman.

"Aye. H-how else?" said Jakey.

He smiled.

"Look at the th-things. The gorgeous beautiful tender b-bairns."

Norman stubbed out his cigarette.

"We find them everywhere we gan," he said. "It's doon to me to dae the deed. Forgive me, mice. You come into a wrong and very bliddy rotten world."

And stamped three times with his steel-capped boots and dragged a boot-length of waste across the mess.

"Now g-gan back to the Lord," said Jakey. There were tears in his eyes. He made the sign of the cross above the scene of death. "Be b-born again in a b-better world."

We worked on.

I reeled at the ugliness, but felt a weird joy in it, a weird joy in being with these others so unlike myself but so like myself, a weird joy to be down in the depths with that shaft of light falling so beautifully from far above, a weird joy to be lost in work, to be becoming lost in memories and thoughts, a weird joy in just being a being on the floor of a tank on the bank of the river at the foot of the hill at the foot of the town.

And then came the moment when Jakey screamed.

"B-body!" he yelled. "B-bliddy body!"

Everything stopped. Even the din of the caulkers seemed to stop.

Then I climbed with Norman through the litter to where Jakey stood in shock.

The corpse lay in a spotlight's glare, with the hatched shadow of the net across it. It lay face-downward in the shadows between two struts.

"B-body!" Jakey screamed again.

The voice of Blister fell from high above.

"WHAT'S THE BLIDDY HOLD-UP, YOU LOT?"

"B-body," Jakey screamed back at him. "F-faller! J-jumper! S-suicide!"

"WHAT?" yelled Blister.

No one answered.

"W-what's to be done?" gasped Jakey.

I went closer. Climbed over one strut into the space that held the body. Dared to reach out towards the body. Touched. And the body flinched. It moved. It twisted on the steel floor and turned its face and laughed.

"Gotcha!" it said.

I screamed. It was more shocking than a death.

"McAlinden!" said Norman.

"Aye, McAlinden," said the body. "Vincent McAlinden, brung back to life by this lad's tender touch."

It laughed again, slid down from the strut, shook itself, reached out a hand to me.

"How you doin, Dominic?"

I clambered away.

"Thanks for bringin us back from the dead, Dominic!"

The others were edging away from him.

"You've got a good lad here," he told them. "And yes, he has a *very* tender touch. What's up, J-jakey? Did I s-scare you?"

"You b-bugger, McAlinden."

McAlinden's eyes grew cold.

"Take care, lad."

Jakey looked away, shut up.

"I heard you were visitin," McAlinden said to me. "I heard you were ganna grace us with your presence. Thought I'd come doon and say hello. It's a funny place for a brainbox and a bliddy tightrope walker. A funny place to tek your holidays."

"Piss off," I told him.

"Oh, Dominic! And here's these lads thinkin they've got a little angel come down among them. Oh, the things I could tell you bonny lads about this bonny lad. Should I tell them about ye, bonny lad? Mebbe not, eh?"

"Gan on," said Norman. "Bugger off."

Vincent swiped his fist across his face. His eyes glittered in the descending light. He grinned. He came in close. Smelt the familiar breath of him. Set my shoulders, clenched my fists, prepared to fight.

"Course this *is* yer holiday, ain't it, Dominic? A week or so in the yard with the lads. Nae need to get to fuckin hate it. Nae need to think ye'll never get bliddy oot of it. Just enough to get a bit scared and a bit pissed off and then get oot again. Ain't that reet? And then ye'll remember it for evermore and tell yer bonny bairns aboot the days spent in the yard when ye were hardly more'n a bairn yerself."

"Piss off," I said again.

He came in even closer. Suddenly he came at me, took me by the throat.

"Fight back," he growled. "Gan on. I trained ye, didn't I? I trained ye to fight and to learn how to beat a McAlinden. It's true, lads. I did. He beat me, many times. You got your knife with you? You got your knife, eh, Dominic?"

The others came at him. He let me go, he threw them off.

"Oh, lads, don't scare me. You're all too bliddy hard."

Then he held me in his arms and kissed me hard on the cheek.

"Not here, Dominic," he softly said. "Not here, not now."

And he turned, and climbed away, up the ladder, through the net.

"Back from the dead!" he called.

He kept on climbing upwards through the falling shaft of light.

"Naebody knaas what the hell he does," said Norman. "It's like they're scared of him, even Blister."

"It won't last l-lang," said Jakey. "He'll g-get slung oot."

We watched him clamber through the distant hatch.

"There was taalk," said Norman, "after Windy Miller."

"K-keep away," said Jakey.

Blister's yell: "GET BLIDDY ON WITH IT!"

We got on. We cleared the depths. I had to keep pausing, had to stop myself trembling. Late afternoon, we climbed away towards the light. I fell, before we'd even reached the net, just a few rungs, just a few feet, but far enough to break my leg, to be annihilated for an hour.

My memory is of being fastened to a stretcher, of being raised. I'm horizontal, rising through the middle of the tank towards the light. I recall the birds. I recall the dust. I recall the light falling on me as I rise. I can't fit through the gap. I'm being tilted. There's a fear that I'll slide right off and fall the full way. Someone grips my shoulders. Norman, whispering comfort, guiding me out.

"Come on, Dom," he murmurs. "I won't let ye faal again."

Then I'm hauled out, tipped down on to the deck.

"Who the hell put him doon there?" is asked.

CHAPTER
FIFTY-SIX

I was young. I came round fast. I was in hospital for just a few hours. They put on a plaster and took me home. They soon had to take the plaster off again, for the wound in the flesh was oozing pus.

"Nae wonder," said Dad, "considering the place the faal occurred."

He muttered about compensation, but it only made him laugh.

"Compensation? For a temporary worker? For a lad on his first damn day? Not a hope in bliddy Hell. It's hard enough to get it for the folks of them like Windy Miller. And Blister? He's spreading the tale that you were messin aboot like kids doon there. He's askin what was *I* diyin sending a lad like you to work like that? He's yelling what did I *think* would bliddy happen?"

He wanted to know if I blamed him. Should he not have sent me down? Was this all his stupid fault?

I told him I was pleased I'd gone into the tank, that I'd felt weirdly at home.

"You could have died," he said.

"It was just a few feet."

"That's aal it teks."

He kissed me and I felt his tears on my skin.

"We didn't even get that pint in the Iona Club," he said.

The damage was slight. I had to rest the leg. I lay on the sofa, kept up with reading, prepared for A levels. Chaucer, Herrick, Milton, Donne. I chanted the words to learn them. I read them in my own voice, and in the voice of Norman Dobson, in Jakey's stammer, in McAlinden's snarl.

Dr Molly visited each week, bringing in the familiar smell of dog with her. Dad cared for me, cooked for me. He left me lunch when he went out to work each morning. He sat with me at evening time. He changed the dressings on my leg.

"How did it come to happen?" he asked one night.

"Eh?"

"All the ways you've turned out not like me."

"But look at us. Two peas in a pod."

"But it's the inside things. The things you knaa, the things you think, the things you want. The things I haven't got a clue aboot."

Coals cracked and shifted in the grate.

"Born at different times," I said, "I'd have been exactly you and you'd've been exactly me."

"Can that be reet?"

"And born at different times I'd be your dad and he'd be me."

"And who would I be?"

"His dad, or his dad's dad."

"Or your son, or your son's son."

I laughed. He laughed.

"Can that be true?"

"I divent knaa."

"And nor do I. I divent knaa."

"It's aal a mystery, eh?"

"Aye, aal a mystifyin mystery."

"Let's have a drink."

"Aal reet."

Holly came, of course. We made love on the sofa and on my bed as the autumn winds strengthened outside, as rain pattered on the windowpanes, as autumn sunshine shone through the thin curtains.

"Me leg!" I'd gasp.

She'd laugh, and touch me gently, and breathe into my ear, "Relax, me poor bairn. It's not a broken wing."

CHAPTER
FIFTY-SEVEN

Dad came home one evening with his eyes glittering.

"McAlinden," he said. "He's a goner."

"A goner?"

"Got the push. He went for that lad Norman with a hammer. Reet in front of everybody."

"But why?"

"Why d'ye think? Nae reason at aal, except the stupidness of him, except for Norman being a canny lad, and him being the stupid bliddy beast he's aalways been."

"Is Norman OK?"

"Oh aye. He swerved oot the way like a dancer. And his mates were with him, and they went for McAlinden aal together and got him doon. Who'd've thought them capable of such a thing?"

"Wonderful!" I said.

"Aye. Reet oot on the open deck. Even Blister couldn't turn his face from that."

"So they sacked him straight away?"

"Aye. Give him his cards reet there and then and sent him oot the gates."

I smiled at the image of it.

"I'm amazed he's lasted this lang," said Dad. "But how's the poor mother ganna manage now?"

I closed my eyes. Imagined McAlinden walking through the gates, leaving the river and the yard behind, climbing homeward towards the pebbledashed estate, seething with rage.

CHAPTER
FIFTY-EIGHT

I tottered on crutches and got back to school. In the depths of a deep dark sleety winter we read about the universities that we might go to.

Creel called us both to his office one day. Joyce was with him. They were smiling.

"We thought that perhaps you should try for Oxford, Holly," said Creel.

"Not out of the question for you, too, Dominic," said Joyce.

"It would be quite a triumph for the school," said Creel. "And for yourselves and your families, of course."

I thought of how awkward Dad had been on his visits to the grammar school. What would he be like in Oxford, in any university? I thought of my own awkwardness, my self-doubt. I thought of my thieving, my killing, my lying, my mask.

Holly was already shaking her head.

"No. Thank you. But I want to go to a modern place, a newly built place. And I think you do, too, Dom." She turned and looked at me. "Don't you?"

"I do," I said.

"We'll be the first of our families ever to go to university," she continued. "We don't want to live our lives according to ancient expectations." She started to grin. "We don't want to lose our northern souls!"

She paused. The teachers smiled.

"Go on, Holly," Creel said.

"We don't want to be chucked into some lovely stony place and steeped in years of history. Don't want to wander through ancient courtyards, dine under portraits of ancient graduates, start an English course with *Beowulf* and end at Yeats. We don't want to be seen as disadvantaged. We want to embrace our disadvantages and turn them into privileges."

Creel laughed now. He beamed at her.

"Don't we, Dom?" she said.

"Yes."

"We are the children of our time," she said. She laughed, and spread her arms wide. "We want to be free to dance the dance of ourselves, to sing the song of ourselves, to be northern and flamboyant and touched with northern grace."

We all laughed with her.

"We'll pebbledash the world!" I said.

"Yes! We'll fill it with the call of larks and din of the yards and the bitter coldness of the sea, with the poetry and music of the North! Won't we, Dominic? Won't we!"

"Yes!" I answered. "Yes!"

"Yes," said both the teachers.

We both put UEA as our first choice.

306

★   ★   ★

I laid out the application forms on the kitchen table and told Dad where he had to sign.

"You really want to gan, son?"

"Yes, Dad."

"And you really think you'll get there?"

"Yes, Dad. I really will."

He took the pen from me and made his clumsy, hardly-ever-practised signature.

"That's that, then," he said.

He cracked a can of beer, lit a cigarette.

"I'll keep on coming back," I said.

"Will you?"

"Yes, Dad. I really will."

CHAPTER
FIFTY-NINE

We heard the battle in the McAlinden house: yelling voices and howling dogs and screaming kids and breaking glass. Bill and Dad went down. Vincent strode out of the door as they entered the gate.

"What you buggers after?" he snarled.

Bill looked towards the door. Mrs McAlinden came out.

"You all right, love?" said Bill.

"Aye," she gasped.

She watched Vincent muscle through the gate.

"Divent worry," he said to her. "I'll not be back."

He slung a sack across his back and moved off down the rocky path.

"Better if ye'd died in me womb," his mother sobbed. "Better if ye'd not been born."

"You're reet!" yelled Vincent as he walked away. "That's the truth of it. I should've never been here. And now I'm off to bliddy Hell at last!"

He became a thing of rumour. There were tales of him carrying a soldier's knapsack, dressed in a massive ripped greatcoat with dangling sergeant's stripes on the shoulders. He led his sick dog on a rope. His hair grew long, matted, tangled. A scrawny beard grew. He was seen to sift through the rubbish in the town's bins. There was talk of him drinking meths. When he was heard to speak, the sounds seemed formless, as if he was losing the power to form words at all.

In the estate, I'd hear children chanting beneath a street light as darkness fell, chanting their dread of Vincent just as we had once chanted our dread of his father.

Vincent Mac is coming up from Hell.
Vincent Mac will walk these streets this night.
Whose door will he enter?
Whose life will it be this night?
Who will Vincent gobble up tonight?
Which child will he carry down to Hell?
Will it be you, will it be you?
No, it will be Y-O-U!

I dreamed that he wandered through me as I'd once dreamed of wandering Jack Law. Sometimes I woke with a start to the sudden scent of him, to the sudden touch of his lips on mine.

Holly drew new pictures of him. Almost-abstract charcoal sketches of a dark jagged figure crossing the landscape with his shadow before him. Pencil drawings of a tiny figure below a heavenly sky. Abstract patterns of a troubled soul en route through deeply darkened spaces towards another deeply darkened space.

He went from view as winter came. The story was he slept in ditches, in the remains of the hovels down on the Tyne. There were reports that he sometimes took a

309

room in Simpson's dilapidated hostel down by the yard. We heard that he spent a couple of weeks in Durham Jail for drunkenness and thieving. There was talk he tried to get a job in the tanks again. Fat chance of that. And there was talk that he began to change himself, that in setting out on his homelessness and wandering, he had discovered his roots, his travelling heritage. He became a wandering man. Home and work could have no place for him. The world must be his roadway and his wilderness in which he could lose himself and be himself. We didn't know for sure. He was said to wander the northern beaches, the tracks of old mineral railways, the slopes of the snowy northern fells.

I dreamed of him fading into misty nothingness, into his own Ultima Thule.

CHAPTER
SIXTY

It was Easter Day when we walked uphill to prune the hawthorn trees. There wasn't much to do: some dead wood clinging on from last year, a few unwanted thorns. The wire was beautiful, had become more flexible, like rope. We attached it to the trees. Tightened it with the tightening winch and it became a clear dark horizontal line against the Easter sky.

Holly danced across it through the air as if she needed no wire at all.

Then me, the chimpanzee.

"Make shapes!" she said, as she had all those years ago as we walked the garden wall. "Be beautiful!"

I spread my arms and crossed again, and she told me I was lovely. We crossed a few more times. We laughed. We could do this so easily now.

The factories and yards were silent. The song of the larks like the singing of angels or the music of the spheres could fill the sky and us.

We kissed on the grass below the wire, the trees and the astounding sky. Then walked away from the wire. Kissed in a copse of birch trees. Kissed at the edge of a flowered meadow. There was no sign anywhere of Jack Law. Walked hand-in-hand across the speedwell, primroses, wild garlic and abundant grass towards his Heaven in the rock.

We knelt and peered in. No candles burning and Heaven in deep shadow.

"Do we dare?" said Holly.

I went in first, shuffled up to the rock, made space for Holly to follow. The earth was soft. We giggled and hugged each other tight and kissed again, giggled again.

Our eyes adjusted to the light.

I pointed into Heaven and showed my mother there.

She said it was beautiful.

She put up her hand to cover my mother's eyes.

"She's watching us!" she whispered.

"And she's happy for us."

"Who could I put there?"

"Us?"

"But we're not dead yet, Dom."

"But sometimes we're in Heaven."

"That's true."

She took my pen and drew us in a space alongside the saints, close to my mother and not too far from God. We held hands, as if we both floated in mid-air.

"Lovely," I said. "We'll have to go to Miss O'Kane and say, Please, Miss, we made it into Heaven!"

"Blasphemy, she'd say! Go away with my curse upon thee!"

The place was still and warm, as shallow as a double hull. We saw the graffiti underneath the blue. And there were bodies lower down on the walls: dark jagged figures with spears or swords. Warriors of the earth, or devils on the brink of Hell yelling curses up to Heaven.

312

Maybe they'd always been there. Maybe Jack Law had recently put them there, in his endless, onward-moving, ever-changing artwork.

We told each other that we loved each other. We entangled our limbs and moved across each other's skin with hands and tongues. We moved away from being one to being each other. Forgot about Heaven, forgot about Earth, forgot about protection, entered each other, interpenetrated, sighed, disappeared, dissolved, moved into the silence.

McAlinden grabbed my throat. He dragged me from her, dragged me headfirst to the opening. He yanked me away into the light. I was halfway in, halfway out of the rock. He already had the wire wrapped around my chest beneath my armpits, and it was tightening.

"Yell and I'll do you now," he said.

He punched me, punched me.

"I messed with you," he said. "Let you think ye were up to playin and fightin with Vincent McAlinden. What a joke."

He tied my hands with wire behind my back.

"Shut up in there," he snarled.

He gripped me tighter.

"And then ye thought I was finished, didn't ye? And I keep on comin back. What a joke."

Holly tried to squirm past me.

"You're locked in, pet," he laughed. "There's nae way oot."

He spun another loop of wire around me, yanked it tight.

"They telt me I need a war," he said. "This is it, then."

He pressed his wet lips to mine.

"Or mebbe I'll mek love not war," he grunted.

He laughed and drooled.

"Let's fight," he snarled. "Let's kiss. Let us see you, Dom. Oh, let us touch you."

He licked my face. Then he punched me hard, and again.

"Keep still," he said. "I'm ganna hang ye now."

He yanked the wire tighter. He hauled on the loose end and I was dragged out of the place. The wire was looped around the bough of the tree above. I slithered over the rock towards it. Holly burst out of the rock after me. McAlinden turned from me. He punched Holly in the face, once, twice. She fell, and he laughed. He kicked me in the head and stunned me. He stood up on the rock and pulled the rope. The wire pulled me into the air. I knelt, I kept on rising. I stood. I stood on tiptoe, and then I was off the ground, and the bough lurched with the weight of me. And McAlinden laughed at me, and kissed me again, and thumped me again, and pushed me softly, to make me sway and dangle as he dragged Holly back into the rock.

CHAPTER
SIXTY-ONE

Dazzling shafts of light through the foliage. Songbirds singing and the distant engine din. The creak and sway of the bough and the tree. The wire tightened, tightened, the agony of it as it digs into flesh. Blood running down my face from where he thumped me. The pain of that, of bones that are surely broken in my face. The kicking and squirming for relief just making it worse. The gasping for breath, the mouthfuls of slaver and blood. The certainty that I'll die this day, that both of us will die this day. And the grunts and screams and snarling from below. The imagining of what is happening down there. Trying to scream for help but giving out nothing but splatters of blood and snot and strangled squawks. Trying to call her name to let her know I'm with her even though I'm dancing useless in the air above. Knowing she can't hear, knowing that she's fighting all alone, suffering all alone. God, what is he doing to her down there? But who is this now coming from the hedgerow, running through the dazzling light? Jack Law. He stoops as he runs. He has a great knife in his hand. Doesn't look at me. Runs to Heaven in the rock and plunges to the entrance and McAlinden protests and howls. Jack Law backs away and now here's McAlinden, crawling out. Blood running from his shoulder, curses from his mouth. Jack holds the knife, body so still, eyes so still as he waits for grunting McAlinden to come at him. McAlinden doesn't come. Wipes the blood, looks at the wound beneath the pierced shirt. Winces, but laughs. "Good shot, Jack! Ouch!" Coughs and spits, pulls his clothes around himself. "You could've got me right, though, Jack. Could've brung it to an end." Spreads his arms, presents his body to the tramp. "So do it now! What better time to bliddy die than after what I've just done. Come on, Jack. Fuckin finish me." He steps forward. "What's wrong? Too scared? No killin instinct in ye? Come on, Jack. This is war. A lad like me needs war. Do it. At least come close and bliddy try." Now Holly's crawling out. Her face all bloody. The falling tears, the gasps of pain, the struggle to slither out of Heaven. "Kill him, Jack!" she snarls. "Finish him." He won't. He can't. He shifts sideways, makes sure he stands between Holly and Vincent. McAlinden sighs. "Listen to that from the lips of Holly Stroud! You could give the knife to her," he says. "She might do it, the state she's bliddy in. Would ye, Holly? Naa. Too much peace and love in ye even now. Need another one to do your dirty work like all the conchie crew. Him dangling in the tree there mebbe? All right up there, Dom? Still with us? Aye? What d'you think, Dom? You up for a bit of killin? Mebbe not. Ah well." He backs away from us. "I'll be off, then. I've done what I come to do. Now it's time for movin on. See you later. I mean, won't see you later." And turns, moves through the abundant grass,

316

the wild garlic, the primroses, the speedwell. Leaves hardly a track behind. Steps through a row of gnarled and ancient hawthorn. Turns northwards and is gone.

CHAPTER
SIXTY-TWO

"They talk about peace, Dr Molly, but this one seems to be forever in the wars."

She smiled at Dad's words. I winced as she asked me to breathe in deeply and breathe out again. I had a broken rib, a broken nose, a lost tooth.

"He's healing," said the doctor, "as is Holly."

"On the outside, Doctor."

"Yes. But we're a tough species, Mr Hall. We have to be."

She touched my cheek gently.

"We've come through worse than this. And how are you these days?"

"Canny, Doctor."

"That's what I mean."

She closed her bag, adjusted her green jacket.

"They haven't found Vincent?"

"No," said Dad.

"Let's hope he isn't causing mayhem somewhere else."

The police came a couple of times to take down details. They were different days back then. Even with the wounds on us, they hinted at collusion, at teenagers' games gone wrong.

PC Romero turned up one day when Dad was in the yard.

He stood bulky in our little living room with his helmet in the crook of his arm.

"I telt them I'd come out and check the facts again. Telt them we know each other from the past and we have an understandin. Telt them I know the laddo that we're lookin for. I've come to clarify the tale so we can see what's what."

"There's no sign of him?"

"The world is big. A lad is small. You've no idea where he's gone?"

I shook my head.

"Strange. Two peas in a pod, you were."

"Back then. Not now."

He looked through the window across the street.

"She's a very nice lass by all accounts. And clever with it. And bonny, of course. But weird, eh?"

"Weird?"

"A bit of the hippy, eh? Free love and whatnot?"

"What?"

He grinned.

"Isn't that what they call it? Free love? Not like my day, anyway. Smoke?"

He took a pack of cigarettes from his pocket and held them out to me. I shook my head. He lit up, blew out smoke, picked a fragment of tobacco from his lip.

"The word is," he said, "that both you lads have been tied up with her."

"What do you mean?"

He smoked again.

"Shagging her, Dom. Both of you."

"What?"

"Howay, Dom. You know what I mean. You're hardly a bliddy innocent."

He laughed.

"It's all right," he said. "Anybody'd understand. The bonny lass across the street. Who could blame you? But you're not so happy when your pal gets his eye on her and all."

I said nothing. He went on.

"So you get to battlin over her as you lads do. Fists at sunset! That's the story, eh? And off he scarpers like the tinker that he is."

"The story is he raped her," I answered.

"Aye."

"What do you mean, aye?"

"So this is his comeuppance, eh? Get him back, good and proper."

"I was there. Jack Law was there."

"Now you have a sane and eloquent witness there, lad! And what about your father. The caulker. What's he make of all of this?"

"He makes the truth."

"The truth? That's very good. Tell you what. Now I'll go and get it from the horse's mouth."

He lifted his helmet to his head, adjusted the strap under his chin.

"Best to sort it all out now," he said. "And then we can move on."

"I'll come with you."

"No. No, you won't." His face hardened. "That's not the way these things is done."

He crossed the street, knocked at Holly's door, leaned back and gazed up at the open window above his head, and the door opened, he stepped inside.

Out he came fifteen minutes later, walked through the garden gate, squeezed himself into his small blue car and drove away.

Then Holly came.

She stood in the living room and wept.

"You're sure you didn't lead him on, he said! There's talk there was a thing with you and him before! When you were hardly more than a bairn they say! And you're still just kids! Thing is, there's too much of this freedom thing! Specially for them like you from a place like this! I could have killed him, Dominic! *Should* have killed him! Got a kitchen knife and oh! Got a hammer oh! And anyway what you doin up there in a place like that and all alone with lads like that, he said! What did you think would happen, pet? Die, you stupid policeman! Die! And all the time she's up there listening! All the time she's doing nothing but listening to the bliddy angels! Die, you stupid woman! Die! Having a bit of fun, eh? he said. Havin a little cuddle and shag, eh? That's right, ain't it, pet? You were messing about like kids from the pebbledash will! Yes! No! What? And oh the daft tramp seen it, did he! Now there's a one we can put some trust in! Or mebbe — and I would only whisper it, pet — he stuck his oar in too! Eh! No!"

She went on weeping.

"So what did you think would come to pass? he said. What did you think would happen, petal? Petal! Oh, Dominic! Oh! Oh! Oh! Oh!"

And we raged and wept together, then calmed, and sat together on the sofa, wincing with our wounds.

And we said afterwards that we both knew, as we joined our hands upon her belly, that everything had changed, and that there was a child growing in her.

CHAPTER
SIXTY-THREE

"You don't *know?*" said Dad. "You don't bliddy *know?*"

"No."

"You've chucked it all away for the price of a blob?"

"Would you *prefer* it to be a McAlinden?"

"I'd prefer it to be nowt."

"So would I."

"All for the sake of a tuppenny blob. All cos you can't keep your cock in your pants!"

He stared through the window, then clicked his fingers in relief.

"Abortion!" he said. "It's legal now!"

"*Abortion?*"

"But no, we can't do that, not here. Or can we? Could we? But what if the child is yours and not that git's? Then we're murderin one of us. Oh, bliddy hell. Oh, Dominic, man!"

"Or there's adoption," I said.

"Oh aye? Your mother's grandkid and you send it straight away?"

Holly said she wanted to die. She wanted to plunge a knitting needle into herself and spew the baby out. Her mother knew nothing, said nothing, did nothing, as always. Her father said that he'd give love and support whatever she did. The word got out. Camilla Muldoon from Stoneygate Lane appeared at the door like a joke from the past and said she'd get rid of it nice and silent and quick and cheap. Bill Stroud guffawed and sent her on her way.

A levels approached.

A bunch of parents went to Creel. They'd heard the news.

Was he going to let this happen in his school? In a Catholic school?

What did they suggest? That she disappeared? That he kicked her out? That he ban her from the exams she'd been preparing for all her school life?

Yes!

But she was raped.

That's the story, is it?

The story?

Well, she's hardly an innocent! Putting herself in a place like that with lads like that.

She's a child.

What kind of message does this send to the younger ones? How can it be right for her to swan into school, to sit her exams, to get a reward?

And the boy?

The Hall boy? Punish him.

How?

However you see fit.

Not in the same way?

The child may not be his . . . and he is a boy.

And the other boy?

Castrate him if he's caught. Lock him up and throw away the key.

And you? What would you do if they were children of yours?

They are not, thank God.

And Jesus?

Jesus?

What would he have said?

We lay on the field beneath the larks.

"How can I have a child that was conceived in violence?"

"It might be born of love. The father might be me. And whoever's the father, you'll be the mam."

"So I should have it, then?"

"I don't know, Holly."

No way to know.

She laughed.

"I was to be the first of my family to go to university. If I want to do that, will I have to be the first to have an abortion?"

Martins swept over us, screaming.

We went to Dr Molly.

The two dogs watched us from below the desk.

"I could sign the papers," she said. "You'd go to the clinic in Durham and it could all be over within the week."

She rested her chin on the arch of her fingers.

She pondered. She reached down to stroke her dogs.

"The things that are absent in the world," she said, "are often as potent as the things that are here. The dead, of course. Your mother, for instance, Dominic. All those young lives lost in Burma or in France. My brother Robert killed at Monte Cassino at eighteen years old. They linger endlessly, the dead. You could be free of this mess. You could go forward with your life and go to university. You could have many children later. Balance this against the thought that you might be forever haunted by the dreams of how this child might have been, how its face might be, how its voice might sound. But maybe that's the price to pay. There are no answers, Holly. That's the only answer. And it's your body, your child. You are the one who has to choose."

She smiled.

"And I could help to arrange adoption, too."

She looked down at the dogs at her feet.

"What do you two think?" she asked.

They growled fondly.

"Ah," she told them. "How very wise."

We lay on the sofa in her living room.

"How strange. I've been dreaming of university, of New York, California, and I find that the undiscovered world is right inside myself. Hello, my little one. Not yet born and you're already changing the world!"

She laughed.

"How could I abandon you?" she said.

I put my ear to her womb, and heard gurglings and groanings and the endless din of running blood.

"Hello, little'n," I whispered.

"Jesus Christ," Holly whispered. "I'm really going to do this, aren't I?"

"Seems so."

She put her hands across her belly. She closed her eyes.

"Can you hear, little one?" she said. "I promise I won't let you go."

Holly and I held hands as we walked into the examination room. Her belly was already as taut and smooth and beautiful as the curved shell of an egg. Creel greeted us. He guided Holly to her desk, then stood at the front of the room before the time to start.

"Work hard," he told us. "Work hopefully. Be modest but aim high. We are proud of you all. Remember that you carry the aspirations of those who have gone before and that you create the world for those yet to come. You may begin."

CHAPTER
SIXTY-FOUR

We were both accepted by UEA.

"You could go," said Holly. "You *should* go."

Dad said the same.

I imagined striding away alone along the wire, turning back to see where Holly was, but knew it shouldn't be me, it couldn't be done.

We wrote with our explanation. We said we'd love to come later if we could. Later? we asked each other. When the baby was at school? When we were old? When we were retired?

A response came back. They were sorry to hear about this. Yes, they'd consider another application in the future, perhaps in a few years' time. There was a leaflet with information about a small number of rooms for families on the campus: normally for post-graduates, but one or two exceptions had been made.

"What's it now, then?" sighed Dad. "Wedding bells?"

It's how things were usually done. A quick wedding, a night's honeymoon at Whitley Bay, a narrow bed and a hand-me-down cot in the spare room of a pebbledash house, then two skinny kids pushing another kid in a worn-out Silver Cross.

"*Shall* we marry?" I asked her, as her mother wailed upstairs and Bruce Forsyth pranced on the TV. Bill and Dad were at the Three Tuns, exclaiming in their different ways at the weirdness of the world.

We talked of marrying on the hill, beside the heavenly rock, with Jack Law as silent minister and skylarks as the choir. Or on Beadnell Beach between dunes and surf, with moon above, bonfire blazing, lighthouse turning, the songs of Joni Mitchell. Or we'd wait until the baby came and have her christened at the moment we were wed.

We did it in Gateshead Register Office on a rainy Wednesday morning. Holly was five months gone. She wore a white Laura Ashley smock. We both wore silver rings and strings of dyed sunflower seeds around our necks. Our dads were there, and Dr Molly, Creel, Joyce, Tash McGuire, Tonto Flynn and Bella Carr. Afterwards, in the office lobby, Bella sang "Morning Has Broken" in a high and lovely voice.

We had chicken in the basket and bottles of Valpolicella at the Springfield Hotel on Durham Road. We all got tipsy. Bill and Dad put their arms around each other's shoulders, told Geordie jokes, sang Northumbrian songs.

"Keep your feet still Geordie hinny,
Let's be happy through the neet
For we may not be sae happy through the day . . ."

They left arm-in-arm and took a taxi back across the hill to the Iona Club.

Holly and I stayed in the hotel that night, in a soft warm bed in a room with red velvet curtains and red flock walls. We drank a little bottle of champagne. We made love carefully, tenderly, the first time we'd been together in a bed like this, the first time we'd been properly three.

Next day we went to the council offices, filled in an application for a flat in Buckingham House 1, one of the almost-completed tower blocks that rose in the eastern sky.

CHAPTER
SIXTY-FIVE

A new start. A bed from the Shephards of Gateshead. An electric cooker from Swan's Used Gold. An ancient leather sofa and cracked Victorian desk from Howie's Yard. Blankets from my house. Pillows from Holly's. A pine table and a pair of stools made in the back garden by Bill Stroud. A bookcase made by Dad. Kettle, pans, a medley of crockery and cutlery.

Bill talked of hiring a Transit, but the roads weren't finished yet. And there wasn't much, and it wasn't to be carried far. We strapped it to our backs, balanced it between us, spent a whole day tramping back and forth like refugees: away from our houses, through the estate, across the lower wasteland, past the Queen's Head, across the top of the square, past Buckingham House 2 and Buckingham House 3, past the bulldozers and kerb layers and road layers and cranes, across the field of rubble leading to the wired-glass entrance. Through the wide door and into the lift. Press 11. The lift shuddered as it rose, jerked as it stopped, creaked as it opened. Number 116. Three large rectangular magnolia rooms and a kitchen opening to a balcony right on the corner of the building.

When the moving was done, I went back for Holly and asked her to accompany me into the sky.

We arranged our books on the shelves. We Blu-tacked our A-level certificates on the wall alongside posters of City Lights bookstore, Dylan, *2001* and Holly's paintings and drawings of us all.

We hung thin net curtains across the wide windows. We put Pink Floyd on the record player, we laughed and sang and danced and swayed through the rooms to *Ummagumma*. Stood on the balcony. The other blocks were fifty yards or so away. We saw the great grey cement sheets that formed each one, the lines of black tar in between, the steel rods, straight steel girders, the multitude of windows. There were people on other balconies, unknowable faces at other windows. We gazed at each other across the gulfs between. Beyond the great bulk of the blocks, beyond their sharp vertical edges, we could see the ring of pebbledash in which we'd grown and the playing fields and wastelands all around.

"Welcome to your new home," we whispered to the hidden child at the heart of everything.

We felt it kick. We laughed.

Workmen dangled in a cage from a crane on the roof and pressed loud pneumatic hammers at great rivets or bolts in the walls. A cockerel called from a balcony close by. The wind rose and spun through the canyon between the blocks, and the whole of our building shivered in response.

CHAPTER
SIXTY-SIX

"You're *back?*" said Blister.

"You're *back?*" said Norman Dobson.

"You're bliddy *b-back?*" said Jakey.

"The word is it might not even be *yours!*" said Silversleeve.

"Get a *move*-on!" shouted Blister.

"And ye *married* her?" said Silversleeve.

"We're trainin up *the new lad!*" yelled Norman.

"Is that *r-reet?*" said Jakey.

"NOW!" yelled Blister.

"Aye," I said.

"B-bugger me," said Jakey.

"The word is it might be Vincent *McAlinden's!*" said Silversleeve.

"Aye," I said.

"Here's your mask," said Norman. "Here's your brush."

"B-bugger *me!*" said Jakey.

"And there's your shovel," said Norman.

"Ye *married* her?" said Silversleeve.

"Aye."

"NOW!" yelled Blister.

"AAL REET!" yelled Norman.

"NOW!"

"WE'RE COMIN! LOOK! WE'RE BLIDDY *OOT!*"

"Bugger *me*," sighed Silversleeve.

"B-bugger *m-me*," sighed Jakey.

"And I thought ye were Einstein," sighed Norman.

"More like Coco the Clown," said Silversleeve.

"Bliddy Coco," said Norman.

He sighed.

"So much for the eleven-plus!"

Out we went. Up on to the ship we went. Stopped on a ledge of scaffolding halfway up.

"In we gan," said Norman, clambering through a hole in the steel.

"You're in luck," said Silversleeve.

"Luck?"

"Confined space *and* f-filth allowance," said Jakey.

"So tek it slow," said Norman.

We slithered in.

"If ye find ye cannot breathe, give us a yell," said Norman.

We laughed.

"At least ye cannot f-faal," said Jakey.

We slithered down through the double hull, clambered past welders and riveters, through the din and stench, slid on our backs through another narrow gap into the double bottom.

"Ee," said Silversleeve. "It's just like bein back inside your mam."

"ARE YEZ IN?" yelled Blister from somewhere far away.

334

"Get brushin, lads," said Norman. "But not too fast."

"Ye *married* her?" said Silversleeve.

"ARE YEZ IN?"

"NO!" yelled Norman. "WE'RE ON THE BLIDDY BEACH!"

I fell easily into the rhythm of it, as if I'd been born for it. Wake early, kiss Holly, murmur greetings to the invisible child, make tea and a bacon sandwich, make bait, leave home, descend in the wobbly lift, walk down through the streets towards the river, down towards the gates, the huge half-built ship. Carry a notebook always, scribble lines in it, scribble notes about the sights and sounds. Write that a new world is dawning as the baby grows.

These were end times on the Tyne. Falling orders, closing yards, men laid off. Ships being built more quickly and efficiently in Korea, Japan, Taiwan. It didn't seem to matter to the cleaning gang.

"There's always a place," said Norman Dobson, "for them that's happy to deal in dirt."

The year declined. Mornings darkened. Wind whipped along the Tyne and rain and sleet began to fall. On dark days the shipyard sparkled with welding rods, oxyacetylene burners, braziers, arc lights, torches, with the strip lights that illuminated the wide windows of the drawing office. Foghorns and river bells sounded. I wore layers of pullovers beneath my boiler suit, woollen hat, thick gloves. I crawled through filth, through fallen birds, nests of mice. I grew closer to my

335

companions. At break times we huddled around braziers or inadequate electric fires in draughty sheds.

I scribbled in my book.

"He's putting us in a b-book," said Jakey.

"Or he's a gaffer's bliddy spy," said Silversleeve.

"No," said Norman. "He always was a good lad. He'll always be against the gaffers and the teachers."

He leaned close, shyly, afraid to be intrusive.

"Are you trying to *copy*, boy?" I whispered.

"Hell's teeth," he answered. "I remember that."

I touched his arm, pointed to his name, then showed him Jakey's and Silversleeve's. They shuffled closer, looked as well.

"T-telt ye," said Jakey.

"ARE YEZ OOT?"

"Bugger off!" I muttered.

I copied his words in capitals.

ARE YEZ OOT?

They watched.

"Keep on the lines," whispered Norman.

"I will," I smiled.

"AA SAID ARE YEZ OOT?"

I wrote his words again. They watched.

"Bugger off," I muttered.

"Tell him proper, man," said Silversleeve.

"BUGGER OFF, BLISTER!" I yelled.

I wrote it as I yelled.

BUGGER OFF, BLISTER!

We giggled as we stood up to go back into the cold.

"That's better, Coco," said Silversleeve. "You're gettin the lingo reet at last."

"See what diligence and care and attention can do," said Norman.

We went out.

"ARE YEZ OOT?"

"ARE YE BLIND?"

At shift's end we'd line up at the gates till they creaked open at last. Sometimes I'd meet Dad in the Iona Club, where the bar would be lined with freshly drawn pints as the men poured in.

"This isn't it, is it?" he said one dusk as hailstones clattered against the windowpanes.

I swigged the beer, felt its lovely bite as it fizzed past the sediments in my throat.

"It?"

He lit a cigarette. He glared at it.

"I'll get the better of these buggers yet," he said.

He inhaled, breathed out, sighed in satisfaction and frustration. I swiped my lips and drank again.

"For you," he said. "Is this *it* for *you?*"

"Course it's not. Just till the baby comes. Just till we're on our feet."

"Ye could gan to the ministry. Start at the bottom, work your way up. Even gan to the shipping office in the yard. Or some bliddy other office somewhere bliddy else. Somethin that's not cleanin the tanks like yer grandfaather did."

I shrugged.

"Don't want to work in an office, Dad."

"So ye gan reet back to the bliddy start?"

"It feels right, Dad, for now."

"Life slips by, ye knaa."

"We'll still go on. It's just we'll have a bairn to take with us."

He grunted. He stubbed out the cigarette.

"And what kind of a burden will that turn out to be?"

"The same burden I have been to you."

He shook his head. He admired his glass against the strip light in the ceiling.

"Beautiful," he murmured.

Then tipped the beer to his mouth and drank.

"I sometimes think you've got a bliddy death wish, lad," he said.

"I knaa. Let's have another pint."

CHAPTER
SIXTY-SEVEN

Ice floes on the river, ice on the decks, ice on the rungs of the ladders. Frozen filth in the tanks and in the double hulls. Frozen sandwiches, frozen half-eaten pies, frozen scarves, newspapers, cigarette butts. Bodies of birds like feathered rocks. Mouse babies turned to stone within minutes of their birth. All of it frozen, coagulated and congealed. We wore gloves, hats, balaclavas, scarves. We put newspaper into our boots. We carried hammers, chisels, crowbars to break the ice and wrench it away. We were scoffed at by the other workers as we went down into the depths to perform our filthy tasks and as we came out again. But we were grinned at as well. We were the tank lads, the double-bottom lads, the dirty lads, the scum. Often it seemed that the colder and filthier it became, the happier we were. We grunted and screamed like wild things, we wielded our tools like ancient weapons. We clapped each other's cheeks to bring back the warmth and to chastise and to play and in among it all to dare display affection. We giggled as we called each other love and petal and dickhead and hinny and cunt. We cursed our fellow workers. We yelled that they were a bunch of bliddy wasters, that they had the life of bliddy

Riley, that they were the bosses' spawn, the gaffers' pets. They didn't have a c-clue what proper g-graft was. We made obscene gestures and threw curses towards the windows of the drawing office and the barred windows of the owners and managers higher up. We told Blister to get lost, to go to hell.

Fairy lights shone from the jibs of cranes. Scrap-metal Christmas trees stood on the decks. Baubles and tinsel dangled and swayed. We swigged from hip flasks of cheap whisky and brandy to bring the illusion of warmth and to toast each other and to filthily start our Christmas celebrations. It was Christmas Eve morning and I was curled up in the depths of the hull when the message came. How had it got to me? I never knew. The message came from the outside, was passed across the yard, on to the ship, down through welders and caulkers, down through the confined spaces, the tangle of men and cables and oxygen tanks and filth.

Is Coco doon there?

Coco Hall?

Aye, him!

He's doon there somewhere with the dirt monkeys.

Tell him his lass has gone in!

Eh?

His lass! She's gone in!

Coco! COCO! COCO HALL!

I clambered out. Out towards the hole in the ship's side, out through the hole, down the ladder. I heard Blister yelling something after me but I didn't turn.

Hurried across the yard towards the locked gates, went to the gatekeeper's hatch.

"I've got to gan," I said.

"Oh aye?"

"Me baby's on the way."

"Oh aye?"

"I've got to be there."

"Oh aye?"

"Let me oot."

He pointed to his clock.

"Wait twenty minutes, son, and ye won't get docked."

"Let me oot."

"I cannot. Not without a . . ."

I turned away. I climbed the gates. He came out after me, yelled after me, cursed me. I dropped down on the other side and ran.

Ran uphill towards the town. There was ice on the pavements, slush thrown from the roadway. Dark clouds hung heavy and low over everything. All sound was muted. Lights dimly shone. The summit of the town and the summits of Buckingham House 1, 2 and 3 were lost in the sky. The hospital was nothing but a bulky shadow in the gloom. Sleet started to fall. Kids and drunks were singing carols. I passed a priest who called out, "Blessings upon you, Dominic!" Someone else called something to me but I couldn't turn. I hurried towards the towering hospital past an ambulance with its amber light spinning and with a body on a stretcher illuminated inside. Through the door.

A nurse was instantly before me.

"May I help you?"

We were in a brightly lit and disinfected corridor. The sign that hung over her pointed to Maternity.

She asked again.

"I've come to see my baby being born."

"Your *baby*?"

An older nurse came to her side.

"He's come to see his baby being born, Matron."

"Not like that he's not. Go home, get scrubbed, get changed and then come back again and we shall see."

"But I might be late. I . . . I think the mother's already here."

"Then that is all that matters. Off you go."

And she turned, hurried away.

"It's for the best," said the young nurse. "Just think of the germs that are . . . Dominic? Dominic *Hall?*"

"Maria?"

Maria Lewandowska, from Miss O'Kane's class, Maria Lewandowska whose family had fled from Poland in the 40s, prim and pretty Maria Lewandowska who knew the names of the sorrowful mysteries and glorious mysteries, who was one of those like me who was never caned for not knowing the catechismic truths.

"Maria *Lewandowska?*"

"Yes. And yes, Holly is here. I took her along myself. But *really*, Dominic. What might the poor baby *catch?*"

She glanced over her shoulder.

"Quickly," she said.

She took me through a yellow door, into a room with a shower, a toilet, a narrow bed.

"It's for the about-to-be-bereaved," she said. She clapped her hand across her mouth. "Sorry! But it is. The ones whose relatives are about to die in the middle of the night and who won't go home. Maybe not the best thing. Maybe you should get home and get back here again."

"No."

"And we have clothes . . . Is this *mad?*"

I shook my head.

"You won't *tell?*"

"Hardly!"

"Quick. Turn the shower on. Get those off and get in and I'll bring the stuff." She laughed as I waited for her to leave. "I'm a *nurse*, Dominic. You wouldn't *believe* the things I've seen."

She giggled and left. I dumped my clothes in a heap on the floor. Scrubbed myself in the shower, saw the dirt draining from me, scrubbed fast and hard until there was hardly a mark on me, until my skin was shining, as if a whole layer of it was gone.

I stood wrapped in a white towel, waiting.

She laughed when she came back.

"Like a newborn babe yourself," she said.

She had some old man's clothes: beige trousers, beige nylon shirt, blue velvety slippers. "The height of fashion in here," she said. "And these?" She pointed to the heap of clothes on the floor. They lay like something hauled in a bucket from the depths of a tank.

"Chuck them."

She stuffed them into a disposal sack.

"They'll get torched with the medical waste."

"OK."

And then she opened the door and showed me the way. I ran, with the too-big slippers flopping on my feet. I took a lift up to the maternity ward, stepped out.

Another nurse was before me.

"Can I help you?"

"I've come to see my baby being born."

"This way. My name is Claire."

She took me through some doors.

"This is your mask," she said. "These are your scissors."

She put these things in my hand. She laughed.

"Put that on. The midwife will tell you what to do with those."

More doors, then there she was, lying on a bed with a midwife at her side.

I moved the mask aside and kissed her. I held her hand. Through the window I saw that the world up here was lost in cloud. Soon the window reflected only us, the midwife, the lights around. Holly sobbed and gasped as the baby made its hours-long ten-inch journey. We were there for the length of a complete shift.

The baby slithered out in the middle of the night, a bloodied, sticky, red, grey, blue, black thing. How could it have fitted in there? How could it have been so close, so hidden, and seem to be so far away? How could it take so long to come? How could it appear so fast?

"A lovely girl!" said the midwife.

She turned to me.

"Would you like to cut?" she said.

She laughed.

"The cord, my dear," she said. "Would you like to cut the cord between your daughter and your wife?"

I cut the cord, felt the scrape and vibration of sharp steel on flesh.

The baby screamed.

"Girls are gorgeous!" the midwife said, then lifted the child to Holly's breast.

CHAPTER
SIXTY-EIGHT

We named her Elaine.

We took her when she was just a few days old to the McAlinden house.

Mrs McAlinden gave us tea and biscuits. The endless fire blazed in the grate. A boy sat silent against the wall in a corner, reading a *Superman* comic. There was a faded black-and-white photograph of a woman standing before a turf cottage holding a basket of fish. There was a map of the peninsulas of southern Ireland on the wall. There were tears in Mrs McAlinden's eyes as she took the baby on her lap.

"So beautiful," she murmured.

She touched the trace of a widow's peak on the baby's brow.

"She's nowt like us, of course," she said.

She sighed deeply.

"It's clear as day," she said. "She's the spit of you both."

She leaned down to the baby's tiny ear.

"I'm not your gran," she whispered. "Though I'd love to be the grandma of a lovely thing like you."

She told us to have more tea.

"You'll look after her," she said.

"Yes," we told her.

"And you'll bring her back to see me sometimes, won't you?"

"Yes, we will."

"That's grand. That's wonderful."

She kissed the baby gently, then let us lift it away.

"Welcome to the world, Elaine," she breathed.

Another place I'd never entered was the bedroom of Mrs Stroud. It was Elaine who gained me entry. The curtain fluttered in the draught of the half-open window as we stepped in. Mrs Stroud was sitting up in bed, pillows arranged around her. The wavering light exposed her pale face, her strange smile. All around the walls were Holly's paintings and drawings.

"Which one are you?" she said to me.

Holly clicked her tongue.

"Mam!" she breathed.

"Dominic," I answered.

"I get mixed up. And is that the bairn?"

"Your grandchild," said Holly.

"My?"

"Yes. Her name is Elaine."

We laid the baby on the bed beside her. I looked at the portraits of Vincent, the portraits of me, at Mrs Stroud's own indecipherable marks and swirls and letters and gaps.

Mrs Stroud touched the baby's kicking legs.

"Does it walk?" said Mrs Stroud.

"Mam!" said Holly.

"Not yet, Mrs Stroud," I said.

"That's good. I heard her coming before she came. Yes, she was with the angels. She was singing with them."

The baby cooed and gurgled.

"Yes!" said Mrs Stroud. "Like that! But much more beautiful, of course. Are you going now?"

Bill was simple in his love.

"You," he'd whisper, and he'd gaze into her eyes and she'd gaze straight back at him, "are the most gorgeous beautiful lovely thing in the whole wide lovely world, and you have the very loveliest parents in the whole wide world, and we all love you very much, and we are very pleased that you came to us!"

He'd hold her tight, and ask her, "Do you know this one?" before breaking out into a sweet singing of "Waters of Tyne" or "Felton Lonnen". "Get ready for the ride," he'd say, and would rest her upon his knee and begin to bounce her gently to "Bobby Shaftoe".

Dad was slow. I saw him searching her features for the shapes of McAlinden. He may have found some, he may have not, he did not speak of them. Then I found him in tears in our high living room one day. Elaine lay on her changing mat, waving her hands before her face. Dad looked down upon her.

"You're just like your grandma," he told her. "You're just like my very own Elaine."

He lifted her to himself.

"Oh," he said, "she would have loved you very very much."

The baby sang as she had sung for Mrs Stroud, and Dad laughed through his tears, and started singing, too.

348

We took her to the grave, of course.

"This is where your other grandma is," I said. "And she's also up in Heaven, and she looks down on you and loves you, and she always will."

CHAPTER
SIXTY-NINE

We took her to Morden Tower and she sat on our laps while poets read and raved and teetered on the high wires of verse. I read there myself, from the first photocopied pamphlet of my first awkward poems, poems about wires and cables and stitch marks and tanks, about bonfires on beaches and Heaven in rock. In spring we carried her across the fields. We showed her allotments and greenhouses and the curving river and the distant sea. We spoke of skylarks and circuses and of the tunnels beneath the grass and the endless sky above. We showed her rabbits, beetles, rats and birds. We whispered of secret nests and nestlings. We told the tales of miracles — of flight, of eggs, of trembling leaves, of opening blooms. We came to our two hawthorn trees and told the tale of those. We lay on the earth beneath, with her between us. We put her fingers to the miraculous shapes of every single blade of grass. We told her of this world that turns and turns and turns beneath us, this light that pours eternally upon us. We showed how light and shadow shift and flicker across our skin. We told her of the other turning worlds beyond this world and of worlds beyond those worlds. We told her of the miracle of herself, how she came from the great gulfs of space and time to become an almost-nothing inside her mother's womb, how she had grown and would grow, how she would walk and dance, how she would walk across the sky with us one day. We told her that new bodies would be born from hers one day. We told the miracle of all of us. She kicked her feet through the air and the light. She waved her hands and looked at them and at us in giggly wonder. We sang together, there beneath the upturned nest, a weird cooing gurgling trio accompanied by the birds.

We lifted her again and wandered on. We told her of the gentle silent wandering tramp, Jack Law, and we took her to his rock. A candle burned in there today. We slithered in, for there was room for two bodies and a tiny one. We gasped. Everything had changed. The sky was freshly painted blue, but there was no Heaven in it, no God, no angels. There was the sun, a flight of silhouetted birds. There were two trees with a cord between, two smiling dancing figures balancing on the cord with a baby held between them. Lower down were many figures, individuals and little groups, all human, wandering beside buildings, or through patches of bright green. There were boats on a river and on a distant sea that blended with the sky. And there was Jack himself, in mid-stride, heading upwards, bowed forward with his little rucksack on his back.

We sighed. The baby cooed.

We moved out of the rock as Jack came to us.

We lifted the baby into his arms. He smiled. He raised her high and gasped at the beauty of her in the light.

He brought her close to his scarred and gentle face.

He sang his high wordless note.

"E-u," he said to her.

And then he became still and held his breath and shaped his lips.

"Good," he said. "G-good."

"Goo," replied Elaine. "Goo-goo."

He smiled and sighed.

"Goo," cried the bairn. "Goo-goo."

The Tell-Tale Heart

Jill Dawson

Patrick, a 50-year-old professor of American Studies, drinker and womaniser, has been given six months to live. In a rural part of Cambridgeshire, a teenager dies in a motorcycle accident. When his heart is transplanted into Patrick's chest, the lives of two strangers are forever conjoined.

Patrick makes a good recovery from surgery, but has the strange feeling that his old life "won't have him". He discovers that his donor's name was Drew Beamish, a local boy who had been expelled from school following a scandal, and becomes intensely curious, not only about Drew but what shaped him: his family and culture, the ancestor who took part in the famous Littleport riots of 1816, and the bleak yet beautiful landscape of the Fens. Patrick longs to know the story of his heart.

Gone are the Leaves

Anne Donovan

Feilamort can remember very little of his childhood before he became a choir boy in the home of the Laird and his French wife. Feilamort has one of the finest voices in the land. It is a gift he believes will protect him . . .

Deirdre has always lived in the castle. Apprentice to her mother, she embroiders the robes for one of Scotland's finest families. But with her mother pushing her to choose between a man she does not love and a closed world of prayer and solitude, Deirdre must decide for herself what her life will become.

When the time comes for Feilamort to make an awful decision, his choice catapults himself and Deirdre head-first into adulthood. As the two friends learn more about Feilamort's forgotten childhood, it becomes clear that someone close by is intent on keeping it hidden.